Plague in Paradise
The Black Death in
Los Angeles, 1924

Families in the Mexican community of Los Angeles are getting sick. Some are dying. Has the Spanish Influenza returned as some suspect? Dr. Matthew Thompson, the most skilled diagnostician at Los Angeles County General Hospital, fears something even more deadly. When patients develop boils, their skin darkens, and they start coughing up blood, his worst fears are confirmed: Plague—the Black Death—has taken root just a few miles from the hospital and main center of commerce of the city.

Some in civic government and even a few high ranking medical officials would like this outbreak kept quiet, even if the secrecy costs the lives of those presently afflicted. The reputation and future of a whole city is at stake. It is more important to protect "The Paradise of the West," as Los Angeles is now known for its healthful climate, beautiful beaches, and bountiful opportunities.

What happens when a plague hits a minority group whose welfare is of little concern to government and medical leaders? Dr. Thompson, Nurse Maria McDonnell, and Fr. Medardo Brualla of Our Lady Queen of Angels Parish decide to fight for the welfare of all, but they find themselves facing much more than a medical crisis: fear, racism, and greed.

Plague in Paradise

The Black Death in Los Angeles, 1924

by

Jeffrey S. Copeland

PARAGON HOUSE
St. Paul, Minnesota

First Edition 2018

Published in the United States by
Paragon House
www.paragonhouse.com

Library of Congress Cataloging-in-Publication Data

  Names: Copeland, Jeffrey S. (Jeffrey Scott), 1953- author.
  Title: Plague in paradise : the Black Death in Los Angeles, 1924 / by Jeffrey
    S. Copeland.
  Description: First edition. | St. Paul, Minnesota : Paragon House, 2018. |
    Includes bibliographical references.
  Identifiers: LCCN 2018016582 | ISBN 9781557789358 (pbk. : alk. paper)
  Subjects: LCSH: Black Death--California--Los Angeles. | Diseases and history.
    | Black Death--Social aspects. | Racism.
  Classification: LCC RC172 .C67 2018 | DDC 616.9/23200979494--dc23 LC
    record available at https://lccn.loc.gov/2018016582

The paper used in this publication meets the minimum requirements of American National Standard for Information Sciences—Permanence of Paper for Printed Library Materials, ANSI standard Z39.48-1992.

Manufactured in the United States of America

10 9 8 7 6 5 4 3 2 1

For current information about all releases from Paragon House, visit the website at http://www.paragonhouse.com

For my wife,
Linda Marie
And to the memory of
Father Medardo Brualla,
Our Lady Queen of Angels—"La Placita"

Contents

Author Note

When first researching this story, I learned that much of what took place in Los Angeles in October and November of 1924 was still shrouded in mystery and intrigue. I combed archives and records centers to gather as much information as I could uncover, but one fact immediately stood out. Descriptions of the events seemed to differ to some degree, some in small details while others hardly seemed to be describing the same events at all. Some also seemed to have *too many* details, perhaps added in an attempt to cover up or create a different light on activities that many had not been all that proud of at the time. Perhaps this makes sense because feelings and tensions also ran incredibly high at this time for all involved, from those in city government to the individuals living in the Macy Street District. As a result, variations in reports occurred in the writings depending upon from which perspective it originated. Compounding this was a virtual media blackout that kept many of the region, in multiple ways, in the dark. As a result, we may never know everything that happened during those fateful days. However, after studying the broad range of accounts, I have attempted to present the story as I believe the events transpired—and as completely and as accurately as possible.

It should also be noted the time period involved was compressed to allow the story to unfold as presented. Also, for the obvious reasons, some of the names have been changed—to protect the innocent *and* the guilty—and other characters are composites of several.

JSC

1349 London

Ring around the rosies,
A pocket full of posies,
Ashes, Ashes,
We all fall down!

1918 New York City

I had a little bird,
It's name was Enza,
I opened the window,
And in-flu-enza!

1924 Los Angeles

In went the doctor,
Out went the nurse,
She sent in,
The man with the hearse!

CHAPTER 1

Arrival

Port of Los Angeles
September 23, 1924
6:20 A.M.

The crew of the *Lin Su* of the China Sea Line, registry Shanghai, hurried about making final preparations for the initial inspection to be carried out at the recently christened West Port of Los Angeles.

First Officer Forrest Anderson, now serving as Ship's Captain, could not outwardly present even the slightest hint of the secret sorrow burning within him. Just two days before, Captain Marua, his dear friend, and three members of the crew had succumbed to an illness unlike anything anyone aboard ship had ever encountered. The men had writhed in agony as thick yellow bile oozed from gaping sores under their arms. They were wracked with fever so high their eyes clouded over, turning dull and lifeless. Stabbing pains shot down their backs and into their legs. Most coughed so long and hard that their breaths came in short gasps and black blood built up at the corners of their mouths. For these men, death brought a welcome relief. Immediately after they passed, they were swaddled, weighted down, and given to the sea after a simple ceremony held amidships.

Anderson was an American, as were most in positions of authority aboard the ship. The company put Americans in charge of its vessels to lessen suspicion and to help build stronger ties with port authorities, especially on the West Coast. Just thirty years old, he was already a veteran of over two dozen ocean crossings, and the company considered him a fine candidate to have his own ship, something he strongly desired. To earn the company's favor, Anderson knew he must protect the shipping line's interests at all costs.

As the *Lin Su* neared Los Angeles, all crew members were sworn to secrecy and informed that any word leaked to the harbor authorities about the illness and deaths would result in an immediate quarantine of the ship. And, because the deaths were of an undetermined cause, the ship's cargo would most likely be burned or taken back out to sea for disposal. Anderson reminded crew members of the company's unforgiving policy: if cargo wasn't delivered, all would lose their shares and wages for the entire voyage. That would be devastating enough, but the crew also knew if anyone slipped up and caused a quarantine, that man would be immediately blackballed and never allowed to work again for any shipping company on the seas. Understanding the situation, the crew went about their work as if everything aboard ship was as it should be.

For the past thirty years, the *Lin Su* had been one of the most popular, and profitable, ships of the line, regularly carrying wealthy travelers and tens of thousands of immigrants between China and western U.S. cities. However, just a few years before, immigration laws became so strict the number of those coming to America dwindled to a dozen or fewer each voyage. At the same time, because of changing economics worldwide, ocean travel simply for pleasure began to lose its appeal. Now, more often than not, the *Lin Su's* luxury cabins housed additional cargo rather than well-to-do passengers.

The combination of these two dramatic changes and resulting loss of revenue left the shipping line in woeful financial straits. The line faced a hard reality: stay the course and eventually be forced to shut down operations or find other means of securing revenue. Those with controlling interest in the China Sea Line understood that creditors would soon be upon them and panicked. Even though the risk was great, they joined with those who had discovered the easiest means of generating profit and thus staying afloat: illegal contraband.

Ready buyers awaited shipments of ammunition and weapons, narcotics—especially opium—stolen art, jewelry, antiquities, and counterfeit currency. And because of the U.S. Prohibition Act of 1920, trade in illegal alcohol became the most profitable venture of all. The sale of these goods would keep the line solvent; the problem was how to do so without being caught. This, too, was finally figured out. Legitimate cargo, such as furniture and textiles, crammed as tightly as possible in the holds served as decoys for the illegal items hidden below them. It was not unusual for the same *legitimate* cargo to be loaded, unloaded, and shipped multiple times while serving as cover for the more profitable goods.

Such was the case aboard the *Lin Su*, one of the most profitable ships in the line.

Not only did Anderson have to worry about concealing the deaths, he also had to make sure the harbor officials did not find the "special" goods hidden throughout his ship. As he watched the port's Marine Superintendent, Barton Turnbull, flanked by his Supervising Engineer and his Port Steward, walking up the gangway, his mind raced, trying to keep the web of lies straight, so he would be granted permission to unload his cargo to the dock below.

Once at the top of the gangway, Marine Superintendent Turnbull requested permission to come aboard. Anderson granted this and walked over to introduce himself.

"I'm acting Ship's Captain Forrest Anderson. I'd first like to say I'm deeply honored to be at your new port and would like to wish you the very best of commerce here."

"It is my pleasure to meet you, Anderson," Turnbull replied, reaching out to shake his hand. "I welcome you and want you to know we will do all possible to make working together smooth and efficient."

He motioned to the men standing behind him. "I'd like to introduce Thomas Gall, our Superintendent Engineer, and Elston McDaniel, the Port Steward. They will be helping with the initial inspection of your ship."

Anderson saluted them, then waved over his second and third in command. "Superintendent Turnbull, I'd like to introduce Joseph Armistad, my Chief Engineer, and Chin Lee, our Boatswain. I've freed them from their immediate duties to be of service to you in any way you wish as you begin inspection."

All shook hands and exchanged greetings. Once the introductions had taken place, Superintendent Turnbull turned more formal as he asked, "You said you are the *acting* Ship's Captain. I must ask you what has happened to your captain. Is he ill?"

"I assure you, Sir, there is nothing more Captain Marua would like than to be here with us."

Armistad and Lee gave each other a quick sideways glance as Anderson continued, "He was ordered by the company to remain at our last port of call to help develop new routes for the line. He is the most experienced of all our captains, so his knowledge and experience were desired—and justifiably so. Poor man. I can only imagine what he is going through now away from the ship he so loves."

"I'm sure it will be uncomfortable for him to…" was all Superintendent Turnbull could get out before Anderson cut in and said, "I know your time is precious. Our time is precious as well, especially as it is my understanding dockage and wharfage charges and brokerage fees here are nearly double what we are accustomed to at our other ports. The longer we are here, the more the company will be unhappy with me. I want to make a good first impression acting as Ship's Captain, so I'd be most grateful if we can begin the inspection now."

Here he paused. "But before we do, even though it will take some extra time, which will translate into more expense, I have a favor to ask of you three."

"What is this favor?" Superintendent Turnbull asked. "I've never had anyone ask for *more* time in port than absolutely necessary. You have my curiosity, Sir."

"It will only take a moment, but I want to ask your advice about something."

Anderson grabbed Turnbull's arm and urged him along as he walked quickly toward the far port side of the main deck, the location of a few of the cabins for the wealthiest of travelers.

The others followed as Anderson continued, his words coming so fast it was at times difficult for all to understand him. "You may or may not know we are soon going to stop passenger service. Just no profit in it any more. More and more lines going that direction these days. I know my best way up the ranks is to find new ways to increase profits, so I have an idea, and I'd appreciate your thoughts on it."

When they reached the door of Cabin 4, Anderson stopped, unlocked the door, and motioned for all to file in behind him. The room was nearly full, but there was still space to stand comfortably at the center.

His voice rising with excitement, Anderson said, "This cabin was once reserved for our wealthiest or most prominent traveler. Now look at it. Just another cargo space."

Clearing away a few boxes, he pointed to the rear wall. "Look at this. Beautiful mahogany, padded behind with layer after layer of oak and pine to insulate passengers from the sounds of the ship and the sea. Now, it seems to me, just nothing but wasted space."

Superintendent Turnbull started to say something, but Anderson quickly continued. "Here's my plan. There are twenty cabins similar to this in just this section of the ship, and seventy-five more below. I say remove all the wood, cut through the steel behind all side walls, and create new holds. But my concern is about structural soundness. Could removing the wood and the extra support it provides be done without compromise to the ship? My Chief Engineer says he thinks it can be done, but I told him I'd ask for another opinion, so he won't take offense by what you have to say. Please, gentlemen, your thoughts? You are all experts and vastly more experienced than I. I'd be most grateful for your comments."

Thomas Gall, the port's Superintendent Engineer, stepped over to examine the wall, knocked several times on the mahogany, and spoke first. "This ship is of a Three-Island design, with its main structural supports at the bow, amidships, and the stern. As long as the door walls in each cabin are left intact, I see no reason why new holds can't be created. It should work fine."

Superintendent Turnbull barely looked at the walls. He removed his watch from his vest pocket, studied it, and said, "If both engineers are of a mind it will work, I suppose I'd go along with that."

He paused briefly and stepped toward the door. "I appreciate your asking for the advice, but we really must be moving along. After all, this is, ultimately, a decision for the company to make." He motioned for everyone to follow him back out of the cabin.

"I apologize," Anderson said as they moved back across the deck. "I shouldn't have taken the time. It's just that I know the line will be replacing two captains who are retiring this coming year, and I'm trying to figure out a way to gain an upper hand. Please, let's get to the inspection."

"Well," Turnbull replied, "can't blame a man for wanting to better himself." Then, turning to Gall and McDaniel, he said, "You know what to do. I'll look around and then meet you back at the gangway. Let's be at it."

As soon as they were out of sight, Armistad and Lee walked over to Anderson, both shaking their heads. Armistad said, softly, "I still can't believe you did that. That was quite a chance you took. The alcohol and opium were right there. He knocked on the wood right over the top of 'em. And now they'll probably be knocking on the walls in every cabin on the ship, and our cargo is behind every one of them. That carries too much risk."

Anderson smiled. "Don't worry. They'll never guess we've already made hollow recesses behind all the outer layers of mahogany. They'll be thinking instead of ways the walls could be altered to make more holds.

That's what I *wanted* them to be thinking about. The puzzle I gave them will keep them preoccupied. Trust me—it will work."

Armistad and Lee looked nervously around the deck. Lee finally muttered, "Better be right."

Anderson spoke even more softly, "Now it's time for *us* to go to work. Get a man down to the docks and get the bribes taken care of. I want to be ready to start unloading as soon as the Superintendent and his men finish the inspection. We'll wait for nightfall for the important goods, but we need to look busy during the day. Concentrate on the furniture today. Tell the men to take a long time. A *long* time. Do I make myself clear?"

"Understood. It'll be done," Armistad replied. With that, he and Lee left to set their plan in motion.

....

11:23 P.M.

Jack Reynolds, Chief Dock Foreman at the West Port of Los Angeles, had twenty-one ten dollar bills, well over a month's pay, rolled tightly and tucked in his front right pocket. The Purser of the *Lin Su* gave him the money in exchange for rounding up a few men who, without asking questions, would offload some of the "special" cargo from the ship, place it aboard a truck, and then deliver it to a secluded warehouse several miles from the harbor.

The men Jack usually employed for this duty had been loaned the day before to the East Dock, where three large ships unexpectedly arrived within two hours of each other, causing a frantic rush to find enough able-bodied men to help with the tremendous amount of work this created.

Most of the men working the docks were what Jack called "wharf rats." They were day-workers, transients who had come to Los Angeles from all over the globe: Australia, China, the West Indies, Poland, South

Africa, and Mexico. Many were here illegally—and would do anything asked of them to keep from being sent back to their home countries. Still others were hiding from the law or had little education and few skills, so their opportunities were limited. Whatever their circumstances, Jack trusted few of these men because he knew if they were caught while breaking the law, most would turn in their own mothers if they thought it would be of advantage to them.

As Jack studied the motley assortment of men before him pushing carts and hauling heavy bundles to the train cars on the spur off to his left, he noticed two brothers who had impressed him with their strong work ethic—exceptions among those typically found at the docks. They didn't apply for work every night, but when they did show up, they kept to themselves, didn't cause trouble, didn't take long breaks, and never complained, no matter how deep into the night they were asked to stay. Other than what he had been able to observe directly, Jack knew little about them other than they had come from a small town in northern Mexico to live with relatives. Once when Jack had asked to see their work papers, both immediately started backing away from him and offered to leave. Jack told them to stay, and even though nothing else was said, the looks on their faces indicated what he was hoping to see: they knew they owed him.

With no better options in sight, Jack called them over. "What are your names again?" he asked.

The older and taller of the two replied nervously, "I'm Alejandro. This is Antonio. Can we do something for you, *Señor* Reynolds?"

"Maybe you can." Jack studied them closely. "Relax, boys. You're not in trouble. I have a small job, and I think you two can do it the *right* way. It pays five extra dollars each. Interested?"

The brothers looked at each other before Alejandro replied, "We will do whatever you ask."

"One more question," Jack added. "Can either of you drive a truck?"

Antonio nodded that he could.

"Good! Now come over here and I'll explain exactly what you are to do."

They followed him across the pavement to a large truck, where Jack motioned for them to sit on the running board. Walking back and forth in front of them, he explained the plan, which was simple enough if there were no glitches.

Special cargo would be brought down from the ship, and they would load it into the back of the truck, covering it all with a thick tarp. Then they were to drive to the harbor's south gate, where the guard would let them through without inspection. From there, they would drive the main road about a mile, cross the Southern Pacific Railroad tracks, and turn right onto the first road after. After driving two miles more, they would come to an abandoned warehouse district that had been mostly destroyed by fire a year before. Trucks would be blocking the road there, and those men would help Alejandro and Antonio unload the goods and take them to one of the few buildings still standing. After that, all they had to do was bring back the truck.

Jack went over the plan twice, the second time stopping after each detail to make sure they understood everything. When he was sure they were ready, he asked them to stand.

"Before we begin," he said, sternly, moving closer to them, "I want to make one more thing very clear. If you get stopped by anyone before you get there, you don't know anything about the cargo. You tell them you found it on the side of the road—and stick to that story. Do I make myself clear?"

The brothers stared at him blankly, neither completely sure of his meaning. However, what Jack said next they did understand.

"You are living with relatives here in Los Angeles, right? It would be sad if something happened to them because you weren't able to follow directions. I know you would feel terrible. Isn't that right?"

Both nodded.

"That's fine," Jack said, patting each on the shoulder. "Let's get to work."

Fifty minutes later, Alejandro and Antonio made it through the South gate and headed down the main road.

"What do you think we are hauling?" Antonio asked his brother as he shifted to a higher gear. "There were holes in some of the crates, and I saw small candlesticks in the straw. But I am confused. The crates are too heavy to have just those."

Alejandro responded, "When I moved the boxes to the front, and when I was sure no one was looking, I stuck my hand all the way in one of them. Behind the candlesticks I touched bottles."

Antonio thought for a few seconds, finally asking, "Whiskey?"

"I am sure of it." Pointing to the side of the road, which was completely deserted along this stretch, he ordered, "Pull over here. Do it— right now! Then get out and help me."

Antonio pulled over. "Why are we stopping? What are you doing?"

Alejandro put his hands on his hips, turned to his brother, and said, "Five dollars each is not enough. We will take the rest of what we are owed now. One crate. They will not miss it, but even if they do, they know this will buy our silence. We will hide it here in the ditch and come back later to get it. Jesús' neighbor has a Ford. We will pay him five dollars to borrow it, and he will be happy."

"But where will we take the crate?" Antonio asked. "No one must ever find it."

Alejandro thought for a minute. "When Jesús is at work, we will place it under his home. Only the dogs go under there."

"I don't know . . ." Antonio said, shaking his head. "What if we are caught?"

"My brother worries too much," Alejandro replied. "If Jesús discovers it before we can sell it, he will not do anything but drink it. That is the worst that can happen."

"The worst that can happen?" Antonio questioned. "I do not think so. I fear bad things may come from this."

"It is as I said," Alejandro responded, playfully slapping his brother on the arm. "My brother worries too much."

Both laughed and moved the crate to the ditch.

....

CHAPTER 2

The Smell

October 18
11:23 A.M.

The Lajuns were at it again.

Every Sunday for the past three weeks, immediately after church services, Jesús and Carlita Lajun discussed the condition of their home loudly and passionately enough that all passing by could hear them clearly through the thin walls of the house they rented at 700 Clara Street.

"Your brothers—they stink like goats!" Jesús shouted so shrilly a family walking past stopped suddenly and wondered if someone within the house was being hurt.

"You are one to talk!" Carlita shouted back. "Your skin is like rotten vegetables every day you come home from the fields. I almost die every night in bed from the smell!"

By this point, as was now the new weekly custom in the neighborhood, a small crowd started gathering in the front yard, waiting to see just how long the shouting would continue.

"What is it this time?" Mrs. Mendez, the neighbor across the road, asked no one in particular as she tried peering through the Lajun's front window.

"Same as always. It's her brothers again," came an exasperated reply from someone in the back, bringing laughter from everyone present.

Jesús' voice rang out to the street. "They eat like pigs! They sleep in my home! My children sleep on blankets by the front door because they have taken their room! It is not right!"

He paused to catch his breath. The crowd inched forward. "Our own daughter, our dear Francisca, has just had the Quinceañera and is presented to the community. She is a woman now and, God willing, should have a husband soon. But who would take her? I hugged her yesterday, and her beautiful hair smelled like, like . . . *them*! I ask you—who would want her that way?"

Francisca had been working in the kitchen, trying to ignore her parents, but now she moved to look out the window at the gathering crowd. She prayed silently that Esteban was not there to hear what her father had just shouted. Another quick prayer asked that no one in the crowd would carry the news to him that her own father said her hair smelled like . . . goats!

Jesús' voice rose yet again as he continued, "And do your brothers help put food on my table? Do they pay rent? No! They are filthy and have such a smell our dogs will not sleep with them in that room!"

The crowd outside burst into laughter just as Carlita shouted, "It is not them! Smell them!"

"Smell them? I wouldn't go near them if their hair suddenly turned to golden braids. I want them out of here!"

At that point, most of the crowd applauded and erupted into cheers in support of Jesús. Peering out the window, Carlita said, dryly, "You did it again. Our friends, our neighbors, they think we are loco."

Jesús faced her, slouched his shoulders, and replied, "If we don't get rid of them and their smell, I *am* going to be loco."

Carlita shook her head, opened the front door, stepped onto the porch, and said to all present, "I am very sorry—again!"

Before anyone could reply, she turned and walked back through the door, closing it tightly.

Pointing to her husband, she said commandingly while pointing to the table, "Sit down! Now!"

Jesús started to speak, but her eyes told him to remain quiet. He sat down, heavily.

Carlita's brothers, Antonio and Alejandro, who had still been sleeping because they didn't get back from their work at the harbor until daybreak, sheepishly entered the small kitchen.

"And you, too!" she shouted at them. "Sit! We are going to get to the bottom of this."

She walked behind her brothers, bent down, and sniffed loudly. Smugly raising herself back up, she said, triumphantly, "I told you. It is *not* them! Smell for yourself!"

"I am not going to smell them," Jesús replied, frustration coming to his voice. "If it is not them, then what is it? What could it be? You tell me."

Antonio yawned, then said, "I was not sure before, but I am now. I believe it is coming from under the house because the smell is worse during the day and when the weather is warmer."

"I say it is *you*," Jesús growled. "After all, you are from Hermosillo, and everyone knows all from that town are unclean and slow to think."

Before her brother could defend himself, Carlita walked in front of Jesús and said, loudly, her tone as sharp as he'd ever heard, "I, too, am from Hermosillo. Have you forgotten that?"

Jesús had gone too far. He leaned back in his chair and said, calmly, hoping to buy time for his wife's anger to subside, "Okay. I'll go outside. I'll check under the house. But I know I will not find anything there. I know this. It is those . . ."

He pointed again at Antonio and Alejandro but didn't finish his thought. The look in Carlita's eyes told him it was time to move toward the door. Carlita picked up the broom next to the sink and held it above her shoulder. "Outside," she ordered. "No more talking."

When Jesús opened the door, those in the crowd who had lingered clapped and whistled. He bowed slightly and walked down the steps toward them. As soon as Carlita stepped out, everyone became completely quiet and started moving back.

Jesús looked at the crowd one last time. He shrugged, sighed dramatically, dropped to his knees and crawled under the house. The foundation was nearly three feet off the ground, held up by hefty brick supports spaced evenly every eight feet all the way to the back of the structure.

Raul Cano, who lived two houses to the west, was seated on an orange crate near the back of the crowd. He stood up and said loudly enough for all to hear, "This is better than going to the fights at Naud Junction. I look forward to this every week."

Still aware of Carlita's presence, few laughed out loud, but everyone around Raul nodded in agreement.

As Jesús finally disappeared from view, every few feet he would shout, "Spiders! Nails! Glass! Ouch!"—much to the approval of the crowd. Carlita just rolled her eyes, raised her broom, and looked to the heavens.

Soon, however, all was silent. Carlita knelt beside the steps and shouted to her husband, "Jesús, everything is all right?"

No reply came. Instead, almost two minutes later, Jesús crawled slowly forward until just the top of his head could be seen. The crowd moved closer so that all were now standing just behind Carlita.

"I am coming out," Jesús finally said.

As he stood up, he was holding both hands stiffly behind his back, hiding them from view.

"What is it? What is the matter?" Carlita asked, stepping toward him.

"Yes, tell us. The suspense is killing us, too," Raul shouted from his orange crate.

Everyone laughed again and moved in closer.

Jesús slowly and deliberately drew his left arm around and raised it high above his head. In his hand he held a large clump of straw, which he immediately flung at those in the crowd closest to him. Instantly covered, they all flinched, groaned, and stepped back. However, it was what was in his right hand that caused loud gasps to ripple all the way back to the road. As he slowly and dramatically raised his right arm, all could see he was clutching a light gray and terribly bloated dead rat.

A woman near the front shrieked loudly, and others recoiled in horror. Most of the men laughed and applauded. That is, they did so until Jesús grabbed the rodent firmly by the tail and started swinging it wildly round and round his head. All immediately scattered, many dropping purses and hats as they scrambled back to the road. Jesús stopped when he stepped on a shoe that had been left behind in the flight.

"Found it!" Jesús finally called out, proudly. He looked over at Carlita, then back at the crowd, smiling to himself. "Still say her brothers caused this somehow. Poor creature was probably drawn to their smell, probably thought they were relatives. And the oddest thing—a box full of straw right under their room, like they made a bed for him."

A few smiled, but at this point no one laughed. The light morning breeze carried the pungent odor directly into the crowd, causing many to gag and pinch their noses. A few swore loudly, "*Santo infiereno—sálvanos!*"

Carlita rushed toward her husband and shouted, "Enough! They all see who is the foul one here now, Jesús. It is not always required you be crude. Get rid of that . . . that *thing*. Take it to the back. Burn it—now!"

She playfully swatted at him with her broom. There was one more outburst of laughter before the others headed toward their own homes. One woman called back, "Carlita, go ahead. Hit him. My nose is dying!"

Carlita pointed the broom toward Jesús and said, "See. What must everyone think of us now? Because of you, we will be known as 'rat family.'"

Jesús laughed and swung the rat overhead one more time.

"It is not funny," she said, her voice now quivering.

Jesús immediately threw the rat into an empty oil barrel next to the porch, drew her firmly to him, hugged her, and said, "I am sorry, my wife. Sometimes I become loud, but I mean nothing by it. After all these years, you must know this. You do, don't you?"

A tear slid down her cheek. She playfully asked, "Do you still love me, even though I am from Hermosillo and am smelly and slow?"

He laughed again and drew her even closer. "It will always be so. And of me, do you still love me—even though I too often reek of rotten avocadoes?"

"I do, my husband. And I always will."

Jesús leaned down to kiss her, but she quickly backed away. "The rat!" she shouted. "First get rid of the rat. Then, maybe if you are lucky, you will have your kiss."

Jesús knew it was time for her to have the last word. He walked to the oil drum, picked up the rat, and walked to the back of the house.

....

CHAPTER 3

Summons

October 28

1:07 P.M.

"Whoa—slow down, Father," I said, moving the phone tighter to my ear. "You're talking so fast I'm getting only every other word. What's this all about?"

Father Medardo Brualla, one of my oldest and dearest friends in Los Angeles, was not prone to emotional outbursts. By the tone and speed of his voice, I knew whatever he was calling about must be terribly serious.

I could hear his rapid breathing as he paused to collect his thoughts. "Matthew, I . . . we need your help. Can you please meet me now? A family in my parish, they're . . ."

His voice trailed off, and for a moment I thought the line had gone dead.

"Hello? Father? You still there?" I heard him say very quietly, as if trying to console someone near him, "*El medico es mi amigo. Por favor, no se preocupe.*"

"Father, what about the family? Is someone ill? If that's the case, I can send a doctor immediately."

"No, Matthew, I don't want another doctor. I want . . . I need *you*. Please, can you come?"

I glanced at my watch. It was just past noon. Rounds with my interns would start in just over an hour, but I doubted the walls of Los Angeles County General Hospital would come crashing down if I missed an afternoon with them. Most of them seemed like they couldn't tell the difference between a boil and a blister. I could give someone else the pleasure of their company and ignorance for an afternoon—a thought that made me smile.

"Of course. I'll be right there, Father. Where would you like to meet?"

In almost a whisper he replied, "Bless you. I'm at the church now. I'll wait here for you, and then I'll take you to the family. I don't think you'd be able to find their home otherwise. Please hurry."

"I will. I'll get my bag and be on my way."

As I hung up the phone, I realized Father Brualla was as important as any instrument I had in my medical bag because he spoke Spanish and I did not. Many of the families in his parish had come from Mexico seeking jobs in the produce fields or on the docks at the Port of Los Angeles. Most of them spoke English about as well as I spoke Spanish, which made the good Father essential to my excursions into their community.

However, more often than not, he didn't give me the best translation of the symptoms the patients shared with him. Over time I finally understood why. As their priest, he administered to their souls above all. While doing so, he stressed the positive, quite overtly and dramatically at times, comforting patients in ways I couldn't begin to approach with my medical knowledge. At the same time, he believed the power of prayer could trump anything I could pull out of my bag, so he didn't always provide the minute details of a case that could influence my diagnosis.

Through the years, we often had friendly, and lengthy, debates about which of us was more important to the community. In the end, we usually ended up agreeing we both had our limitations, but the lives of the people were much better for tolerating us both. Our friendship was forged even tighter when we concluded that when both of us appeared together— one who had the skill to tend to the sick and the other with the power to deliver the Last Rites—we were the last people on earth those who were ill wanted to see standing over their beds. Arriving individually, each of us was welcomed with open arms by the people of his parish, but when arriving together, we represented something akin to an open grave.

For these reasons, I had learned a long time ago my diagnoses and treatments were much more accurate when I took along someone else who could translate for me, someone who could stick to the pure medical aspects of each case. As soon as I finished checking my bag, I picked up the phone, tapped the switch hook several times, and asked the hospital operator to connect me with the nurses' station.

Our nursing supervisor, who everyone joked came with the building—and I couldn't swear she didn't—answered, "Station One."

"Nurse Adams, this is Dr. Thompson. I can't recall her name, but I need that Spanish-speaking nurse to make a house call again with me. Is she around today?"

Never one to mince words, Nurse Adams immediately shot back, "Doctor, don't you ever pay attention to anything around here? Nurse Soto has been gone for over six months. Married that rich appendectomy case we had last spring. You know, the gentleman who owns all those avocado farms just the other side of the county line."

She paused for a minute. "You don't have a clue what I'm talking about, do you?"

"Sorry, I don't. All I know is I need a nurse whose Spanish is good, and I need her right now. I mean *right* now. Got anyone for me?"

She laughed. "Oh, I have one all right, but I'm not sure I should do this to you. Ever heard of Nurse McDonnell?"

"Can't say as I have. What's wrong with her?"

At that point, Nurse Adams started laughing so loudly I had to move the ear phone away from my ear.

"She's the most know-it-all, contrary, rule-breaking, short-tempered nurse I've ever known, and I bet I've worked with nearly a thousand through the years. Nobody'll work with her, and I don't blame them one bit. You know we rotate our nurses through every part of this hospital. Well, she's already been rotated through every station *twice* because the doctors keep moving her right along. A regular hot potato."

"If she's that bad, then why don't you just fire her and be done with it?"

"Can't. Her father is Dr. Seamus McDonnell, as in *the* Dr. McDonnell who practically runs Massachusetts General Hospital. He's also the one who designed the new retractor being used in abdominal surgeries and several other instruments as well. And if that weren't enough, he was a classmate of not one but *two* members of our hospital's Board of Directors. No, Nurse McDonnell would have to burn this place to the ground before we could shove her out the door, and I'm not completely sure we could do it even then."

"Maggie, in all the years I've known you, I've never heard you give a glowing rebuke like that to anyone, not even for that knothead ambulance driver we had last summer. Is there any good to her at all?"

"That's the problem. She's also one of the most skilled and knowledgeable nurses I've ever worked with. I've heard through the grapevine she followed Papa around like a puppy since she was old enough to hold a stethoscope. It rubbed off on her. She knows more about medicine than any of the new residents we got this year. And one more thing. One minute she's a witch on wheels and has people fuming, and the next she steps in and helps everyone from orderlies to the interns keep from making huge mistakes that might cost lives and their positions. And won't take a bit of thanks for it.

"Someone ought to whack her with a stick every morning—knock some sense into her. One minute I admire her, the next I can't stand to be around her. Her biggest problem is she just can't keep her trap shut, so *nobody* wants to work with her. Believe me, if you want to take her out of here, you'll be the new hero to everyone in this wing."

I looked at my watch again. "Well, thank you for being honest with me, but I wish you'd have sugar coated at least some of this. I don't have any choice. Go ahead and track down Miss Wonderful and tell her I'll meet her at your station in five minutes—and tell her not to be late."

"I can't do that."

"Why not? She can't be *that* difficult."

"In case you haven't noticed, intercom's out this morning. Maintenance is still working on it. She's down in the nursery today. Probably making all the newborns scream and cry. I'm busy, so if you want her, you'll have to get down there yourself."

Before I could remind her that was her job, I heard a loud click and the line went dead. That wasn't the first time, and likely wouldn't be the last, that Nurse Adams would have the last word with me. I grabbed my bag, coat, and hat, and headed down the east steps to the nursery.

As I entered the room, three nurses were standing together next to a row of newborns. It took just a few seconds for me to pick out Nurse McDonnell. She was standing in the middle, roughly pushing the others to the side as she swung around to face them. Her expression was one of complete disgust.

"Just where did you go to nursing school?" she admonished the others loudly enough to be heard over the shrill cries of the babies. "Study with some quack? You do *not* give them bottles when their heads are tilted down. Not unless you want to drown them!"

Just then she spotted me, put her hands on her hips, and said, sternly, "Hey, Bub. Can't you read? No fathers in here. You're a bag of germs. Get out before I have you thrown out."

Before I could respond, the shorter of the other two nurses stepped forward, and said, "Dr. Thompson. Good to see you. What brings you down here?"

She looked at Nurse McDonnell before continuing, "Anything I can do for you?"

Her expression and the way she asked the questions almost made it seem like she was pleading with me.

"Thank you, but not today. I need a word with Nurse McDonnell." I pointed toward the door. "McDonnell, please come with me."

Once we were in the hallway she asked, "Am I in trouble again?"

"Probably, but not with me. I need you to come with me to a house call. I need one of your skills. Go grab a first aid kit and meet me at the main ambulance entrance as quickly as you can."

She didn't move. She just stood there, staring at me. Finally, she asked, squinting her eyes as she shook her head, "It's my Spanish, right? *¿Usted no habla Español?* That's the skill you need?"

"Look," I said, "you don't object to going to help some people who are ill, do you? Last I checked, that's our job. If you do object, say so now and I'll find someone else." I pointed to the window of the nursery. "Time's wasting. It's them—or me."

The door was closed, but muffled cries could still be heard. "But I'm supposed to be stationed here all day."

"I've already cleared it with Nurse Adams. Are you coming?"

With one last glance at the nurses rocking the babies, she said, "In that case, I'll go. I'll get my bag and meet you downstairs."

Before I could say anything else, she turned and walked quickly down the hall.

"Short straw," I muttered to myself. "Looks like I drew it today."

....

CHAPTER 4

The Ride

October 28
2:03 P.M.

I had been standing outside the emergency entrance for nearly five minutes and still no Miss Wonderful.

I was just about to go back inside to look for her when Ed Armbruster, our most senior ambulance driver, motioned for me to move away from the back of the vehicle. "Dr. Thompson, if you'll just stand over here a minute, I'm going to spread some blankets on those wooden benches in the back. If I don't, there'll be a splinter with every bounce on the road."

Rubbing my behind, I said, "Thanks, Ed. We really appreciate it."

He smiled broadly and climbed in the back of the ambulance.

"What exactly is this thing?" I asked, walking over and placing my hand on the enormous fender at the rear.

"Just got it. Supposed to be some kind of experiment, I think. It's an old military truck. They took the bed off and replaced it with what looks like half the emergency room. Got all kinds of medical supplies in back, even oxygen tanks and a portable operating table. Can you imagine that? The only real problem I can tell so far is this thing weighs a ton and doesn't like to take corners too fast. I hear tell one over at City Hospital rolled on its side last week. Driver broke his arm. Wouldn't doubt it. Thing drives like a damn tank. So, don't be mad at me if it takes us forever to get where we're going." He stepped back out and sighed, "Doc, I swear I'll get us there quick as I can."

"You always do. We're headed to Our Lady Queen of Angels on

North Main Street in the Macy Street area. I hope my nurse gets out here soon. We've got to get going."

At that moment, Nurse McDonnell rushed out the door and towards us. I wasn't happy she took so long, but I did my best to hide it in my voice. "Nurse McDonnell, we're lucky today. This is Ed Armbruster, the best ambulance driver we've got. He's going to—"

Ed removed his hat and bowed slightly, but Nurse McDonnell didn't acknowledge him. She walked right by, without saying a word to either of us, and climbed into the back of the ambulance.

"I think she's new," I said, trying to cover for her rudeness. "Probably shy, too."

Ed glared at me, shook his head, and said, "I know her. Want to ride up front with me today?"

Caught in my fibs, I smiled weakly. "No. Thanks anyway. I think I better jump in back and go over with her how these house calls are handled."

"I wish you luck with that," he said, still shaking his head. "But I'll keep my offer open just in case."

I climbed in and moved to the front of the bench so I could talk to Ed through the open window there in case the need came up. Just as I started to sit down, the ambulance lunged forward, flopping me back right onto Nurse McDonnell's lap. She grabbed me tightly and kept me from rolling all the way to the floor.

"Thanks," I said, righting myself. "Ed's right. This thing does drive like a tank."

"Think nothing of it," she replied, avoiding my eyes. "Just didn't want you hurt—didn't want to go back to the nursery so soon."

My mouth dropped open, but before I could say anything, she smiled and said, "Just foolin'. Glad you're okay."

When I was finally seated, I smiled back and said, "I'm in your debt."

"No, you're not. You got me away from those screaming babies. How about we call it even for now?"

"That sounds like a deal to me, but I'd gladly go into your debt again if you'd help me retrieve the contents of my bag."

During the initial commotion, my medical bag opened when I fell, and now nearly everything I had inside was rolling back and forth across the floor. I half expected her to scold me for being so clumsy, but she didn't. Instead, neither of us spoke as we did our best to stay upright while chasing bottles and instruments, which kept changing direction with each hard bounce in the road. At one point, our heads tapped together slightly. I apologized. She didn't.

When we had finished gathering the last of the items, we each sat back down. However, this time I moved to the bench running along the other side so we were facing each other. Nurse McDonnell turned her attention to her own bag, one very much like mine. Just as she started checking and rearranging its contents, she very matter of factly said, "I didn't recognize you in the nursery, but I know all about you, Dr. Thompson."

"You do?" I responded, leaning forward. "I'm sure we've never met before, so what possibly could you know?"

"If you really want to know, I'll tell you. Still, you might not like everything I'd have to say."

"You're teasing me now," I said, leaning back again against the side of the ambulance. "If you've got something to say, if you think you really know me, then let's hear it. This should be amusing."

"You asked for it," she said, snapping her bag shut. "Here goes. I hear you are the best diagnostician in this hospital. Many say the most skilled in Los Angeles."

"Thank you. You flatter me."

"No, I don't," she continued. "Just stating the facts as I've heard them. However, it's a good thing because . . . " Here she paused before adding, her voice rising, "Look, I'm not going to be at the hospital very long, so I can tell you this. Someone *should* tell you this, so I'm going to do it. It's a good thing you're such a fine doctor because I heard you have as much bedside manner as a tree stump."

"Oh, really," I said, crossing my arms. She looked at me closely, as if waiting for me to rail at her for making such a blunt comment. Instead, I shocked her. I laughed and said, "That's nothing new. I've known that for a long time. Just not my long suit. Is that all you've got, or do you have any other juicy morsels to share?"

She studied me closely, smiling broadly. She genuinely did look like at least some of the frankness had been taken out of her sails. This time she sat back before continuing. "I've got more. You sure you're ready?"

I nodded.

"Remember, you asked for it. You're a good-looking fellow. I'll give you that. What—about six feet tall? I'm five and eight and you go some over me, so maybe six and two? Not a bad face either, except for that pitiful moustache. It's too thin. Let it sprout out some. I'd also say about forty, give or take a year or two. You're too good for being so young, and some of the older doctors still try to beat you down when they get the chance. Right? You know you're good at what you do, but you don't flaunt it. I respect that. My father is the same way. And you've never been married, but that's the biggest problem of all with you. Why? Because you're already married to the job. You don't have time for people who aren't sick, and that's eventually going to haunt you."

She bowed slightly toward me and asked, "Close to home, was I?"

I hated to admit it, but she was right more than she was wrong. My work at the hospital *was* my world. It wasn't even halfway through my residency at St. Louis City Hospital when I knew I was blessed with diagnostic ability others around me didn't have. I also knew it wasn't because of innate smarts on my part. Half of it was mostly because I could still see in my mind whole pages of medical books long after reading them. While others rushed to their medical libraries to help with a diagnosis, I knew what they were looking for before they left the room.

The other half came from my father, a veterinarian, who taught me that it was always wisest to have "patience with patients," whether they be animals or people. That was his not-so-subtle way of telling me that the best medical people took the extra moment to think before acting, to act upon a combination of careful observation and the best available knowledge. I always took that extra moment right from the beginning of my residency, and in doing so, I also built the reputation of someone who had the communication skills of, well, a tree stump. I didn't mind, though. If I appeared to be distant while observing and taking the extra moment, I always felt that was a small price to pay for being successful with all those I'd been able to help.

I grinned and said, "Anything else you'd like to add—or is that it?"

"That's it for now. I'll hold back judgement on some things until I see them first-hand."

"Fine. Now it's my turn. Can you take the criticism as well as you can give it?"

"Fire away. Don't hold anything back. Let's see just how good of a diagnostician you truly are."

I tilted back my hat, sighed for effect, and leaned forward once again. "I didn't know you from Eve earlier, but I think I can place you pretty well already. Here's what I think to be likely. You are just about thirty. Maybe a year or two more. You're too old to be acting like such an irritant around the hospital, yet you still do. And, you're a very attractive young woman, but you don't like that fact much. Not much at all."

"What do you mean?" she interrupted.

"You don't get to say anything yet. Remember, it's my turn."

"Go ahead," she said, softly, appearing not to be so sure "my turn" was going to be such a good idea.

"You're tall, and I can imagine that didn't play too well with boys when you were growing up. At the same time, your features—your eyes, nose, mouth—make you quite pretty when you aren't making a face or saying something to get someone's goat. Oh, you could shoot Cupid's arrows at men if you wanted to and they'd gladly be struck, but you hold back because of your complexion."

"Now wait just a minute," she said, her tone approaching anger. "I don't think—"

I cut her off as quickly as I could and mimicked her earlier speech. "You're not going to be at the hospital much longer, so someone *should* tell you before you leave—and I think I'll do it. So you just sit back and listen."

Before she could say anything, I, again mimicking her, raised my voice and said, "Your complexion is too dark, even for someone living near the ocean here in California. I'd say one of your parents, probably your mother, was from another land. Probably Latin. You're not ashamed of this in the least, but you perceive people look at you differently because of it. And you strike out at people because of it. I'd say you always have."

She started to speak, but I waved her off and continued, "But it isn't your looks that completely define your behavior. No, you can be, how should I say this, *difficult* at times because of your medical knowledge. You know more than most other nurses, and your skills are probably close to those of many doctors, right? And this bothers you tremendously because you could be helping people a whale of a lot more than you are allowed to right now. That makes you angry and bitter, and you haven't yet figured out how to control that."

She was tapping her left foot on the floor and looked like she was about to move to the attack, but I wasn't going to let her. "Look, I have no doubt you have plenty to say about my diagnosis, but we're *not* going to talk about it now—and I want that understood. We've had our introductions, albeit more direct ones than I'm used to, but it's time to go to work. If you want to give a counterpoint later on, fine. I'll listen then. But not now. And I don't care if you sit there and fume the rest of the way as long as you pay attention to what I'm going to say now. Do I make myself clear, Nurse McDonnell?"

Much to my surprise, all she said was, "Yes, Doctor," before looking toward the rear of the ambulance. For an instant I thought her eyes might have been wet, or it could have just been rage building up. Either way, I thought it best not to mention it.

As we approached the spot where the Southern Pacific Railroad tracks intersected Macy Street, Ed slowed us to a stop, turned his head, and spoke to us through the window. "Doc, train's going by up ahead. Looks like a long one, so better settle yourself in. Sorry about this. Nothing we can do now but wait."

"Fine—thank you. You're doing your best. Don't worry about it."

I actually didn't mind the delay. I knew I needed some time to let Nurse McDonnell know what I wanted her to do once we arrived.

"When we finally get there, we're stopping first at Our Lady Queen of Angels Church to talk to Father Brualla. He's a dear, dear friend. He's also very direct. Not as much as some," I said, looking directly at her, "but close—so don't go jumping down his throat if something comes up you don't agree with. Father's completely devoted to his parishioners in the Macy Street area and would do anything to help them—and I mean *anything*. Most in his flock shouldn't be in this country. They've come up to work in the produce fields and at the harbor because life was falling apart around them in Mexico. Father Brualla knows the right people, especially those who own the farms, so getting jobs isn't a problem.

"His biggest challenge is keeping everyone away from the immigration officials. I don't know how he's done it, and I really don't want to know the details in case I'm ever questioned, but he's figured out a way to rotate people from job to job so that the same person doesn't stay in one position long enough to attach suspicion. One week a man will be working tomatoes—the next week he'll be unloading cargo from a ship. There's some kind of 'new arrival' document that gives a person several weeks to get the rest of the proper paperwork in order, and somehow, he has a whole stack of them. I mention this only because I want you to know what is in his heart—and how serious this must be if he has sent for me."

Nurse McDonnell, who had finally faced me again and appeared to be listening intently, interrupted me. "Explain that, please. What makes you think this is so serious?"

"Because I'm what's called a 'necessary evil,' and our patients are going to look at you the same way. They need us to keep them healthy, but nobody in this area completely trusts us. They know we could turn them in to the authorities if we had a mind to, and if we did that, they'd be sent packing and their dreams would go up in a puff of smoke. They're going to watch you today like a hawk."

Here I smiled. "There's something else you should be prepared for. These are very proud people. Most don't have the money to pay for the care, but they insist upon what I suppose we'd call 'in-kind' compensation. That is, I've taken back with me chickens, canned preserves, and a lamp that I'm pretty sure followed someone home from the docks. So, if you are offered something today, take it. It's important to them. If you don't, they'll feel disgrace."

Neither of us said anything for a couple of minutes as our drive resumed, and we bounced up and down and side to side with every bump in the road. Her silence surprised me. She had been listening, expressionless, but I could tell she had taken in everything. Finally, after one particularly nasty bump that had us both standing for an instant, she asked, "Do you have any idea why we've been summoned? Someone in your position doesn't typically make calls like this. I get that this priest is your friend, but even so, this makes no sense to me. Why *you*?"

"That's a fair question," I replied. "The short answer is you were pretty close in some parts of your diagnosis. I *don't* make friends easily, so I treasure the ones I have. I met Father Brualla about ten years ago when I took out his appendix, which was close to rupture. Know how he paid me? He put me to work. He wanted first-aid stations at a few of the large produce farms in the area. If anybody got hurt, the rule of thumb was 'rub some dirt on it, and you'll be fine—if you don't die.' So he had me talk to the owners. They said as long as I came up with the supplies, they wouldn't have any objections. Care to guess who ended up paying for those supplies? When we had the last of the stations up and running, I said to him, 'Some way to repay me for the surgery.' I'll never forget what he said to me: 'You are being compensated the best way I know how—and payment will continue as long as we are friends.'"

I shook my head. "At first I was confused, but eventually I understood. I *did* need to get out of the hospital more and see the world past my nose. So, ever since, I get a call and more payment from him about once a month or so. I haven't been able to go myself as often as I'd like the past year, but I always make sure someone gets there to help out. And, well, that's why you and I are dodging splinters on these seats right now."

Nurse McDonnell studied me a few seconds before asking, "If you've been sending others, what makes this time so special? Why today?"

"The tone of his voice. I haven't a clue what we're getting into. Could be a gunshot or knife wound. Those'll happen a couple times a year. Could be someone dodging the law was hurt badly while working. Could be just about anything, but I know he wouldn't have been so insistent that I come unless he felt it was very important."

Looking out the front window, I could see the grove of palms I knew were just down the street from the church. "Just one more thing. We're *not* the police. We treat—and then we move on. If something needs to be reported, Father Brualla will do that. Here in Los Angeles, doctors typically have to report within twenty-four hours any treatments that may have been related to serious crimes, but the police look the other way for me because they know Father Brualla will do it. He didn't like it at first, but I insisted he take that responsibility, so I could distance myself at

least a little from the regular authorities. Just another *quid pro quo* I felt
necessary, and it *has* made a difference."

"You're still taking an awful risk. In your shoes, I'd just report everything—and right away."

"Right," I said, smiling again. "A rule follower like you would *never*
break the law, right?"

I saw just a hint of a smile back before she quipped, "Rules are rules.
I hear that from everyone all the time."

We looked at each other and laughed. That is, we did until Ed swerved
hard to the left, mashed the brakes, and skidded to a stop. Through the
front window I saw the entrance to the church. Standing, I said, "Stay
close, and please . . ."

I let my voice trail off and didn't finish my plea on purpose. She
looked at me, smiled once again, and shook her head slowly. As I helped
her to the street, she turned and said, "I'm just the short straw. What
could I possibly do?"

I had the feeling I'd soon find out.

....

CHAPTER 5

Fever Dreams

October 28

2:44 P.M.

No sooner had we stepped out of the ambulance when Father Brualla rushed down the steps of the church to meet us.

"*Gracias, mi querido amigo*," he said, out of breath while reaching to shake my hand. "Matthew, we must talk privately. Please come with me."

Before I could return the greeting, he grabbed my arm and started pulling me toward the rectory. An instant later he stopped short when he spotted Nurse McDonnell. "Where is Nurse Soto? Who is this?"

"Father, Nurse Soto married away. I'd like to introduce you to Nurse McDonnell. She'll be a good help to us. We can trust her, so I want her to hear whatever you have to say."

He walked toward her, took her hand in his, and said, "I am Father Brualla of *Nuestra Señora, Reina de los Ángeles*. Trust is earned, but time may be short here. You are Catholic, yes? That is enough for me now."

Nurse McDonnell jerked her hand away, stepped back, and blew out a breath before responding, loudly, "Oh, I see. Brown girl must be Catholic, right? You should—"

Father Brualla cut her off and said, "I only meant . . . *McDonnell*, that is Irish, yes? I've known very few of that country who weren't of my church. And you *are* Catholic, yes?"

She just stood there staring at him, clearly upset but also looking as if she didn't quite know how to respond. I turned slightly to my right so she couldn't see my smile. Father Brualla continued, "And I will venture one more guess. By the quickness of your response, I would say your teachers were Jesuit? They are definitely the most direct in their speech, and the pupils end up the same."

"Are you finished now?" she said, the irritation clear in her voice. She stepped toward him. "I'm here to help. And one more thing for *you*. Jesuits don't make immediate judgments about people. They know better. They're smarter than many *other* orders."

Unfortunately, she saw me smiling. "So, you think this is funny, do you? Everyone around here thinks he's a diagnostician. This is just great."

"Come on, you two," I gently scolded both of them. "Enough of that."

I headed for the rectory. They followed close behind, silent at last.

....

As soon as we were in the rectory, Father Brualla motioned for us to sit in the chairs in front of his desk. He sat down, placed his palms firmly on the desk, leaned forward, and began.

"I pray I am wrong, but I do not think so. I think . . ."

His voice trailed off as he picked up his rosary and drew it to his chest. It had been many years since I had seen him so full of emotion.

"Please, Father, tell us what this is about. I will do all I can to help— no matter what it is."

He remained silent for a few more moments before finally speaking. "Half a dozen years ago, you and I helped care for those with the influenza. I fear it is back. That is why I did not say more when I called. I believe two of my parishioners have this awful illness, and I do not want it to hurt others. I'm afraid—"

Nurse McDonnell interrupted him, irritation clearly forming in her words. "But you are not a doctor. You can't possibly know what afflicts these people. It could be dozens of illnesses that appear similar. I'm surprised at you, Father. You should know better than to jump to a conclusion like this."

Father Brualla didn't reply. Instead, he looked at me as if asking for support, so I spoke up. "Nurse McDonnell, during the Great Influenza

Outbreak of 1918 millions of people died, as we all know. Here, most of Los Angeles was hit very hard by the illness, but in this neighborhood, because they are so isolated, only four became ill. Father Brualla and I cared for them as best we could, but they were already too far gone when we found out about them. All four died. So, you see, if he says he even has the slightest of suspicions, I know I need to look into it as well."

Father Brualla kept staring at his rosary as he spoke, his voice now very calm, "Dr. Compton was here yesterday. He said the father has a . . . venereal disease, and the daughter has a bad cold. He gave the father an injection and the daughter a vial of some type of grease to rub on her chest. He said they would soon be better. I do not think that will be the case."

Nurse McDonnell leaned forward and said, "You mean another doctor has already been here? Then why are you wasting our time? This is ridiculous. These people are . . . He probably does have—"

His demeanor changing quickly, Father Brualla interrupted her and shot back, "These are your people. You should care more what happens to them."

"These are not *my* people. My mother was from Madrid, a world away from here. I'm not like . . . *them*."

"Now who is it who is so quick to judge?" he said sternly. "We are all God's children. *All* of us."

"I believe that, too," she said. "We don't disagree. I'm just not one of *these* children, so you can stop trying to shove guilt to me."

"One can only feel guilty if—"

I had had enough and stopped them both. "Look, this ends now. I don't want to hear this. If you two want to chew at each other some more, fine. But stay here and do it. I'm going to try to help some people."

"And one more thing," I said turning to face Nurse McDonnell. "This *Dr.* Compton is known as the 'undertaker's friend.' He was drummed from the profession years ago and now preys upon those who are frightened and suspicious of the authorities. Now, we should be going. "

"You are right, Matthew," Father Brualla said. "We should be going."

"And I," she said, "I'll come along. It's my *duty*. I'll help."

I could tell both weren't happy with what they had said to each other, but neither apologized, which really didn't surprise me. I was just grateful we could at last put our attention to the matter at hand.

"Before we go, what can you tell me about them?" I asked Father Brualla. "Please tell me all you can."

"It is Jesús Lajun and his daughter, Francisca. The Lajuns are a *good* family."

It was clear his last comment was made specifically for Nurse McDonnell. Before she could say anything, I said, "Please . . . go on."

"Jesús works for the Southern Pacific Railroad, taking care of the tracks, when there is work. At present he is working in the produce fields. He works very hard and provides for his family. They eat well, they come to Mass, they are proud. Francisca has just become a woman. She has been in the fields with her father and mother. She is kind and gentle."

"When did they become ill? Do you know?" I asked.

"I do not. I was called to their home only yesterday when they sent for Dr. Compton." He paused. "But . . . they did miss Mass last week. They could have been ill that long."

"Thank you. The ambulance is outside. If you'll guide the driver, let's get to their home."

"After you, Father," Nurse McDonnell motioned toward him. "Please, you first."

I had the feeling that was as close to an apology I would hear this day.

....

When we arrived at the Lajuns' home, I instructed Ed to stay at the ambulance and told him I would call for him if he were needed. Father Brualla led us up the front steps and knocked solidly on the door. When Mrs. Lajun appeared, she welcomed us warmly and urged us inside.

As soon as Father Brualla had taken care of the introductions, I said, "Mrs. Lajun, I'd like to see your husband and daughter now."

Obviously distraught, Mrs. Lajun clutched my hand and spoke in careful English, so I would not miss her meaning. "Please help them. I have never seen them so, so . . . *enfermos*. So sick."

"We will do what we can," I promised.

We went down a short hallway to a small bedroom at the back of the house where Mr. Lajun and his daughter were sleeping in beds on opposite sides of the room. No sooner had we entered when Nurse McDonnell pushed out her arm and held me back, which caught me off guard.

"Doctor, it's time for your gloves," she said, calmly, matter-of-factly.

She opened her bag and withdrew examination gloves. While handing me a pair, she leaned closer and whispered, "Some blood on the sheet where it's folded next to his mouth. Better put these on."

I hadn't noticed the blood yet, so I was grateful for her diligence. I nodded my thanks. Father Brualla waved off the gloves offered to him and stepped closer to the bed, finally kneeling next to Mr. Lajun. Mr. Lajun was a large man with deep, irregular wrinkles on his forehead, no doubt the result of many years working under the sun. His arms, folded at his chest, appeared quite muscular and powerful.

I bent down on the other side of the bed and began my examination. I first noticed his forehead, face, and neck were drenched with sweat. His breathing was rapid but shallow. Lifting his wrist and checking his pulse, I found it to be very fast.

"Nurse, please, my stethoscope," I said without looking up. Nurse McDonnell placed it in my left hand. Using the stethoscope and listening carefully confirmed for me the heartbeat was regular but, indeed, quite rapid. I next checked his eyes and was surprised to find the pupils cloudy. I also examined the lymph nodes and found those in his groin significantly enlarged, the symptom which I imagined led Dr. Compton to his venereal disease diagnosis. Finally, I gently opened his mouth and placed a thermometer under his tongue. At point of register, his temperature was one hundred three and a half degrees.

"I hate to wake him," I said, "but I need to know what he alone can tell me."

I shook his arms gently and patted his chest until he finally opened his eyes. Father Brualla moved closer to him and said, "*Jesús, por favor, es el Padre Brualla. Debe despetarse ahora.*"

After a few moments, he slowly opened his eyes then blinked rapidly. The sight of so many people standing over him must have frightened him because he suddenly tried to roll over the side of the bed. Father Brualla stopped him and gently pushed him back toward me.

"We are here to help you," I began, trying to keep my voice as calm as I could. "Mr. Lajun, I must ask you some questions. I need you to tell me how you are feeling and if anything hurts."

When he didn't respond, Nurse McDonnell stepped forward and said to him, "*Por favor, conteste estas preguntas para mí.*"

Turning to me, she said, "I'll gather the symptoms. I know what to ask."

Continuing in Spanish, she asked question after question, pausing occasionally to jot notes on a small tablet she held in her hand. When she finished, I could tell she thanked him and asked him to try to get back to sleep.

"I have what you need," she said, finishing her notes. "Now the daughter."

She motioned for Father Brualla to join her as she knelt next to Francisca's bed, gently woke her, and began asking questions. Francisca didn't appear nearly as ill as her father, but she was obviously feverish and had a very bad dry cough. I noticed she was nearly as tall as her father but thin as a rail. Her features, especially her nose and mouth, were also delicate, in stark contrast to those of her father's heavily weathered face. She had long, curly chestnut hair that clustered around her neck so that

Nurse McDonnell had to brush it aside as she checked the lymph nodes.

When Nurse McDonnell finished, she stood up and motioned me forward so I could examine Francisca. Her lymph nodes weren't swollen, but other than that, the symptoms were identical to her father's. Discovering that, I needed to know what Nurse McDonnell had learned, but I did not want to speak in front of the others.

"Father," I said, "I need to get some medicine from the ambulance. Would you please remain with them as I do so?"

He nodded, sat lightly on Francisca's bed, and started praying, softly.

"I'd like you to come with me, Nurse McDonnell. I'll need your assistance."

Before leaving the room I removed my gloves, took Mrs. Lajun's hand, and said, "Please try not to worry. We will do all we can for your husband and daughter."

Once we were back to the ambulance, I turned to Nurse McDonnell. "What did they say? Leave nothing out, no matter how small you think the detail might be."

"I'm *thorough*," she stated, emphatically. "I never leave anything out. First, Mr. Lajun. Mild symptoms started nearly a week ago and quickly accelerated. Extreme pain in the joints when moving both the arms and legs. Muscle ache in shoulders and calves. Headache for the past two days. Throat feels raw. Some vomiting. I was unable to determine by his description whether the blood came from his nose or up from his chest by coughing. Mild dizziness when standing. Urination infrequent. That is all the information he could provide."

"Excellent report," I said. "Conclusions? Diagnosis?"

Her expression bordering on disbelief, she responded, "You're asking *me*? Are you making fun of me, or are you really interested?"

"Interested. Talk to me."

"The Spanish Influenza," she said without hesitation. "I think Father Brualla is right. I helped treat about a hundred patients back in Eighteen, and this is what I saw then. I've expected it to return. I'd say this is it."

"I was hoping you would say that because that was my first inclination. Could be . . . but I don't think so," I said, shaking my head.

"But the symptoms," she said, "are too close to the same. The fever, the pain, especially the blood."

"But there are differences here," I said, pointing to the house. "First, the heart rate was too rapid, ninety-two for the father, eighty for the daughter. Also, the respiration was too high. None were present in the daughter, but he had enlarged lymph nodes, also not common with influenza. Finally, I know the light wasn't the best in there, but did you notice the bluish tinge to the skin of their face and shoulders? I never saw that in Spanish Influenza. Not once."

"Then what do you suspect?" she asked, finally removing her gloves and folding her arms. "Your diagnosis, Doctor?"

I smiled and replied, "Not until I have more information. However, I do have a theory."

"You won't share this theory?" she asked, clearly annoyed.

"No. But, we need to get them out of here—to the hospital. I want to put them in isolation while we run some tests—blood, saliva, urine, and more. If my suspicions are correct, we better do this at once.

"You were good in there, Nurse McDonnell. If you've no objections, I'd like to keep you with me for this. I believe you may be able to help me a great deal, and not just with the language. I also have the feeling Nurse Adams won't object. If I can arrange it, are you willing?"

"I am," she said, "but for my own reasons. I still think I'm right, and I want to be there to say 'I told you so' when you discover that."

"I pray you get to tell me that," I said.

Looking back at the house one more time, then knocking loudly on the side of the ambulance, I said, "Ed, let's get to work. Let's get these people out of here."

....

CHAPTER 6

Isolation

October 28
4:21 P.M.

Before Ed stopped the ambulance at the Emergency entrance, I asked him to continue forward to a parking area about fifty feet ahead.

"But we can roll them in right here," he said, confused.

"Not yet. You and Nurse McDonnell will need to keep them in here until I can make some arrangements inside. And one more thing. Ed, I have a favor to ask. I'm going to put them in isolation. Can I rely on you not to say anything—to anyone?"

"Sure, Doc. You can count on me," he said, as he pulled forward and parked.

"Thank you. This is important." I turned to Nurse McDonnell. "And thank you for watching them. I'll hurry."

"I'll be here," she said, a wry smile coming to her lips. "I'm staying around for the 'I told you so,' remember?"

I smiled back, shook my head, and headed for the entrance.

Once inside, I immediately tracked down Nurse Adams, who was reading a chart while making her way down the hallway toward her desk. I frightened her slightly when I reached for her arm and, without saying anything, steered her a short distance into an empty conference room.

"Maggie, I need a favor—a big one," I began.

"What is it?" she asked, dramatically rolling her eyes. "What on earth this time?"

"This time it's serious. I don't want to get you in trouble, but we're going to have to stretch the rules a little here. I hope I can count on you."

"Maybe," she responded, quickly. "What's it about?"

"I've two patients outside in an ambulance, and I need you to set up an isolation room for them. This is a special case, and I'd like them taken there *immediately*. Skip the admissions forms and all the regular paperwork. Normally something like this would first take an administrator's approval, but my gut tells me we can't take the time for that. My instincts tell me we need to act quickly."

Pausing only for a moment, I continued, choosing my words carefully, "It could be a rare form of pneumonia, one that is highly contagious. Or, it could be something similar, but until we run some tests, I don't want to risk exposing anyone else to it—whatever it is.

"And there's something else. They can't pay for the treatment I'm going to order. That means there's a possibility it could come out of our hides if I can't fix it with the higher-ups."

"Mexicans?" she asked, quietly.

I nodded.

She stepped back from me slightly, studied the chart in her hand again, and said, without looking up, "Well, I haven't been in trouble yet this month, so I'll gamble my luck will continue. Give me about five minutes and then bring them in. The room will be ready."

I started to thank her, but she waved me off. "If push comes to shove, I'm just going to say I misunderstood what you requested and put them in isolation until I could get it all sorted out. I'm getting old and forgetful, you know. Ask anyone. Or, I'll just pin the tail on you."

"You're a dear is all I know," I replied. "Maggie, this really could be trouble. I'll do my best to protect you as much as I can if this turns bad."

"I know that," she said while turning to go back down the hall. However, before she could take two steps I said, a little too loudly, "There *is* one more thing."

This time she blew out a quick breath and said, "More? You're joking, right?"

"If you've no objections, I'd like Nurse McDonnell assigned to me through all of this. Think that can be arranged?"

"Does a bird fly?" she responded, just barely breaking a smile. "Take her—*for as long as you want*. If you'd asked for that first, I'd have given you a dozen isolation rooms without blinking an eye."

"Oh, come on. I don't think she's as bad as what everyone seems to think. As a matter of fact, I find her refreshing, in an odd sort of way."

"Odd *is* a good word for her. But you go ahead and take her. She's all yours. With my blessing—and, I've no doubt, the blessing of everyone else in this hospital."

Before I could respond, she began walking away. "I've work to do. Five minutes. When I'm ready, I'll send someone out to the ambulance to guide you to the room. In the meantime, tell Nurse McDonnell what treatments you want started."

"Maggie, I—" was all I could get out before she threw up a hand to hush me and headed back down the hallway. At that point, all I could do was shake my head and smile.

....

It was exactly five minutes later when two very young orderlies carrying stretchers approached the ambulance. When they stopped, one said to me, "Nurse Adams told me to tell you she's ready. We're also supposed to help you with the patients if you want."

"Thank you," I said, "but put these gloves on before you do. You two will take one patient, and Ed and I will take the other. Don't touch them—and don't touch anything but the handle of your stretcher. Understand?"

Both orderlies looked confused but immediately put on the gloves. At that point, Ed and I gently placed Mr. Lajun on their stretcher and asked them to stand to the side. We put his daughter on ours and lifted her out of the ambulance.

As we started toward the door, Nurse McDonnell whispered to me,

"I'll keep an eye on them and will make sure the stretchers and gloves stay in the room when we get there." I nodded my thanks.

Once inside, with the orderlies leading the way, we moved quickly past the Admissions Desk and down the hallway to the last room on the right, Room 117. Nurse Adams was waiting for us and waved us inside.

Once we had Mr. Lajun and Francisca safely in their beds, Nurse McDonnell moved forward, took the gloves from the orderlies, and asked them to leave the room. As soon as she was finished, I said to her, "We discussed the treatment outside, but I want you to have the floor now. Please explain to Nurse Adams what we are going to do. I want to hear you go through this so I can make sure you understand everything perfectly."

She glared at me, but before she could speak, I added, "You are going to be in charge here when I'm not around, and there can be no mistakes. None. So, please begin."

When she turned to face Nurse Adams, I could see in her expression the irony of the situation had immediately struck her. Earlier in the day she was the proverbial hot potato. Now she was going to be giving orders to her supervisor. She looked down at her notes briefly, then said, "Since *some* of us aren't sure exactly what this is, we're going to take a middle of the road course and initially do standard treatment for both pneumonia and influenza. First, everyone who comes in this room, without exception, must have mask and gloves. *Everyone*. Next, temperature and pulse rate must be charted every half hour, around the clock. We may have to turn to intravenous delivery later, but for now they are to have three to four quarts of water or fruit juice every day to promote kidney function. Let's try a glass every half hour when they're awake. I'm sure they won't want it now, but let's see how soon we can get them to eat some oatmeal or rice to help the bowels. Let's also start with high dose Salacin and aspirin to try to do something about the fever. I'd say every four hours. Do you concur, Doctor?"

I nodded. Nurse Adams was furiously taking notes and finally interrupted her, "Slow it, please. I need time—"

Nurse McDonnell didn't break stride. "Ice packs over the heart every
two hours to help lower heart rate. That should also help some with the
fever. Also, as soon as possible, let's culture urine, swab their noses to
check for bacteria, and also do sputum cultures."

Turning to me, she asked, "Anything you'd like to add?"

"No, you've covered it well. We'll start with this course of treatment
and adjust accordingly as we see changes in their vital signs. Nurse Adams,
we're going to need other nurses to spell Nurse McDonnell, so please see
if you can round up a few for her to instruct about correct procedures
inside this room. Get them here as soon as you can."

I looked at my watch and realized I'd have to hurry if I was going to
catch the hospital's Assistant Administrator before he left for the day. "I'll
have to excuse myself now," I said to both of them. "I know you two will
take care of what needs to be done, so I'm going to try to catch Charles
Hornbeck. Might as well face the music right now and see if I can smooth
out a storm before it hits. I'll check back in as soon as I can."

Nurse Adams started to say something, but Nurse McDonnell cut
her off. "On your way, Doctor. We'll see it done."

"Wish me luck," I said, turning and moving toward the elevator. "I
have the feeling we're going to need all we can get."

....

Charles Hornbeck, the new Chief Administrator of Los Angeles County
Hospital, was seated behind his desk and fiddling with the tuning knob
of his radio when his secretary led me into the room. He didn't look up
as I entered.

Our former Chief Administrator, Dr. Wendel Brown, had turned
over the day-to-day operations of the hospital to Charles six months
before. One would have been hard pressed to find someone who didn't
both respect and adore Dr. Brown because of his kind heart and the sense

of community he had built for everyone, from the cleaning people to the most highly skilled surgeons, inside the walls of the hospital. However, it was a mild attack in this kind heart that made his decision to step away from the pressure-filled job of running the hospital one all who cared for him understood and agreed with. Now, when feeling up to it, he served as our spokesman and the "face of the hospital" everywhere from charity events to political functions. I knew he missed his old role at the hospital, but I also knew if ever a man was born to spread goodwill and trust, Dr. Brown was that man.

The same characteristics, however, could not be used to describe Charles Hornbeck. He was known throughout the hospital as "Bottom Line Hornbeck," a moniker he knew about and relished. The highest officials in all the hospitals where I'd previously served were either practicing or retired physicians, which made sense because they understood the delicate balance that always existed between the need to acquire revenue to keep the doors open and the challenges associated with bringing first-rate medical care to all in the surrounding community. Charles, on the other hand, was an accountant, plain and simple, with numbers the driving force in his life and in the code he followed when making decisions about every branch of the hospital.

On one side, he was a fair man who played no favorites. He treated everyone the same—like a digit on a budget sheet. On the other side, he did know the importance of at least making it appear like the hospital cared for those in the community, no doubt because he also believed that would help keep a positive flow of revenue coming into the coffers. I knew if I had any chance at all of selling anything to him, it was this last area I was going to have to build upon now.

He was still playing with the radio when I stepped forward, extended my hand, and said, "Good to see you again, Mr. Hornbeck. I'm sorry to interrupt you, but if you don't mind—"

"Piece of junk," he said, first shaking and then setting the radio roughly on his desk. As he did so, music suddenly blared loudly from the speaker. "Well, look at that—finally. Bought this thing second hand, but I fully expected it to be reliable."

As if talking more to himself than to me, he continued, "I'm still not convinced radio isn't just a passing fancy, but with the price of recording disks constantly going up and music on radio being free, I'll take my chances and see what happens."

Charles was a short man, just barely over five feet tall, with a rather round midsection that seemed significantly larger every time I saw him. He was also bald, save for small patches of gray hair just above each ear. His fiftieth birthday party had been held in the hospital cafeteria just a month before, and everyone I knew had either attended the event or sent a present, not out of any love for the man, but more to keep on his good side. I was on rounds at that time so couldn't be there myself, but I did send along a gift, a hastily purchased comb and brush set, which in hindsight probably wasn't the best choice.

Just a few seconds after the music started, it stopped, and only a slight crackling sound continued through the speaker. At that point, he finally looked up and appeared to notice me for the first time. He didn't reach out to shake my hand. Instead, he shrugged his shoulders, motioned for me to sit down, and said, "Know anyone who repairs these contraptions—inexpensively?"

"Sorry, I don't," I replied. "But I'll ask around and let you know if I come up with someone."

He turned off the radio, clasped his hands together, leaned forward, and asked, "And to what do I owe the pleasure of the company of my best diagnostician?"

I knew I had to choose my words carefully. "Mr. Hornbeck, we have a special case downstairs, and I felt it my duty to tell you about it. I have two patients in isolation, and I'd like to—"

"Isolation?" he interrupted. "Very expensive. Must it be done?"

"Yes, I believe it must."

I knew that Charles, even with all his time spent in the hospital, still had very little medical knowledge and liked it when he was presented such information in plain language. So, I put on my best serious face and continued, "It is entirely possible this is a very rare form of pneumonia or influenza, one that could be highly contagious. I felt it best to bring them here for observation and treatment."

"Who are they?" he asked.

I knew the question was coming and was prepared for it. "They're from the Macy Street area." I paused and waited for his response.

"Mexicans?" he asked. "Why, they can't pay for . . . Why didn't you just isolate them at that church there? Isn't that what's usually—"

I interrupted as quickly as I could and said, "Don't worry—I thought about that but decided against it, and here's why. I believe payment will come back to the hospital many times over when people find out this was done to help protect the *white* community. After all, if what they have spreads through the Macy area, think of the number of Mexicans who come into the city to work as housekeepers, custodians, maintenance men, and even in all that new construction going on. If this is as contagious as I think it to be, we could be talking about widespread illness among those who care the most about this hospital. That's what I was thinking about. Think of their gratitude. Think of how they will show that appreciation once they find out what you have done for them."

I knew I had him with that last bit of reasoning. His ego was legendary, deserved or not. And, if there was a way to enhance his reputation, I guessed he would take it. He sat back in his chair, folded his arms, and stared at me without blinking. As I stared back, I imagined numbers crashing into each other inside his head.

Finally, he spoke. "But they *are* Mexicans."

"They are. But remember this—the greatest endowments can come from the simplest acts of charity. This is a case where you—I mean the hospital—stand to profit on all sides. Think of what a humanitarian and hero you will be once the Mexican community finds out about the help the hospital has provided. Then, think also of the value of the publicity gained by a carefully positioned article or two in the papers about how action was taken to protect the citizens of this city. And who would they say was responsible for everything?"

I paused for a moment and picked up his wooden nameplate from the desk. "Why, that would be you, Sir."

He scratched his chin and asked, "And what do you get out of all of this? It's been years since I've been buttered up this much, like an ear of corn. I'm not stupid. I know there must be something else going on here as well. It's time to stop playing around. Tell me the truth."

That was the opening I was hoping for. "You, Sir, are correct that I'm buttering you up. Everything I said to you can happen, but there *is* more. I'm a diagnostician, and only once in a blue moon does a case present itself that has as much mystery surrounding it as this one does."

I leaned forward. "Look, in the same way a businessman aches for the chance to solve a seemingly impossible financial situation, those of us in my profession pray for an opportunity to solve the most difficult of medical puzzles."

"I can understand that," he said. "But you're asking me to let you solve your puzzle on the hospital's dime. That doesn't seem like good business to me."

"In a way that's accurate, but in this particular instance, the more I profit from solving this puzzle, the more the hospital will profit—as I've already explained. Plus, if this illness turns out to be as contagious as I think it could be and we stay ahead of it, the hospital wins all the way around. On the other hand, if I'm wrong and it isn't as serious, then I'm the one with the egg on my face, and everyone else is off the hook. But, the hospital will look good no matter what."

Charles didn't respond. Instead, he reached for the radio and turned it on again. This time music instantly played. I smiled at him and said, "They also have news regularly on that thing now. I could see positive publicity flowing from there as well. How are you in front of a microphone?"

While drumming his fingers on the desk, he said, "I may regret this, but I like your style—and the way you think. We may have a lot more in common than I thought when I first met you. If I agree to this, what do you need?"

"Thank you, Mr. Hornbeck," I said, reaching again to shake his hand. This time he took my hand, firmly, and gave a good pump. "I'll do my best to keep expenses down at every turn, but I'm going to need to reassign a few nurses to help maintain isolation. There will also be extra tests, and the room may be needed for quite some time. And, for reasons I'm sure you'll understand, this must be kept under wraps as much as possible while we find out what this illness really is. These days, any time the words 'highly contagious' are used around an isolation room, people start to panic. They remember what happened back during the great influenza epidemic, and their emotions run amuck. I don't want that, and you don't either. We'll keep this quiet for now as much as possible, and I promise I'll keep you informed."

I stood to leave. "This is a good decision. A good *business* decision."

"It better be," he said, turning off the radio. "For the hospital's sake—and for yours."

I nodded I understood and left the room. As I headed toward the elevator, I realized I should have felt terribly guilty for baiting him so. But I didn't.

....

CHAPTER 7

Post Mortem

October 29
4:49 A.M.

I didn't know how long the phone had been ringing before I picked up the receiver. Still groggy, I said, "Hello. Dr. Thompson here. Who is this?"

"Doctor Thompson, this is Nurse McDonnell. Sorry to wake you so early, but I thought it best to call you at once."

She paused only briefly before adding, her tone calm, even, "Francisca just died. Respiration crashed suddenly, and there was nothing that could be done about it. I called for an oxygen tent, but she went before it got to the room. Happened that fast."

While flinging back the covers and throwing my legs over the edge of the bed, I replied, "Get her down to autopsy right away. I'll take the responsibility for this. Call Dr. Jacobs, our new pathologist, as soon as we hang up. Tell him I have full authority from hospital administration to call him in. Tell him I want him there so we can look at the lungs as soon as possible. But tell him to wait for me. I'll be joining him soon as I can. Got that?"

"I do. Consider it done."

"And what of Mr. Lajun?"

"Stable. Fever down slightly, but no other significant change. Still asleep. When he wakes up, I'll break the news to him. I'll take care of that."

"Yesterday she wasn't nearly as ill as her father. Doesn't make much sense at this point. I have to be at that autopsy. If I'm right . . ."

I purposely let my words trail off. I still didn't want to say out loud what I was thinking, not even to Nurse McDonnell.

She said, "I saw it happen this quick back in Eighteen. I'm not going to say 'I told you so' just yet, but I'm getting closer."

"I still don't think so," I replied. "Hopefully, we'll have more answers after the autopsy."

"Anything else?" she asked.

"Yes. Don't go near Mr. Lajun without gloves *and* mask. I'm sure you're already doing that, but don't forget and slip up. Not now."

"I know that," she replied, clearly irritated. She also sounded dead tired.

"Maria, when's the last time you got some sleep? Have you been at the hospital this whole time?"

I hadn't realized it until right after I said it, but that was the first time I had called her by first name, and by the silence on the other end of the phone I think it surprised her.

Finally, she replied, "I sleep when I need it. Don't worry about me. I'll see you when you get here."

I dressed quickly as my thoughts raced. Without tying my shoes or grabbing my hat, I opened the front door and raced across the lawn to my car.

The whole time I kept thinking to myself, "It can't be. It just can't."

....

It took me a lot longer to get to the hospital than I had hoped. A Southern Pacific Railroad train had broken down right where the tracks crossed Alhambra Avenue. It took a good thirty-five minutes before it was underway again, and then just before the caboose crossed the track, it stopped again for about five minutes. At that point, drivers in nearly every car both in front of me and behind started honking their horns. Straight ahead of us a worker for the railroad climbed up on a flatcar, smiled, and bowed dramatically toward us several times. The sight was so absurd that under other circumstances, I might have laughed. Other drivers may have been amused because the honking stopped. However, I still gave serious thought to parking my car at the side of the road, climbing through the train cars, and walking the rest of the way. If the train hadn't started moving shortly after that, I might have.

When I finally pulled into the doctors' parking lot, I decided the journey had taken so long it wouldn't matter if I took a couple extra minutes to check on Mr. Lajun before heading down to the morgue. As I entered Room 117, Maria, in full hospital gown and wearing gloves and mask, was sound asleep in a chair by the window. I didn't have the heart to wake her, so I stepped quietly toward the bed and examined Mr. Lajun, who was also asleep.

As I held his hand to take his pulse, I noticed it was the calloused hand of a man who worked hard in the fields and the train yard doing all he could to support his family, and now we had to tell him his daughter had died. Pulse rate and respiration were still the same, and his chart indicated no change in his other vital signs. In the margin next to the last entry I wrote my initials, added the time, and wrote, "Continue course of treatment" so that Maria would know I had stopped by.

As I was trying to attach the chart to the clip at the foot of the bed my hand slipped, and the chart crashed to the floor. Maria jumped up and said, "What's this?"

"It's just me. I'm sorry. Didn't mean to. It just slipped."

"What time is it?"

"Time for you to get some real rest. Why don't you get someone here to relieve you so you can go home to your own bed? I just checked him, and nothing has changed. We'll just continue what we're doing—for now. So, how about it? Ready to go home?"

She didn't answer my questions. Instead, she asked while yawning, "Headed downstairs now?"

"You *were* able to get hold of Dr. Jacobs, right?"

She yawned again. "Woke him from a sound sleep. Believe me, he wasn't happy. He added more than a few colorful words into his response."

I shook my head. "I can only imagine. He's new here, and I've worked with him only once. I'll never forget that day, though. Even when he appeared to be talking to himself, he swore like a sailor. But I don't care what he says as long as he's good at what he does."

Maria hesitated before responding, "Well, you'll get plenty of debate on that subject. I know I'm not supposed to hear these things, but his reputation isn't very good. 'Shoddy' is the word I've most often heard applied to his work. Supposedly, he was let go at his last two hospitals because of that. Just thought you should know."

"Thanks for the warning," I said. "I'll take it under advisement. Now, do try to get some rest. If you don't do it for yourself, do it for me. I have the feeling we're just getting started with this."

"So, you still think this is something else, do you?"

"I hope I'm about to find out. I'll give you a full report later today. In the meantime, go home!"

"I'll think about it," she said, again yawning, which caused me to do the same. Then, without another word, she walked to the bed and started checking Mr. Lajun's pulse. I knew there was nothing else I could say to convince her to leave, so I quietly left the room.

....

The autopsy suite was at the back of the morgue and, when I entered, I found Dr. Jacobs reading the newspaper. He was also quietly mumbling something to himself.

Maria had been right when she said Dr. Jacobs had been asked to leave his last two positions. The reasons were still unclear, but I had heard he had a reputation for simply not getting along well with others. We hired him because pathologists were in very short supply all across the nation, and we had just lost one of our best to retirement. So, even though Jacobs was well up in age and had more than just a few rumors stuck to him, the hospital decided to risk a chance.

I knocked on the door to get his attention and said, "Hi, Jacobs. Ready to get started?"

"On what?" he replied, not looking up from the newspaper.

"Francisca Lajun."

After turning a page of the paper, he picked up a clipboard and held it out for me.

"What's this?" I asked, while stepping forward to take it.

He motioned for me to look at the sheet on the clipboard. It was an autopsy checklist, with Francisca Lajun's name printed at the top. I scanned the sheet quickly, and it had the standard evaluations at the top: height, weight, notation of distinguishing marks on the body. However, the rest of the checklist was blank, save for the word "Pneumonia" printed in large block letters in the box designated "Cause(s) of Death."

After I had scanned the sheet, I again asked, this time in disbelief, "What's this?"

Still not looking at me, he said, "Your autopsy. Already done."

"But didn't my nurse tell you I wanted to be here—that you were supposed to wait for me?"

"You should talk to her. Nasty woman. Bossy as a cow."

He went back to his reading when I walked to the table, jerked the newspaper away, and dropped the clipboard in its place. "This won't do," I said. "This doesn't tell me anything. Didn't you at least take blood and tissue samples? Where are they?"

"No need," he said, finally looking up at me. "I was told to look at the lungs. This was just pneumonia, the simple garden variety type. Was easy to tell."

"What do you mean easy to tell? On what did you base your judgment? Where are the tissue samples?"

At this point, he took the newspaper back and said, his tone condescending, "I've been doing this since you were in short pants. If I say it's pneumonia, it's pneumonia."

He paused just a moment before adding, "And besides, she was a Mex. I see this in those people all the time. What's the big deal?"

For a moment all I could do was stand there and stare at him. Half of me wanted to pull him over the desk and sock him right in the eye, but the other half knew work needed to be done—and the only way to get to Francisca's body was through him. Even though I felt sick at the thought of it, I knew it was time for some flattery.

"Look, I know you are highly competent in what you do. But, here's the fact of the matter. I have full authority from as high up as it gets at this hospital, from Charles Hornbeck himself, to ask for a 'complete' autopsy in this case. You're probably right. This is probably just pneumonia. What did you call it? A garden variety? But still, I'd like to check a few more things because Mr. Hornbeck and I see this as an opportunity to help the hospital in financial and other areas as well. I can't go into specifics right now, but what we do with this girl is *very* important."

Here I paused and added, emphasizing each word. "I need your help. The hospital needs your help."

"But it's just pneumonia," he said again. "I've seen hundreds of cases just like this." At that point, he looked up at me, his eyes indicating he had just thought of something. "Why so *important*? Do you suspect something else here? If so, I'd like to know. Now."

I knew I had him. The seed had been planted that he might have missed something, and it was clear I had his full attention.

"Oh, you're probably right," I said once again, waving my hand in front of me for dramatic effect. "You've been doing this a long time and have great experience. Your reputation follows you."

He stared at me blankly as I continued, "Still, you know as well as I do if there are other circumstances not known to a doctor when a diagnosis is made, or even when an autopsy is performed, we still might have work to do before we can make complete judgment. I always call it the 'Physician's Puzzle,' and I think that describes it perfectly. We're always striving to get to the solution, don't you agree?"

"All I know is you haven't told me anything. Let's have it. What do you suspect here? Why all this fuss?"

"Well," I said, lowering my voice and motioning him to lean in closer to me. I looked around the room to make sure no one else could hear us before continuing. "I promised Mr. Hornbeck I would keep all this under wraps, but I'm going to trust you and fill you in as much as I can. Here's the story. We have another patient upstairs, in isolation. We're not sure exactly what this is, and you're probably right this is just pneumonia, but there's the thought that there could be a highly contagious illness at play here. And, if it is, we want to be able to take appropriate steps to close the doors on it. Understand?"

Dr. Jacobs was still blankly staring at me, so I continued, "For instance, when you examined the lungs, what was your evaluation? Reflux or aspiration present? Possible bacterial manifestation? Viral? Fungal? How about the air sacs? What type of inflammation in the alveoli? With full knowledge of this, we'd know better what to do next. Or, what *not* to do next."

I could tell by the way he shifted in his chair and cleared his throat my questions were starting to make him uncomfortable, so I added, "I'm to see Mr. Hornbeck again this afternoon. This is already late October, and our annual performance evaluations are coming up soon. I'm sure you'll agree it wouldn't hurt to have Mr. Hornbeck completely happy with us right now. I'll make sure he knows what a help you've been with this."

He didn't smile, but he didn't snarl either. Standing, he said, flatly, "If you want us to look again, I'll pull her back out. But I still say . . . "

I cut him off. "You're probably right. But let's be sure, okay? Let's do some blood and tissue samples. Won't take long."

"Then follow me," he said, shaking his head. He also muttered something I couldn't quite make out. I was glad I couldn't.

After placing the body on the cart and wheeling it into the autopsy suite, he motioned for me to follow him in. He roughly shoved the upper torso onto the marble examination table and flipped the legs over as well. As he did so, I turned to him and said, "Easy!"

I stood there a moment, gathering my thoughts. When I examined her the day before, Francisca Lujan was quite ill, but because of her youth I also saw in her the promise of a future, one that now lay extinguished before me. I had patients pass suddenly before. At times, that just happened, often without the full cause ever being known. But I couldn't let that be the case this time. I had to do everything I could to discover why she was here.

When Dr. Jacobs finally pulled back the sheet, I wasn't surprised by what I saw before me. There should have been a Y or U-shaped incision running from both shoulders down to the bottom of the sternum and then continuing all the way to the area of the pubic bone. This was the standard beginning of the procedure to allow for easy access to and removal of the internal organs. However, no such incision was present. Instead, there was a single, deep incision straight from the bottom of the throat cavity down to mid torso, and it was apparent the ribs had been crudely pried outward to allow access to the lungs. Based on what Maria had said about his reputation, I fully expected as much. However, what did surprise me when he stepped forward and spread the ribs again was finding the lungs still in place. They should have been removed for full examination, but they hadn't been.

I looked over at Dr. Jacobs, who said, "I cut into the left and examined it. Typical mucosa and quantity consistent with pneumonia."

Maria was wrong about one thing. "Shoddy" didn't begin to describe his work. The words "incompetent" and "lazy" seemed much more accurate. I badly wanted to say something to him, but I guessed the look on my face told him more than my words ever could have.

"I see," was all I said. After I paused long enough to make sure he knew what I was thinking, I said, "Let's get some tissue samples, shall we? We'll know much more of the puzzle then. While you're removing the lungs, if you don't mind the assistance, I'll draw blood and the other fluids. Fine with you?"

He avoided my eyes as he nodded approval. Not another word was spoken between us while we completed our tasks.

When we were finally finished, I pulled off my gloves, placed them in the bin, and said, "Please stain the tissue slides now. I see your microscope over there. I'd like to look at them before I leave. The blood and other fluids can wait. I need to see the tissue slides right away."

His voice quiet, his demeanor calm, he grabbed at my arm and asked, "What do you suspect?"

Removing his hand, I replied, "I suspect we are going to be mightily surprised and not in a good way."

I pointed toward the microscope. "The slides, please. As quickly as possible. And be careful handling them. I hope you didn't get any fluids on you earlier. I assume you wore gloves at all times, but I just wanted to remind you again so that there'll be no slip-ups. We still don't know exactly what this is."

He didn't reply. Instead, he stared blankly at me before turning and walking away. I did hear him mutter something the entirety of which I couldn't quite catch, but I did make out a salty expression in there that had me turning my head. At that moment, I had the feeling we'd all be calling up a few of those before this was all said and done. I hoped I was wrong, but I still didn't think so. I shook my head and quietly said to myself an expression my father often used when frustrated or upset, "Horsefeathers and bushwa," which was about as colorful as Dad's language ever got.

Dr. Jacobs turned around and asked, "You say something?"

I didn't reply. I just pointed once again to the microscope.

....

CHAPTER 8

Only Mexicans

October 29

7:25 A.M.

I was still numb, my thoughts swirling, when I got back to Room 117. Just as I reached for the door, Maria stepped out, crashing right into me. I grabbed her gently to keep her upright but didn't say anything.

Stepping back, she looked up and said, "Is everything all right? You look like you've seen a ghost."

She went on before I could reply. "Father Brualla is in there with Mr. Lajun. I thought it best to get him over here. When I told Mr. Lajun about his daughter, he just stared at the ceiling and didn't say a thing. Nothing. At first I thought he hadn't understood me, but when the tears started rolling down his cheeks, I knew someone should be with him this morning. I didn't want to expose his wife and family any more than has already happened, so I decided to call Father Brualla. Nurse Phillips is in there now for her shift, so I—"

I quickly took her arm and led her to the large supply closet across the hall. I opened the door, flipped on the light, and pulled her in while closing the door behind us.

"Why, doctor," she said in mock horror, "I didn't know you cared."

I grabbed two wooden crates from the back of the room and put them next to the shelves of sheets and blankets. "Sit. Please," I said, pointing to a crate.

"This must not be good," she said, her voice now full of concern.

"It's as bad as I originally thought. Keep this just between the two of us for now."

She nodded she understood. "What is it?"

I paused and looked away from her, trying to find just the right words. She reached over and gently touched my hand. "Please go on," she said.

"I just finished helping Dr. Jacobs with the autopsy. It wouldn't have taken so long if you hadn't been right about him. I finally got him to do tissue slides of the lungs. I can't be sure because the slides were so poorly done and I've never seen this other than in medical books, but I'm fairly certain I know now what we're up against. I'm going to call in an expert to confirm it. I hope I'm wrong, but I don't think so."

Maria immediately jumped in, clearly irritated. "I'm not doing this dance again. Either you tell me or you don't. Right now."

"As I said, the slides weren't good, but I saw what appeared to be kidney shaped cells I've seen in drawings before. Ever hear of *Yersinia Pestis*?"

"Can't say I have. What do they indicate?"

I leaned back slightly, looked right at her, and said, "Plague."

"Plague!" she repeated, too loudly.

"Yes, plague. And keep your voice down. Remember after the initial examination at their home when I mentioned Mr. Lajun had enlarged lymph nodes but his daughter didn't? That was my first inkling, supported by a few other symptoms that didn't match influenza. Bubonic plague usually has that type of swelling, especially in the groin."

"But Francisca didn't have that, and she just died."

"Which confirms for me something else I've been thinking. The bubonic form can quickly become pneumonic, which doesn't carry the swollen lymph nodes but does mimic many symptoms of pneumonia. Again, I'm not an expert on this by any means, but I know we'd better get someone in here who is—and quickly."

"How soon will you be reporting this? If we don't do something fast, plague spreads like a forest fire. What do you want me to do?"

"I'd like you to keep quiet."

"Quiet!" she said, again too loudly.

"Yes, quiet. There's still a chance I'm wrong, but it's more than that. Just the word 'plague' has the power to cause a panic, and we can't have that. The very mention of it would cause people to scatter and, if that happens, this could spread so far so quickly I honestly don't know what we'd do."

"Then what do we do now?"

"The first thing I have to do is get this confirmed. One of the foremost authorities in this area is in San Francisco, and I'll try to get him here. In the meantime, I need you to talk to Father Brualla and see if he can find out if anyone knows of others who are ill. While you're doing that, I'm going back to Hornbeck and see about getting the outside help. He won't like it, but I've got to convince him."

"Are you going to come right out and tell him you think it's plague?"

"I'm going to tell him I think this is a highly contagious form of malignant pneumonia. I remember reading some doctors used the term years ago to describe the plague because while that sounds pretty bad, it doesn't send the same shock through people. Hornbeck isn't a doctor, so I think I can get away with that for at least the time being."

"You look so tired," I continued. "You mentioned Nurse Phillips is here, so I'm ordering you to go home and get some rest. I'd like you to talk to Father Brualla first, and then get out of here. I'll need you back here late this afternoon. You are right that we have much to do. So, let's both get moving."

"Plague?" she said while shaking her head. "How'd they get it? Where'd it come from?"

I helped her to her feet and said, "I have dozens of questions, but we'll take this one step at a time. Let's get this diagnosis confirmed, and then we'll draw up a plan. In the meantime, let's hope there aren't any other cases. We might get lucky."

"Then again, we might not," she said, moving toward the door.

....

This time when I was shown into his office, Charles Hornbeck was seated his chair, his back to me and feet propped on the window sill, as he appeared to be looking over the streets below. When his secretary announced me, he didn't turn around. Instead, he raised an arm over his shoulder and with his thumb pointed to a chair in front of the desk. I immediately sat down.

Still without turning around, he said, "I hope you've come to tell me there's no more need for that isolation room. Incredibly expensive."

"I'm afraid not. There's been a new development. I'm here to tell you we have a problem—a *very bad one.*"

He jerked his feet off the sill and spun his chair around. "Don't talk to me about problems. Whatever you have to say can't be as bad as how much I just found out we're over budget on medical supplies around here. This seems to be the day for problems, so let's hear yours."

"Sir," I began, "one of our patients in the isolation room died this morning, a Miss Francisca Lajun. It was the manner of her death I'd like to talk to you about."

Charles opened a small wooden case on his desk, pulled out a cigarette, and placed it in his mouth. He didn't light it. Instead, he pointed first at the case and then to me.

"No, thank you," I said. "Not now."

"You should," he said, finally striking a match.

Then, turning his chair around again so that he was facing the window, Charles said, his voice empty of emotion, "I'm sorry to hear that, but this was only a Mexican girl, right? Then why all the fuss? They're *always* sick with one thing or another. This is their problem, not ours."

I thought of pulling his chair around so that he could see the expression on my face. Instead, I made sure he knew what I was thinking by the tone of my voice. "Only a Mexican? It doesn't matter who she was. Whether Mexican or Anglo, we could be facing one of the most serious problems since the Spanish Influenza of Eighteen."

That last part caught his attention, and he turned to face me again. He quickly stubbed out his cigarette and said, "Whatever in the world are you talking about? Is this the Influenza again? Is that what you're telling me?"

His voice was suddenly tense, his expression as serious as I'd ever seen him.

"No, it isn't the Spanish Influenza. But it could be something equally as dangerous, and we need to take steps right now to protect everyone."

"Well, if it isn't that, then what could be so bad you're back here to see me? I'm a busy man."

I needed to choose my next words carefully. "I know that, and I hate to take you away from your important activities. However, we could be facing something that will affect not only this hospital, but all of Los Angeles—and possibly beyond."

He reached for another cigarette as I continued, drawing out the words, "Malignant pneumonia."

"Malignant pneumonia? What in the world is that, and how could it cause *us* a problem? Just what are you driving at?"

"This could be a highly contagious form of pneumonia that spreads through a simple cough or sneeze. I'm sure you remember how quickly everything happened in Eighteen. The influenza started in Fort Riley, Kansas, and as soon as troops got on trains and moved around the country, new pockets sprang up everywhere. Almost two hundred thousand died in October alone. And let's not forget people all over blamed public officials for not acting swiftly enough. Well, we could be facing the same thing now. We have to take steps to prevent that."

"Now, now," he said, condescendingly. "I know you are our best diagnostician, but let's be realistic. You don't really seem to know what this is, so the odds of it being something as bad as the Influenza again are, what, one in a million? If I were a betting man, I'd say this is something they brought up from Mexico. You already talked me into the isolation room, and the minute I authorized it I regretted the decision. You could be making a mountain out of a mole hill, and all for nothing. From what you've given me, I honestly can't see why we should be doing more."

He had me, and he knew it. True, I wasn't entirely sure. But, I still believed we needed to dig deeper, to make sure I was either wrong—or right.

"Sir, Dr. Jacobs and I have already done an autopsy, and tissue samples indicate enough to me that we can't take any chances with this." I moved my chair closer to him. "Look, it's like I said yesterday, if I'm wrong, I'm the one who will be hung out to dry—not the hospital. When this is over, if I *am* wrong, I won't utter a sound if you tell everyone you have an absolute idiot on your staff who doesn't know hair tonic from blood. After the autopsy on the girl, I'm more convinced than ever we need to do more."

"More? In addition to that isolation room, if I'm being informed correctly, we have staff being reassigned all over the place. Dr. Thompson, all of that is costing us a fortune."

Trying to sound more grateful than argumentative, I said, "And I appreciate your support, but now I'm going to ask for one more thing."

"But first answer me this," he said. "What did Dr. Jacobs find as the cause of death? I'd like to know what he had to say."

"At first he listed pneumonia, but after additional examination he changed that to 'death by unknown cause.'"

"So, I see. You changed his mind, too. Just what is it you're trying to do here? These are Mexicans, for goodness sake. What more do you want from me?"

At that point, my heart started racing, and I knew I had to control the anger I felt building. I reached for a cigarette and started tapping it gently on his desk as I continued, trying my best to keep my voice calm. "Mr. Hornbeck, I'd like to tell you a story. Don't worry—it won't take long, but it's one all of us should be reminded of every once in a while."

He struck a match and held it toward me. I waved him off and began,

"This story takes place in San Francisco way back around 1901, when you and I were just youngsters. A terrible illness was found there. I know you didn't grow up in California, but maybe you've heard about this along the way. Some doctors and city officials didn't think the illness was important enough to deal with because it was almost entirely the Chinese residents who became sick. Over two thousand people died before any serious steps were taken to halt the illness.

"This didn't set well with the medical community at large, and once the newspapers got hold of the story heads started to roll. Hospital administrators and doctors there were called out for their inaction, and quite a few were let go. Even the Governor, who knew all about the illness but didn't do anything, was thrown out of office. Think of that—the Governor of California. And think of this. Instead of losing their jobs, the Governor and the hospital officials all might have well become heroes if they'd taken even the most rudimentary steps toward offering help."

Charles suddenly cut in, "If you're trying to threaten me, you better—"

"No threats here I assure you. My *point* is we all have certain responsibilities that are expected of us now *because* of what happened in San Francisco. It makes no difference what our personal feelings are on some issues. We're now talking strictly about a matter of business, plain and simple. We're in the business of healing and protecting the health of our citizens. It's what's expected of us, and if we don't do it, we'll be booted out, as we should be. That's the lesson of San Francisco."

Looking quite agitated and lighting yet another cigarette, he said, "I still don't understand. Just what is this *malignant pneumonia*? How does this relate to your *story*? Has this just been your long way of saying you think what we have here is what they had in San Francisco? If that's so, spit it out."

I didn't want to answer his question directly. Instead, I said, "I believe this to be something very similar. And, if you please, I'd like to go back to what I was going to ask a few minutes ago. To be sure—to *make* sure we've done everything humanly possible at this time—I want to call in a specialist to look at the case, Dr. James Perry from San Francisco. Dr. Perry's reputation is second to none, and he's one of the world's preeminent authorities on diagnosis and treatment of malignant pneumonia and other related illnesses. He was also in San Francisco during that illness and was put in charge once medical treatment began. If Dr. Perry comes here and says I'm wrong, believe it or not, I'll be thrilled because my worst fears will have been squashed. On the other hand . . . "

His agitation clearly showing again, Charles pushed back his chair as he slammed a fist to his table. "And I suppose you want me to come up with the money to get him up here. San Francisco is a long way away. Do you know what that would cost us?"

"Relax," I said, hoping my tone would settle him down some. "I feel certain that once he finds out why we want him here, he'll pay his own expenses. As I said, he's considered one of the best, and opportunities for him to get involved in these cases don't come along very often. There is always more to learn, and he will jump at the chance to help us out—because it would be helping him out, too."

Charles cleared his throat and said, "Well, that's a different story. Why didn't you say that right away? I just don't know about you, Dr. Thompson. I don't think I've ever run across anybody so, so *windy* in all my days. You're obviously a smart man, but you use too many words. When you talk to somebody, get to the point. Your life will be much easier, and it'll be a hell of a lot easier on anybody who has to listen to you."

He was right. I had heard that before, more than a few times. However, I wasn't upset. I was actually happy the conversation had turned toward me and away from Dr. Perry. My around-the-bush talk had worked after all, and the thought made me smile.

"So, what you are telling me is if I can get him here without costing the hospital a dime, then you're fine with this."

He started to say something, but I didn't want him to think about all of this too much. So, I quickly continued, "I'll get in touch with him by long distance yet this afternoon and see if I can get him here tomorrow. Don't worry. I'll take care of everything."

He actually laughed while saying, "With you in charge of this, I *am* going to worry."

"Try not to. I'll do my best." Turning serious as I stood up from my chair, I added, "Just one more thing."

"Uh, oh—what now?" he asked.

"I was just going to say that for the time being, I'm going to strongly suggest that nobody else other than us should know about this illness and about Dr. Perry coming here. Are you fine with that?"

"Whew—that's a relief. I thought you were going to ask for something else that would cost me more money. I agree with you that we should keep this between us—for now. I hadn't heard about your San Francisco story—if it's true—but if this turns out like you think, then somebody is going to have to blow the whistle. I get that part of what you were saying."

"It's a deal," I said, holding out my hand.

Charles stood slowly and shook my hand. This time his grip was light, a far cry from the iron clasp I had felt the day before. He said, "I still hope you know what you're doing. It's a tough thing to watch a man working so hard to make his own noose."

Rubbing my neck, I said, "I wish you hadn't put it quite that way."

He laughed heartily, shook his head, and motioned for me to leave his office. I did, gladly, and headed straight for my office.

It was time to call San Francisco.

....

CHAPTER 9

Just in Case

October 29
8:37 A.M.

As soon as Dr. Thompson exited Charles Hornbeck's office, Charles moved quickly to his door, stuck his head out, and said to his secretary, Judy Martin, "I need to make a call, and I don't want to be disturbed. It may take some time."

"Want me to connect you with your party?" Judy asked.

"No, I'll do it myself. Again, I don't want to be bothered until I'm finished. Got that?"

"Yes, Sir. I'll keep everyone out."

Back at his desk, Charles opened the top drawer and withdrew a small address book. Thumbing through it for only a moment, he stopped, picked up a pencil, and wrote down a telephone number. After lighting a cigarette and sitting in his chair, he clicked for the operator and had her make the call.

"Hello, Stuart, this is Charles. Have a minute to talk?"

Stuart Bunning was Charles' closest friend. The two had met several years before when both were invited on the same evening to join a private and quite exclusive investment club, the Greater Los Angeles Economic Progression Council. Because of his father's sudden death, Stuart had just become president of the family enterprise, Bunning Construction, a company specializing in building structures for large businesses new to the Los Angeles area. He was to take his father's place on the Council.

Council members asked Charles to join because his reputation with a budget ledger had achieved almost legendary status in the region, and they knew his services could be invaluable to them. After that first meeting, at which both Charles and Stuart were unanimously inducted, the other members of the Council invoked a long-standing tradition: new members were required to stand the bill at a nearby speakeasy for drinks for all other members. It was in the raucous, music-filled back section of the speakeasy that Charles and Stuart first visited and soon discovered they had two things in common that would forge a deep and lasting friendship: a love of managing money and a desire to accumulate enough wealth to afford a luxurious lifestyle. Although they were already moving swiftly toward that lifestyle, both knew membership in the Council would open financial doors for them they could never reach on their own.

The Greater Los Angeles Economic Progression Council was formed by businessmen representing a broad spectrum of companies all across the greater Los Angeles area, ranging from banks to real estate to shipping to the emerging movie industry. They had expanded membership so greatly in the past half dozen years they now had within their group representatives from nearly every corner of business and industry. All members were from Los Angeles, but they did not, in any way, represent the interests of the city, unless that happened coincidentally along the way. Rather, the Council existed for one purpose: to make money for its members.

The Council met the last Monday evening of each month to talk about potential investment opportunities. Each member brought to these discussions his own special expertise, so there were few if any areas not explored in great detail when a potential investment was brought before the group. If the Council decided a particular enterprise seemed worthy of investment, all members were asked to provide a specified dollar amount toward the venture. In this way, all members shared the same risk—and the same profit if positive results were achieved.

Los Angeles was the perfect environment for this club because, as the city grew, so did the possibilities for investment. Los Angeles had just become America's third largest city, and businesses and the people attached to them continued to move into the area at a rate unparalleled in any other city in the country. The Chamber of Commerce took most of the credit for this because of three incredibly successful publicity campaigns they had running simultaneously.

The first campaign touted the city as the "New Port of the Country." With the recent expansion of the Port of Los Angeles, few would argue with the claim. The more the port was advertised, the more businesses that relied on shipping took notice. As a result, the once sparsely developed areas around the harbor were becoming filled with office buildings and warehouses.

The second campaign boasted "Los Angeles: The Most Beautiful Weather, Year Round!" This sunny California city—with very little temperature fluctuation and only occasional precipitation—appeared like heaven on earth to many of those in other parts of the country used to seasonal deep snow, torrential rains, tornadoes, and other natural disasters.

All around the area, billboards displaying pictures of families frolicking happily on the beaches helped to promote the third campaign: "Los Angeles—The Healthy City, the Perfect Place for Raising a Family." The Chamber augmented this campaign with health statistics they had created themselves after meeting with officials from area hospitals. Some local groups may have doubted the accuracy of the numbers, but no one challenged them because newspaper headlines like "9 Out of 10 Doctors Say Los Angeles Is the 'Health Capital' of the World!" made *everyone* look better.

Out of self-interest, the Council supported these campaigns in every way possible. Members knew the better the city did, the more they would profit. The Council's president, Raymond Butler, was fond of saying, "What's good for the goose, is good for the gander." It was a perfect symbiotic relationship between the Council and the city. When the council provided a gift here, a donation there, an endorsement when needed, the relationship tightened. In response, it wasn't uncommon for the resulting action to be a quick permit, a favorable building inspection, a tip about a rezoning plan. Nothing approached the point where anyone was seriously worried about legal consequences, but everyone knew there was more than a shade of "looking the other way" going on. Still, as long as greed didn't exceed need, all profited and were perfectly happy.

It was with the preservation of this special relationship in mind that Charles decided to call Stuart.

"Listen, my friend, we may have a situation brewing."

"Of what type?" Stuart asked. "A business opportunity? If so, I'm all ears."

Charles paused a moment before responding. "I better explain. This may be nothing, but then again it might be time to call the Council together to hear about this. I'd like your thoughts here."

He paused again, lowered his voice to make sure his secretary couldn't hear him, then continued, "It's merely speculation at this point, but I have a doctor here, a good one, who thinks there may be a serious, contagious illness coming toward the city."

"What type of illness? What are you talking about?"

Charles cleared his throat before replying. "He said something about a type of pneumonia that can spread like a fire, but he's not absolutely sure of the diagnosis yet."

"Then why are you worried about it? What does it have to do with us, with the Council?"

"I'm worried about it because, remember, we're the 'Health Capital' of the world, and it would be very bad for all of our business concerns if we are suddenly known as the 'Pneumonia Capital' of the world. Follow me?"

"Not really. We're not doctors. What can *we* do about this?"

"If this turns out to be as bad as this doctor thinks, then we need to cover ourselves."

The confusion clear in his voice, Stuart asked, "What do you mean? Cover how?"

Charles lowered his voice even more before replying, "Look, if there ends up being an outbreak of something serious, that could keep people from coming to Los Angeles, which would halt several of our projects. Projects, I might add, that you and I are invested in right up to our eyeballs. That wouldn't be good, but if things do go bad, I'm sure there would still be money to be made, right?"

Stuart let out a hearty laugh. "Anyone ever tell you you're going to hell? And probably straight there. Take advantage of the suffering? You're horrible, Charles."

"Yeah, maybe so, but I don't lose any sleep over it. I'd rather plan ahead right now and be safe rather than sorry later."

"So, just what plan do you have in mind? If the illness does end up being an issue, how could we profit?"

"Let me ask you this," Charles replied. "What's needed most when people are sick? Medicines and medical supplies, that's what. If this ends up even half as bad as the doctor suspects, and I do want to say I still have my doubts, these would quickly end up in short supply. We have ships coming every day to the docks. Suppliers of these goods from overseas are cheap, a lot cheaper than we can get over here. So, we could be ahead of the game by getting shipments in place if needed. Oh, we don't have to act right this minute, but getting a plan in place might not be a bad idea."

"You may be on to something," Stuart said, the laughter gone, his voice now dead serious. "Let's bring this up at the next Council meeting. I think it's a good idea. I agree completely with you. So, what do we do now?"

"Nothing. At least not immediately. Some expert is being called in to confirm if we have a problem. I think he'll be here tomorrow. If we do have a medical crisis, we'll call a special meeting of the Council as fast as we can. Make sense?"

"I'm with you. All the way. Call me again when you know something definite."

"Will do. In the meantime, I'm not sure which way I should hope, which way to cheer. Seems we win either way here."

"You *are* going to hell," Stuart laughed.

"And you'll be right there with me," Charles shot back. "With a pocket full of cash, no doubt."

Both men laughed heartily—then hung up their phones at the same time.

Charles then yelled out to his secretary, "Judy, I'm free now. I'm open for business."

....

CHAPTER 10

Spreading

October 29
9:46 A.M.

I was pouring over medical books at a small table at the back of the hospital's medical library when I felt a sudden and firm tap on my left shoulder. I was so startled I knocked a whole stack of books to the floor as I jerked my head around.

"Oh, didn't mean to scare you," Maria said. "I'm sorry. I need to talk to you, and I thought you might be here."

She bent down to pick up the books, but I stopped her. "Look at this first," I said, pointing to a drawing in the book open before me. "Say hello to *Yersinia Pestis*. I saw either him or a really close cousin at the autopsy this morning."

After studying the drawing carefully, she said, "It is shaped like a kidney. Is this what you saw in the microscope?"

"I remember a very short lecture about this in medical school, but the doctor who shared the information just skimmed over everything. He laughed and said we needed to know about all three forms of plague, but we'd never see a case of any of them. He said it was a disease right out of the Middle Ages—that nearly half the population of Europe at that time fell to it. I believed him that I'd never encounter it . . . until now."

Maria bent down to retrieve the spilled books as I went on, "I put in a call to an expert, Dr. James Perry. He's in San Francisco, but he promised to be here first thing tomorrow morning. He was skeptical, and I don't blame him, so I promised if this was a wild goose chase I'd buy him the thickest steak in town while I ate crow. Dr. Perry is probably the world's foremost authority, so we'll know if we're facing plague. It'd be a blow to my reputation, but I'm still praying I'm wrong, praying it's something else easier to fight."

While she placed the last of the books on the table, I asked, "What did you want to see me about?"

"I'm afraid I bring bad news. I just talked to Father Brualla. He's found more cases he says are just the same. One of them is a neighbor who took care of Francisca Lajun when she first became ill."

"Oh, no!" I said, slamming my fist on the drawing before me. "So soon? No matter what it is, we've got to figure out a way to stop the spread. Better get back out there and see what we can do."

"I knew you'd say that, so I asked Father Brualla to meet us again at the church. Do you want me to find Ed and the ambulance?"

"No, I don't think so. Better not. There's no way Charles Hornbeck is going to let me isolate more people right now. We'll have to get them to the church and do the best we can for them there. We'll take my Ford. When we get back, I'll let Hornbeck know what's going on and see if I can get some help out there. Even that will be tough, but not as bad as getting him to agree to more isolation rooms. Don't worry. I'll figure out something."

As I stood from the table, I suddenly realized that Maria still hadn't gone home. "Wait a minute," I said. "Didn't I order you to go home?"

"No," she replied sharply. "You ordered me to get some sleep, and I did—in the nurses' lounge on the third floor. I got enough. I'm fine."

"I doubt that very much, but we don't have time to argue about it. You sure you're ready to go?"

"Don't worry about me. I'll keep up."

"One more thing," I said, facing her again. "Whatever this is, it's bad. Dangerous—and to us, too. You've done a great service already, so I want to give you a chance to get out now because I can't guarantee we won't end up the same as Francisca Lujan. If it is plague, the mortality rate is very high. We still don't have a good treatment. You can stay right here and run things while I'm away. Somebody needs to do that, you know. If you'd rather be here, I'll understand."

Her face was expressionless as she put her hands on her hips. "Are you finished?" she asked, quietly. When I responded I was, she said, "Good. Then let's get going. We're wasting time."

"We are at that," I said, waving her ahead of me. "After you."

Neither of us said a word as we walked down the hallway. At the exit door, she held the door handle and said, "You don't need to ask me that again."

Before I could respond, she stepped out into the morning sun.

····· ····· ·····

The drive to the church took us a long time because of work being done on the railroad tracks where they intersected Macy Street. Anyone traveling across this part of Los Angeles knew there would always be a delay of some kind thanks to the Southern Pacific Railroad. That was an absolute and, without much success, I was doing my best to get used to it. Fortunately, this time the wait was only about five minutes, which was much better than usual. When we finally arrived at the church, I parked my car in the alley behind the rectory.

As soon as we stepped from the car, Maria asked, "How are we going to get our patients back here to the church? Your car isn't exactly an ambulance, you know."

"I've already thought about that. A car was donated to the church a few months back. It will probably take several trips back and forth, depending on where we find them, but Father Brualla can take care of that. It may take time, but we'll get it done.

"There is another reason why I didn't ask Ed to come along. People won't take notice of my car or the church's so much, but I didn't want an ambulance seen leaving the homes of so many. We don't want a panic starting here. If people see an ambulance coming and going and start asking questions—and find out a bad illness is spreading—they might scatter. We know what could happen then."

She said, smiling, "I think there's a little conniver in you."

"Oh, you have no idea," I replied, smiling back.

Father Brualla must have been watching from the window in his rectory because he opened the door before I could knock.

"Please, come in," he said, his voice firm. "We must talk at once."

When we were all inside, he began, "Matthew, there are now five more cases. All the same as Francisca and Jesús. I am frightened. If this is the Influenza again—"

"It's not," I interrupted quickly. "That much I'm sure of."

Looking at Maria so she understood I didn't want her to say anything, I continued, "I have a specialist, a very great doctor, coming tomorrow. He should be able to tell us exactly what this is, so, we'll know soon. In the meantime, we need to bring the new cases here to the church—and as soon as possible."

"Why? Why not leave them in their homes with their families?"

"For exactly that reason—their families. We don't want them passing this illness along to others in their homes. We need to isolate them now before it spreads so far we can't stop it."

Father Brualla sat back in his chair, clasped his hands together, and said, "It will be hard on them."

"We must think of the entire community and what's best for everyone."

Maria, who had thankfully been quiet to this point finally jumped in. "I'll be with them, Father. I'm staying here."

He smiled but didn't say anything right away. Instead, he stood, walked to the window, looked outside, and said, "That is very nice . . . considering these aren't your people."

Maria's back snapped straight. "Listen here—" was all she could get out before I interrupted her.

"Father, you're tired and upset. And you," I said pointing at Maria, "You have an inkling of what your next words were going to be, so don't. We've important things to do *right now*."

Doing my best to put focus back where it belonged, I turned to Father Brualla and asked, "Do you still have those Army surplus cots, the folding ones, that we brought here when we had the measles outbreak over on Avila Street?"

"They're in the old storage building out back. We'll have to clean them up, but they will work. I think we have everything we need except enough sheets and blankets. We burned those."

"I'll take care of that," I said. "Basic medical supplies will be brought later today, at least enough to get us through the night. Nurse McDonnell will be here to make sure everything gets set up appropriately. Anything else I've forgotten?"

"I cannot think of anything at this moment. We'll do what we did when the measles came. We'll tack up sheets to close off half the sanctuary and keep everyone inside."

"Good. Then I suppose we better go look at our new patients—and pray that more haven't cropped up."

Father Brualla nodded, closed his eyes, and said, "Prayer is exactly what we need most now."

I wasn't going to argue with that.

....

We took my car and drove straight to Mrs. Samarano's home. I wanted to examine her first because she had taken care of Francisca right after she fell ill. Her home was right next door to the Lajuns, and the only outward difference I could see between the two structures was that the Samaranos had painted their front porch and window frames a light beige, and wooden fencing with a closely formed crisscross lattice pattern extended from the bottom of the porch to the ground all around the home. I imagined the purpose of the fencing was to keep animals and children from exploring underneath the house.

Since Mrs. Samarano had the most direct contact with Francisca, I needed to know if her symptoms were closest to Mr. Lajun's or those of his daughter. That knowledge would greatly help my diagnosis, and it would be one of the first questions asked by Dr. Perry on his arrival.

Mr. Samarano answered the door, greeted Father Brualla warmly, and urged us to enter the house quickly. No sooner had we stepped inside when he stopped, turned to Father Brualla, and said, his voice now cracking, "*Mi Lucena está enferma, pero mi hijo . . . temo . . . Por favor, ayúdelo.*"

Maria immediately said, "Oh, no!"

"What is it?" I asked, leaning closer to her. "What did he say?"

"It's his son. He thinks he now also has it. This could be spreading much faster than we feared."

Mr. Samarano walked over to me, took my hands, and said, his English labored but clear, "Help us, please."

"We'll do everything possible. I promise you. Please, may I examine your wife?"

The layout of their home was nearly identical to the Lajuns', so as we entered the bedroom, I had a chilling "been here before" moment that temporarily stopped me in my tracks. Maria handed me gloves, adding a mask this time as well. She donned the same, but Father Brualla, as he had done at the Lajun home, waved them off.

Mrs. Samarano was under several covers, but she was still shivering, likely as a result of fever. As Maria and I approached the bed, Mrs. Samarano opened her eyes. Her face was tired, drawn, expressionless. I introduced myself and Maria, and then pointed to Father Brualla, who quickly knelt beside the bed, took her hand in his, and said her name repeatedly, softly, "Lucena, Lucena."

While Maria checked Mrs. Samarano's temperature and spoke to her gently in Spanish, I rolled her on her side and listened to her lungs. The crackling and gurgling sounds were much more pronounced than I had heard in Francisca, so it was evident her state was already quite advanced. Pulse rate, as I anticipated, was also quite elevated. I also noted she was expecting, possibly as far as six months along.

"Temperature?" I asked Maria.

"Hundred and three."

"Pupils? Did you check?"

"Cloudy, the right more than the left."

"Other observations?"

"It was only for a moment, but while checking pulse rate I believe I detected some irregularity."

"Palpitations," I replied. "I noticed them, too, likely tied to the blood pressure. I'll check lymph nodes."

I gently eased Mrs. Samarano flat on her back again and checked the nodes at her neck. There was no swelling. However, when I moved the covers to the side and began easing her gown up to continue my examination, she suddenly went rigid, started breathing rapidly, and tried rolling away from me.

"Better let me do that," Maria said, moving closer. "She'll take it much better from me."

"Know what to look for?"

She gave me a sideways glance as if to say, "What do you think?" Then, speaking softly to Mrs. Samarano to comfort her, she checked her neck, under her arms, and then finally the area about the groin. When she finished, she smiled, thanked Mrs. Samarano, and pulled the covers tightly up around her. Finally turning to me, she said, matter-of-factly, "No swelling—anywhere."

Obviously taking that as a positive sign, Father Brualla squeezed her hands and said, "*El examen fue bien. Vamos rezar.*"

Maria anticipated my question and said, "He asked her to pray with him."

I nodded. "Let's look at the son. Where is he?"

Maria turned to Mr. Samarano, who had been standing quietly at the door since we entered the room, and asked him where we could find their son. His answer was long. When he finished, Maria quickly translated for me. "He said his son, Alberto, started a cough yesterday and now has a fever, but he can't keep him in bed. He's seven and is apparently quite an active child. He was playing on the back steps until right before we got here, so he *thinks* he's still there. Should I go get him?"

"That's just great," I said, shaking my head. "We've got to get him in here right away—before he comes in contact with others. That nurse's uniform might scare him off. Let's have Father Brualla look for him."

Father Brualla heard me, looked over, and nodded. After patting Mrs. Samarano on the back of her hand, he stood and left the room.

Mr. Samarano then asked me a series of questions, but his English wasn't clear enough for me to understand most of what he was saying. Maria must have figured this out because she asked him to sit in a chair by the window. Once he was seated, she pointed to his wife, smiled, and then turned quite serious as she spoke to him. I picked up only a word here and there, but understood she was trying her best to comfort him. When she finished, Mr. Samarano, now appearing much more at ease, reached forward, slowly shook her hands, and said, *"Gracias y te bendigo."*

I didn't need a translator for that. The look on his face said everything.

Just then Father Brualla reentered the room with Alberto in tow. Both were out of breath, and the son was gasping for air between deep coughs. He was stocky and had raven black hair that was long at the sides. His cheeks were flushed, and there were slight beads of sweat on his forehead.

"Maria, please tell him I'd like for him to lie on the other bed so I can examine him."

"I can speak for myself," he said, proudly. "I'm Alberto. I was born here."

"Then please forgive me, Alberto," I said, bowing slightly toward him. "I'd like to check a few things because your mother isn't feeling well, and I want to find out if you might be coming down with the same thing. If you are, then we could treat you both. May I please examine you?"

"Sure. Want me over there?" he asked, pointing to the bed.

"That would be fine. Let's begin."

I checked him thoroughly while Maria took his temperature, which registered a hundred and one. His lungs were clear, which suggested he was likely at the very first stage of the illness. He also had no swollen lymph nodes. Still, he would need to be kept away from others.

When I had finished, through Maria I explained to Mr. Samarano that we wanted to come back later and take his wife and son to the church, where they would receive the best care we could provide. I expected him to put up at least a little bit of fight, but word had spread about Francisca's death, and it was clear Mr. Samarano didn't want the same fate within his family. He asked Maria a few questions, and when he seemed satisfied with the responses, he nodded he understood and thanked us both again.

As we walked back out to the car, I spoke quietly to Maria. "Lymphatic system normal in both, which means if I'm correct this has now moved fully to the pneumonic state. By how swollen Mr. Lujan's nodes were, I'd have to say he must have been the first, or at the very least *one* of the first, to become infected, and the progression took off from there. If that can be confirmed, we'd sure be able to trace the spread better. We better act fast. Once it becomes pneumonic . . ."

I could tell by the look in her eyes Maria understood. Rather than saying anything, she gently squeezed my arm. At that point, there wasn't anything to say.

We spent the next hour visiting two other families. Both of their homes were just around the corner on Avila Street. At the Sanchez home, the father felt so terrible he had already taken to his bed. The Milan's lived just three houses away, and in their family the grandmother, mother, and a daughter were ill. All presented symptoms consistent with what we had just found in Mrs. Samarano and Alberto. As we had at the Samarano home, Maria and I worked together to explain we would soon be moving all of them to the church. Again, likely because of the news of Francisca, none of them refused. To my relief, the plan seemed to provide them with great comfort.

Once we were back at the church, Father Brualla thanked us and excused himself after explaining he needed to get down to the corner market to recruit a few people to help him prepare the cots and the section of the sanctuary that would serve as our temporary hospital.

As he left, I asked Maria to sit in a chair next to his desk. She fell heavily back, almost flopping into the chair. She was, plain and simple, dead on her feet. She took off her nurse's cap as soon as she was settled, removed some small clips from her hair, and let her rich, dark hair fall about her shoulders. It was the first time I had seen her attempt to relax—and the first time without full uniform. And although she looked as if she could close her eyes and be off to sleep instantly, I also noticed something else. She was more than pretty. She was quite beautiful.

I must not have realized how long I had been staring. Suddenly, she looked up and asked, "What? What are you looking at?"

Fumbling for words, I said, "I . . . well, I'm looking at someone who ought to be home in her own bed. And when's the last time you had something to eat? And why, of all things, did you say you'd stay here tonight? You need rest more than anything, and on top of that, you and the good Father aren't exactly chums. I shudder to think what's going to happen between you two when I leave."

She laughed lightly, smiled, and said, "Do you have a cigarette?"

"You smoke?"

"No, but I'm thinking this is probably a good time to start. It might help me stay awake."

I frowned. "You don't need anything to keep you awake. Close your eyes and drift off for a while if you really intend to stay here."

Suddenly the phone rang, startling both of us.

She was closer to the phone, but she didn't move. "Well, you going to answer that?" she asked.

Picking up the receiver, I said, "Dr. Thompson here for Father Brualla. May I take a message?"

The connection wasn't the best, but I could still hear the voice on the other end say, "Doctor, this is Nurse Adams. I was hoping I'd catch you there. I'm afraid I have terrible news. Mr. Lajun just passed, not more than ten minutes ago. I thought you should know."

I paused a long time before responding. "I see. Thank you for the call. I'm coming back to the hospital right now. I'll stop by your desk as soon as I get there."

I hung up and stared at the floor.

"And?" Maria asked. "Don't make me pry it out of you."

"Mr. Lajun just died." That was all I could think of to say. I walked around the desk and sat down next to her feet, which were still propped there.

"Oh," was all she said, softly, before closing her eyes and leaning back farther.

Spotting Father Brualla's cloak hanging behind the door, I grabbed it and covered her up. I half expected her to kick it off, but she didn't move.

"There," I said, backing away. "Hard to tell how long he'll be gone. Close your eyes and rest. You look terrible."

"That's what a woman always loves to hear," she said, dryly.

"That's not what I meant," I fired back quickly.

She smiled again and said, "I guess you're right. I could get a few winks *if* you'd get out of here."

"I'm gone," I said, moving toward the door. "Close your eyes."

I looked back, and I could have sworn she was already asleep.

....

CHAPTER 11

The Experts

October 29
5:20 P.M.

I was studying a map of the Macy Street area when Nurse Adams knocked sharply on my office door.

"Here they are, Doctor," she said, stepping back into the hallway.

"I'm Dr. Perry," the older of the two announced as he stepped in. "I brought along a 'second opinion' with me. I hope you don't mind. This is Dr. Robert Miller."

I had heard so much about Dr. Perry I had already formed an image of him in my mind: old, distinguished, prim and proper in his manner. What I saw before me was nowhere near close to that. He *was* older, I guessed somewhere in his mid-sixties, but he had the lean build of an athlete. He was wearing a very expensive and dapper suit with matching vest. No, he didn't look at all like an old, stodgy, microscope gazer. He looked like he might just have done a bout of sparring at the gym before showering and dressing for a formal dinner.

Dr. Miller appeared close to my age. He was tall, thin, with a full head of black hair just starting to lighten at the temples, and had the looks of what my mother called a "fanner," a man so handsome women would reach for their fans when he passed by. It would have been serious under-statement to say these weren't the doctors I was expecting.

"I'm Doctor Thompson," I said, stepping forward to shake their hands. "Thank you for coming—"

Dr. Perry cut me off. "As I mentioned on the telephone, I shouldn't be here. We've scheduled my wife to have her gallbladder removed day after tomorrow, so I'm going to take a look and then head back to the station for the overnight train. That's why I brought along Dr. Miller. I stole him away from Harvard. He's one of the best pulmonary experts in the country—*the* best if you listen to him. He's been through outbreaks several times, so he knows about as much as I do these days."

"He's exaggerating," Dr. Miller said, a thin smile coming to his lips. "It's true I've been around some, but you're looking at the very best in the world in Dr. Perry."

Before I could get a word in, Dr. Perry turned toward me. "That's enough bragging on each other. Doctor, as time is precious, take us to the morgue. While we walk, I'd like to ask you more about your cases here. And, specifically, if there have been any more deaths."

"Follow me," I said, urging them to the hallway. As we made our way to the elevator, I gave a brief update. "Several more cases today, all pre-senting the same symptoms. We have them isolated right now at a church in the area where this started. I decided on overlapping standard treat-ments for both influenza and—just in case I'm right—*Yersinia Pestis*. We're doing our best to keep patients hydrated and as comfortable as possible, given the circumstances."

"Sounds reasonable," Dr. Perry responded. "I would have done the same in your place."

I addressed my next words specifically for Dr. Perry. "We had another death this morning. I suspect he was either the first or one of the first to contract the illness. The body is waiting for us."

Both doctors glanced at each other, but neither said anything. Once the elevator stopped and the doors opened to the morgue, Dr. Miller turned to me and said, "After you get us set up here, stand to the side and let us complete our own independent examination. It's how Dr. Perry and I work together. You can observe, but we'd appreciate it if you don't interrupt. If we want to point out something to you, we'll let you know."

"I understand," I said, nodding to both of them. "I'm grateful for the opportunity to observe and, I hope, learn from both of you."

"Good," Dr. Perry said. "We find many doctors are upset by our routine. It will be nice to work with someone who won't be."

I smiled. "I'm fine with this, but you won't receive the same from Dr. Jacobs, our resident pathologist. He feels this is his kingdom, and he's the king. Good luck with him."

"We've dealt with *royalty* before," Dr. Miller said, smiling back. "Thanks for warning us."

Dr. Jacobs was looking into a microscope when we entered. I cleared my throat, and he looked up. After quick introductions and a reminder from me to Dr. Jacobs that our guests were to have full cooperation, Dr. Perry asked to see the slides and notes from the first case. With a sneer, Dr. Jacobs grudgingly retrieved the slides and, without saying so much as a hello, pointed to a microscope near an examination table on the other side of the room. Just as we headed that direction, he muttered under his breath, softly but with enough carry we could all hear it, "Don't know what you'll see that I didn't."

Dr. Miller turned to me and whispered, "Well, he's quiet royalty—at least for now."

"I'm surprised he isn't following right along with us. He stuck to me like flypaper the last time I was here."

"We always bring out the best in people," Dr. Perry said, laughing softly. "Actually, we usually bring out the green-headed monster *jealousy* in most—or her first cousin *anger*. Whenever we're brought in, for whatever medical malady is present, people always have the misguided idea that we're there to pick up the towel they threw in when they couldn't make a diagnosis. It's true we do some of that, but others don't know it's no disgrace to ask for assistance, and it's our job to pick up those towels to make sure we know what we're fighting."

"That's a fine attitude, Doctor," I said pulling up a chair next to the microscope.

Before he sat down, he turned to me again and said, "Dr. Thompson, your reputation as a fine diagnostician is getting to be known in the medical community. I just may have to steal you away from here like I did-Miller from Harvard," Dr. Perry said.

Dr. Miller shrugged his shoulders. "He had me at San Fran General before I knew what hit me. Be careful around him."

"Slides no good—not stained properly and too smeared to be of use," Dr. Perry said, looking up from the microscope. "We'll make our own. Where's the other body?"

What happened next had the choreography of a fine dance performance. During their autopsy, it was clear they had done this together so many times before that each could anticipate the movements of the other. As one checked weight of the body, the other took measurements. While one conducted a routine external exam of the upper torso, neck, and head, the other checked everything below. While one made an incision here, the other made one there. One examined the lungs, the other the heart. They seldom spoke, but, when they did it appeared they were working their way down a master checklist for the examination. Finally, as Dr. Perry gathered the necessary fluids, Dr. Miller walked over to Dr. Jacobs and asked for some new slides. It would have taken me well over an hour to accomplish what they did in just twenty-five minutes. It would have been incredibly bad form to applaud at an autopsy, but I wanted to do so to express my admiration.

When Dr. Perry finally placed a new slide on the microscope, he fiddled with the focus knobs until he had them just as he wanted. For a long minute, he peered intently through the lenses. Finally, without saying a word, he motioned for Dr. Miller to take a look. Then, at the same time, both said to me, "Your turn. Come and tell us what you see."

The kidney shaped structure I saw was identical to what I'd seen in the medical book earlier in the morning. Without looking up, I said, quietly, "*Yersinia Pestis.*"

"Your diagnosis is, unfortunately, correct," Dr. Perry said. "Full-blown pneumonic state. We lost over twenty-five hundred in San Fran, and I saw nearly double that fall in China a few years after that. The loss of life can be staggering in a very short period of time if *Yersinia Pestis* is left unchecked. Los Angeles is growing by leaps and bounds, which makes the potential pool of victims very deep. *Very* deep."

"I was praying it would be otherwise," I said, looking again at the body. My heart was racing, and suddenly I had a hard time catching my breath. I leaned back against the wall and blew out a sharp breath.

"You okay?" Dr. Miller asked. "You don't look good. When was the last time you ate or had some good rest?"

"Sorry, doctors," I said, standing straight again. "I guess I am a little tired . . . and a little stunned. I'll perk up."

Dr. Perry put his hand on my shoulder and said, gently, "Don't worry, Son. First time I saw Mr. *Pestis*, I fainted dead away. Just flopped to the floor in front of a huge crowd. In an operating theater no less. At least you didn't do that."

I knew it wasn't true, but I was grateful for his kindness. I just nodded and said, "Thanks."

Dr. Miller asked, "Have you notified anyone—any other medical offices—yet?"

"No. I didn't. I wanted to be sure. Now that we are, we should see our hospital administrator, Charles Hornbeck. He said he was going to stay until you could give your report, so I'm sure he's up in his office. If you're both finished here, we'll let Jacobs clean up after us and get upstairs. Fine with you?" They said it was, so we started leaving as soon as Dr. Perry gave detailed instructions to Dr. Jacobs. However, before we could get to the door, Dr. Jacobs mumbled, again loud enough for us to hear, "What do you think I am? Your maid?"

"From royalty to a maid in short order," Dr. Miller said, smiling broadly. "My, how quickly some people fall."

Dr. Perry just shook his head. "People from Harvard have none of the social graces, as you can see in this man. Good thing he's a fine doctor."

"I'll take skill over manners any day," I said, laughing softly.

"Then we'll all get along just fine," Dr. Perry said, urging us ahead of him.

....

I was surprised, and pleased, by how smoothly our meeting went with Charles. When they presented their diagnosis, I half expected Charles to wring his hands over the amount of money all of this would cost the hospital. Instead, he took the news calmly, almost stoically, and asked how he could be of help. I could tell his demeanor even caught Dr. Perry and Dr. Miller off guard because there were several awkward silences at points after they explained all the contacts that would have to be made and the reports Charles would have to complete. I didn't know whether Charles had resigned himself to everything or was in shock.

Toward the end of our conversation, Dr. Perry gave Charles an account of the San Francisco outbreak as it unfolded some twenty years ago. He shared it as a cautionary tale of what would happen if we weren't all forthright in reporting the information to the proper agencies, especially the Office of the United States Surgeon General and specific State health organizations. Charles said he understood and would take care of everything. However, he asked for twenty-four hours so he could inform all appropriate local groups and have plans in place first. He also said that as soon as we left he'd make the necessary calls to get a meeting set up for early the next morning. He'd invite a few key people so at this point secrecy could still be kept as much as possible. Dr. Perry approved, primarily because he said the key to not having a panic erupt on our hands would be for everyone involved locally to be communicating effectively with each other before letting out any information to the general public.

Finally, Dr. Perry spoke of his need to get back to San Francisco to be with his wife during her surgery; however, Dr. Miller would remain to help us through the crisis. Charles thanked him profusely for his help *and* for his loan of Dr. Miller. At that point, Dr. Perry asked if someone could help him get back to the station. Charles called down and secured an ambulance. When Dr. Perry raised an eyebrow, Charles said, "It'll get you there quicker. Consider it a taxi with a siren."

As we left Charles' office, I thanked Dr. Perry for his assistance and gave my best wishes for a speedy recovery for his wife. He thanked *me* for sending for him. He appreciated the opportunity to "get back in the saddle again" and asked that I watch over Dr. Miller during his stay. I assured him I would.

Once we were in the hallway, Dr. Perry turned to me and said, "Doctor, I'm going to sound like an old uncle, but listen to me. You watch yourself. Gloves, mask, and gown at all times. Make sure there's no contact with fluids without the proper precautions, and even then you might want to add a prayer or two for good measure. We've lost too many good doctors and nurses to this monster. I don't want your name added to the list. And one last thing. After my wife has recovered, if you need me back here, just call."

I was caught off guard by what happened next. He stepped forward, shook my hand firmly, and patted me on the back. "You just watch yourself," he repeated. "Never let your guard down. Now get going."

"I understand," I said. "Thank you—for everything."

We stayed with him in the elevator until the third floor, where Dr. Miller and I got out to go to my office. As soon as the elevator doors had closed, I turned to Dr. Miller and said, "I'd rather not take the time for it, but I know I should get something to eat. And I doubt you've had a chance for a bite today, either. There's a little diner across the street that serves mostly our hospital employees. You up for it?"

"I thought you'd never ask," he said, patting his stomach. "I'm empty."

"Just give me a minute to call down and tell my nurse to join us. I *know* she hasn't eaten a morsel in over a day. I also want you to meet her because she'll be with us all the way through this."

As soon as I finished my call to Maria, I turned back to Dr. Miller and said, "Now, I don't want you to run when you see the name of the place. It's called Morg's. And, yes, there are always plenty of jokes that he gets his stew meat from our morgue. Don't be half surprised if you get razzed some. You'll be recognized as a newcomer, and you'll probably get the special menu Morg keeps behind the main counter for just such instances. What it is, basically, is an autopsy sketch with different parts labeled to show the 'Specials of the Day'—like rib roast, rump roast, baked leg, and so forth. First-timers, especially new doctors and nurses, usually get razzed a lot. Crude? You bet. But once you get past all that, the food isn't half bad. And it's cheap and fast."

"Glad you warned me," he said, shaking his head. "I'm still queasy from the train, so I appreciate it."

"Don't mention it," I replied. "Just didn't want you to get sick and ruin my meal."

"Very funny," he said.

....

Morg shook my hand and greeted me warmly as we entered his diner. I introduced him to Dr. Miller and told him that since he had already had a long and bumpy train trip, perhaps it wouldn't be wise to give him the "special" menu. While showing us to our table, Morg laughed and said he quite understood.

Right after our glasses of water arrived, I heard the tiny bell above the door jingle as Maria walked in. I stood and waved her over. Dr. Miller was still looking over the real menu and at first didn't look up as she sat down. Maria promptly picked up his glass and poured about half of its contents right in his lap, causing Dr. Miller to jump up and yell, "What in the—"

He stopped mid-sentence, a look of shock taking over when he saw the perpetrator before him. "Maria!" he shouted. "Now what was that all about!"

Maria roughly shoved her chair back, stood over him, and let loose with a string of insults I hadn't heard shoved together in quite that manner before. All eyes were on her as the other customers stopped what they were doing and focused attention our way. Morg clapped his hands loudly until he had her attention, then shook his head and pressed a finger to his lips. His meaning was clear enough, so Maria slowly, but grudgingly, sat down.

"As if you didn't know," she then shot back. "You're just lucky I didn't break the glass over the top of your skull."

"You two *know* each other?" I asked, still stunned by what I had seen. "Where did you..."

Still under Morg's stern gaze, Maria struggled to keep her voice level. "This . . . this cretin! First, he uses me to get a special surgical internship with my father. Then, the night of the Nurse's Ball he says he'll meet me there, and he never shows up. I was never so humiliated in all my life. I didn't mind being used to get the internship. Deep down I knew what you were up to. But to leave me alone at the Ball like that! How could you!"

Dr. Miller cut in, "I didn't *use* you, and I couldn't help missing the Ball. There was a medical emergency."

"That lasted three years?" she replied while gritting her teeth. "You can do better than that!"

While dabbing at his trousers with his napkin, he sat back heavily in his chair and said, his voice almost a whisper, "I felt really bad, but I just didn't know what I could say that would make things better. I was wrong. I knew it at the time. I should have contacted you, but I received word I had to get back to Harvard as quickly as I could. I knew you wouldn't understand, so I decided it was better to, well, let it go."

"Let it go! Why you—"

This time I jumped into the fray. "It appears you two have some things to get settled, but this isn't the time or the place. You've got to stop this, and if you don't, Morg is going to throw us out of here."

Dr. Miller, obviously upset, his hands shaking, turned back to his menu, but Maria was still fuming and staring at him. "You're going to have to let it go for now," I said, handing my menu to Maria. "This will have to wait. I'm not going to be your referee. I need *both* of you right now, and you know why. *That* is what we have to focus on. We shouldn't even be taking the time to eat. We've got much to do."

Then, looking right at Maria, I added, "It has been confirmed. It is our kidney-shaped friend. So, let's order something, eat quickly, and get out of here."

"Oh, no!" was all she said, shaking her head, then looking down at the table.

Obviously trying to lessen the tension, Dr. Miller turned to me and asked, matter of factly, "It's getting very late. What else did you want us to do tonight?"

I did my best to redirect the conversation. "The last report said there were more cases being brought to the church where we're still isolating everyone. We'll have a quick bite and then drive Maria over there so she can help Father Brualla. The poor man just has to be dead on his feet by now."

I turned to Maria. "I know you're exhausted. Hopefully, this will be the last night we'll need you there. Somehow, we're going to have to get everyone over here."

Maria turned her head to the side, and for a moment I thought she was going to start crying. I reached over to put my hand on her shoulder, but she quickly jerked back.

"I need to get some more medical supplies," she said abruptly. Then, standing, she added, "I'll meet you at your car when you're finished. Eat fast. I need to get back to the church."

Before I could say anything, she was already half way to the door.

"Wow—she is *really* mad," Dr. Miller said, shaking his head. "After all this time. I had no idea. I haven't seen her in it must be three years."

"I don't know what went on with you two, and, frankly, I don't want to know," I replied. "I just hope it can be put aside for now. We *need* her. So let's see if we can avoid a donnybrook, okay?"

"I'll try my best."

As Morg stepped over to take our order, I said, "I'm going to have a steak, rare, and whatever vegetables you have in the pot today. And some coffee—black."

"And this gentleman here," I said pointing to Dr. Miller, "He will be the one eating crow tonight—if you can find one in the back."

Dr. Miller turned to Morg, laughed, and said, "He's right. That's all I deserve."

"I'll see if I can find a nice fat one," Morg said, dryly, while scribbling on the order pad. "We always aim to please."

When he was out of earshot, I said, "Don't worry—you'll get the same as me."

"Just as long as I don't end up with something off his 'special' menu," Dr. Miller said, smiling.

Then, turning serious again, he asked, "It just occurred to me I don't have a place to stay while I'm here. I did bring a few clothes, just in case. Is there a place I can bunk at the hospital?"

"I have a small house near downtown. You can stay with me. That's probably best anyway because I don't think we'll be out of each other's sight much until we get a handle on all this. After we eat, we'll drive Maria over to the church. That is, if you think you two can be in the car together. I want you to see what's over there. Then, we'll get back to my place and rest up a little. Tomorrow is going to be more than full."

"Thank you. I appreciate the offer. Frankly, I'm really tired, but I do want to see the church and how it's being set up for this. But then I'll be ready for the sack."

He paused a minute before adding, once again smiling, "And I'll sit in the back seat of your car. Probably the safest place for me. Would be harder for her to whack me if I'm back there, don't you think?"

"I don't think," I replied. "I know. But if she puts her mind to it, sitting in the back won't save you."

We both laughed as Morg, carrying a large serving tray, approached the table again. He lifted the lid on the tray and there, underneath, was a large paper crow. "Will this do, Sir?" he asked Dr. Miller.

"It'll do just fine," I said laughing so loudly those at the tables around us wrenched necks to see what was going on. Soon, the whole diner erupted in laughter as Dr. Miller's face turned crimson.

"What have I gotten myself into?" he finally said.

....

CHAPTER 12

Plague in Paradise

October 30
8:15 A.M.

So much for secrecy . . .

The mayor's council chamber was so crowded when we walked in there were no seats left anywhere. Close to thirty people were present, many of whom were standing along the side wall under a bank of high windows overlooking the downtown district. Charles Hornbeck, sitting in a chair to the far left of the small dais at the back of the room, saw us, stood up, and waved us forward.

As we made our way through the crowd, I recognized several individuals I knew either personally or had seen quite often in the newspaper: Steven Morton, Chief Officer of the Los Angeles City Health Department; Edward Pogue, Head of the County Health Department; Charlie Barker, Police Chief; Jackson Demeter, Chair of the Chamber of Commerce; Raymond Butler, Chairman of the Greater Los Angeles Economic Progression Council; and several representatives from other hospitals and civic organizations. As I scanned the room, it was clear Charles Hornbeck knew how to call a meeting.

They must have been waiting for us because no sooner had we taken our seats when Mayor Stanley Burgess, whom nearly everyone called "Smoky" because of the ever-present pipe dangling at the corner of his mouth, stepped toward the lectern at the middle of the dais.

"Before we begin," he said, his voice strong, stern, "I want to make something abundantly clear. What we are going to talk about in a few moments will *not* leave this room."

One of the men standing in front of the windows removed his cigar, stepped toward the middle of the room, and shouted out, "Geez, Smoky, what are you up to now? Legalizing brothels? Puttin' a speakeasy in every block?"

The crowd erupted in laughter as two men stepped toward this man and shook his hand. Mayor Burgess was not amused. He just stood there, scowling, and waited for everyone to quiet down. The man who had posed the questions, stepped slowly back to the window and shook his head.

The mayor pounded his fist firmly on the lectern, scanned the room carefully, and said, "That's enough of that. You were called here today because you represent the city in important ways. We've much to talk about, but I want to say something first—and no more funny business. If word of this meeting leaks, I'll find out who did it, and the consequences will be *very* severe. This isn't a warning. This is a threat, and believe me, you don't want to cross me on this. Is that plain enough?"

"Okay, so you're serious," Police Chief Barker said, crossing his arms. "But you still haven't said what this is about. We're all busy men. What in the world—"

Mayor Burgess stopped him in mid-question. "You have no idea how busy you're *going* to be, so I suggest you all keep quiet and listen up. We're facing potentially the most serious threat to this city any of us have ever seen before. This does *not* leave the room. The reason will be evident in a few minutes, so just sit there and shut up for once in your lives."

Except for the slight flutter of a window shade caught in the incoming breeze, the room was absolutely silent. At that point, the mayor motioned for Charles Hornbeck to step to the lectern and, as Charles did so, the mayor walked over and took his seat. Everyone in the room knew Charles and that he represented County Hospital, so a low murmur immediately sprung up in pockets around the room. If Charles was going to speak, what was coming wasn't going to be good.

Charles cleared his throat and looked down at a few notes he had written on a scrap of paper. "First, I am in complete agreement with Mayor Burgess. None of what you now hear can leave this room or . . ."

He paused here, slowly turning his head and taking the time to look at the face of every person in the room before continuing, "Or we could have a panic that would ruin this city forever. *Forever.*"

The murmur of a few moments before suddenly became more like a bank of thunder rumbling across the room. Mayor Burgess stood, waved his arms, and shouted, "Keep your mouths shut—and listen!"

"Thank you, your Honor," Charles said, nodding. Turning to face everyone once again, he said, "Those of you who know me know I don't beat around the bush. Brace yourselves, gentlemen. I'm going to put this in plain English. It has now been confirmed. We have cases of the Black Plague in Los Angeles."

The words had barely left his mouth when questions and exclamations erupted from every section of the room: "What do you mean?" "How do you know?" "This some kind of joke?" "You're out of your mind—can't be plague!" "Charles, what are you trying to pull now?"

Charles spied a gavel underneath the lectern, picked it up, and hammered as loudly as he could until the room had quieted enough he could be heard again.

"I assure you this is no joke. We wouldn't have called you together if there was any doubt at all. I'm not going to ask you to take my word about this. If you'll quiet down, I have right over here one of the world's leading experts on the Black Plague, and I want him to address you. Please, please listen. You have to hear this."

He motioned for Robert and me to step forward. "Many of you know Dr. Thompson from my hospital. And this is Dr. Robert Miller from San Francisco General. They're both going to fill you in, so give them your full attention."

I motioned for Robert to stand right next to me as I began. "I know what you just heard is a shock, and some of you probably still don't believe it. But it's true, and we're going to have to deal with it—and fast."

Many before me appeared stunned, shaking their heads in disbelief. When the room finally became silent again, I saw my opportunity. "I'm going to get right to the point so you'll know how we've reached our conclusions. Two days ago, I was called to the Macy Street area—"

The second I mentioned the Macy Street area loud groans sounded throughout the room. However, I quickly continued, raising my voice, "I went there because of suspected cases of influenza just like those we had back in Eighteen. I examined the individuals, and I was fairly certain right away it wasn't influenza. When one of the afflicted individuals died, we conducted an autopsy, but the findings weren't conclusive. After others in that area became ill—and others died—we sent for experts to help us find out exactly what we were fighting. I'd like to introduce you to Dr. Robert Miller. Those in the medical profession consider him one of the world's leading authorities when it comes to illnesses like this, and I'd like him to say a few words."

Robert stepped forward, but before he could begin, Jackson Demeter, Chair of the Chamber of Commerce, stood and asked, of no one in particular, "And this was in the *Macy Street District*?" As soon as he posed the question, he sat back down, shaking his head as he did so. Others around him, shaking their heads, leaned over and whispered. A lone voice called out from the back, "It figures!"

Robert didn't respond to Jackson. Instead, he picked up the gavel but didn't strike it to the lectern. Holding it for a second, he placed it back down and stood still and quiet, staring pointedly at those still talking among themselves. Within a few seconds, the whispering stopped, and everyone's attention turned to the stern-faced man at the lectern who then spoke. "In my career, I've seen four outbreaks of the various forms of the plague, and I know how to diagnose them. I examined one of the dead here, and there's no doubt in my mind—none at all—that we're looking at the type called pneumonic plague. Pneumonic is the form of plague that spreads the quickest, so if action isn't taken immediately, we could be looking at a city-wide outbreak—and beyond."

Edward Pogue, Head of the County Health Department, stood and asked, "Just how sure are you of this? Think of the consequences if you're wrong. Don't we need more confirmation before we get ahead of ourselves? None of my people were even consulted."

Many called out their support for and approval of Pogue's questions. The rumble in the room started growing again until Robert broke in. "You are correct that additional confirmation is always wise. That's why I came here with Dr. James Perry. I know some of you might recall his work during the plague outbreak in San Francisco about twenty years ago. I'm just going to say it bluntly. Probably the only person who knows more about diagnosing this than I do is Dr. Perry, and he confirmed it as well. You won't find *anybody* more experienced than he. We're sure. This *is* pneumonic plague, and it's right here at your doorstep."

The room was absolutely silent—but only for a moment. Police Chief Barker stood, waved his right arm to get everyone's attention, and said, "I was in San Francisco back in O-Four. I was just a snot-nosed beat cop then, but I remember what the plague did to that city. I don't want to live through that again—and don't want it to happen here. So, I have a suggestion that may save us all a lot of time and worry."

All eyes were on him as he continued, "If the cases are coming from the Macy Street area, we're talking about Mexicans. Most of 'em are illegals and shouldn't be here. They probably brought this with 'em. So, this is their problem—not ours."

There were a few shouts of "Hear, hear!" as Chief Barker picked up steam. "I say quarantine 'em. Lock 'em down. If we keep 'em penned up, we'll keep the disease there, right? It'll just die out when they do. Worked like that with the Chinese back in Frisco. If we do the same here, won't be a problem for *us* then."

About half in the room applauded and cheered. I looked at Mayor Burgess, half expecting him to stand and call for quiet. Instead, he leaned back in his chair, bowed his head, and stared at the floor.

Dr. Steven Morton, Chief Officer of the Los Angeles City Health Department, stood and waved for attention. When the applause had died down enough, he said, "Chief, I can't believe what just came out of your mouth. You're a Christian man, after all. What you're suggesting is that we just give these people a death sentence—that we don't do anything to help them. We *have* to help them. That is our duty. Our duty!"

Leaning over close to my ear, Robert said, "Uh, oh—I better jump in again before it's too late. Get ready in case I need you to back me up."

Just as Chief Barker started to stand, Robert pounded the gavel on the lectern until he again had the attention of all. "Look," he said loudly, pointing the gavel at both Chief Barker and Dr. Morton, "I'm not going to take sides here, and we're not going to have a debate. What both of you just said makes sense, at least on one level, so I want to thank you both—and respectfully ask you to remain quiet while I address what you've said."

Pausing just long enough to check that he had Mayor Burgess' attention, Robert spoke, his voice calm this time. "First, what Chief Barker said is important. In most cases, a quarantine of some type is imposed to contain the spread of the disease. Again, because we're dealing with the pneumonic form, if it isn't contained, the whole city could be at great risk."

Turning to face Dr. Morton, Robert went on, "And Doctor Morton is also right. We *do* have to treat those who are ill because if we don't, I can guarantee you the spread will be dramatic no matter what type of quarantine we have. I've seen it before many times. That's just the nature of the illness."

Before Robert could continue, Jackson Demeter, Chair of the Chamber of Commerce, stood and said, his voice quivering, "Quarantine. Treatments. Mexicans. Quite frankly, I don't give a rat's ass about any of that. You people just don't get it, do you? There's something much bigger here we better talk about or we're all going to be finished. What about our city? What about everything we've done, everything we've worked so hard to achieve these past years? We've built what we've touted as the 'Paradise of the West,' and we've done a damn good job of it. If the word *plague* gets attached to us, that's something we'll never overcome. If that happens and the plague doesn't get us, the city will be dead anyway."

A few people applauded. Others shouted, "He's right!" and "Amen!" I looked at Robert, grabbed the gavel, and said, "Okay, now it's my turn."

"Listen up!" I said as loudly as I could. "Hold on just a minute."

When the roar settled to a rumble, I continued, "First of all, we are not going to use the word *plague* again once those doors open back there and we leave this room. I want that understood. Look at the faces around the room now—and listen to yourselves. The word *plague* causes panic, which we simply can't afford. It could cause people to flee the city and scatter to the winds, which could further spread the disease beyond all control. No, from now on we're going to refer to this as malignant pneumonia, a term often used instead. It doesn't carry the same connotation. It still sounds bad, but people won't know quite what it means. They'll just know it's serious and something we have to stop."

I paused to look around the room. I had the attention I wanted. "And I'm recommending that we have nothing in the newspapers about this. Not a word. I'm fully aware we have an obligation to be honest about all of this, but our first obligation is to stop this illness, and our second obligation is to keep a panic from happening. If we can do both—and I think we can—then we also will have met head-on the concerns expressed by Mr. Demeter."

Mr. Demeter rose again from his seat. This time, there wasn't a trace of a quiver in his voice. He asked, almost commandingly, "Then what exactly can we do? If it gets out there is 'Plague in Paradise,' everything we've worked for will fold like a house of cards. I just don't know . . . "

Robert took the gavel from my hand and said, "My turn again."

"Your Honor," he said, looking toward Mayor Burgess. "I've dealt with outbreaks like this before. With your permission, I have a few suggestions I'd like to put forth."

Mayor Burgess sat up straight in his chair and nodded his approval.

"Thank you," Robert said. "First, I'd recommend we institute a tight quarantine around the area where the cases have come from. *Not* because they are Mexicans—this could be any community in the city. We need the quarantine because we have to make sure we stem the spread of the disease, and this is the best way to accomplish that at this point. Your Honor, I'm sure you can appoint the necessary people to do this—and it needs to be done *immediately*. Second, the people inside the quarantine area need to be told why this is happening to help avoid a panic. Leave that to me and to Dr. Thompson. We're dealing with malignant pneumonia, remember? It'll be our job to sell that, and at the same time, to explain to them why the quarantine is necessary. Don't worry. We can do it."

Robert gathered his thoughts before continuing, "I'm sure you have questions, but please let me finish first. There are a few other matters to consider. For this to work, all of us here will have to be kept informed at all times. So that rumors don't get started and so that we all keep to our assigned roles, I'm going to suggest that Mayor Burgess appoint someone to be the 'answer man' who will be available at all times by the telephone when questions arise. From past experience I can tell you keeping up good communication among ourselves will be the key to everything here.

"Finally, we have to treat those who are currently ill and who will shortly become ill. If we don't, this particular form of plague will keep spreading and spreading. In plain language, that means we'll have to have an 'isolation ward' somewhere where we can do what we doctors need to do. Right now, some who are ill are being kept in a church in that area, but there's no more room there. We need another place—and soon. You also need to know there is a serum available for this. Unfortunately, it hasn't been tested enough for me to put my complete faith in it. We're going to check into it, but I'm not even sure we can get any. In the meantime, we're back to the need for an isolation ward—*right now.*"

I couldn't believe what I heard next. To my utter surprise and shock, Charles Hornbeck stood and said, "Doctor, if I may have a word, I think I can put that concern to rest right now."

Charles cleared his throat loudly and said, "I'm putting myself out on a very thin limb here, but on my responsibility, we'll prepare an isolation wing in County Hospital. Out of what I feel is our duty and responsibility to the city, we'll cover much of the cost of that and the treatment that needs to be given to those who are ill."

Audible gasps filled the room. Charles' reputation as a penny-pincher was legendary. More than several mouths hung open, mine included.

"Why, Charles," Mayor Burgess said, standing and moving quickly toward the lectern to stand with us. "I don't know what to say."

Looking around the room, he added, "I don't think any of us do."

For the first time since the discussion had started, many openly laughed—and heartily.

Charles, smiling broadly, responded, "I *do* hate to part with the money, as it appears many of you realize. I won't lie about that. But, there comes a time when the safety of our citizens and the welfare of our city must be put first. It may shock you, but even a miser like me knows that.

"Plus we're going to have some help with the funds. I knew about all of this before the meeting, so I approached the leadership of the Greater Los Angeles Economic Progression Council—the President, Raymond Butler, is sitting right over there—and they have agreed to pick up the check for anything we can't cover. Apparently, Raymond isn't nearly the cheapskate I am."

This time everyone in the room laughed—and started applauding, the applause building to a near ear-splitting crescendo. Charles bowed slightly, as did Raymond Butler, before both slowly sat back down. My first thought while looking at Charles after the applause wound down was, "Who is this man?"

At that point, Mayor Burgess turned back to Robert and asked, "Okay, now with that taken care of, Doctor, is there anything else we should know before we get to action? Do you have any other advice?"

"Just a couple more things. I'd like to reiterate what I said before about the quarantine. It must be done as quickly as possible. And once it's established, we'll have to send in doctors and nurses to do a house-to-house inspection to find all residents who are exhibiting symptoms and isolate them. That's a must. We'll never get ahead of this if we don't. Dr. Thompson explained to me a little about where the cases are clustered, but I'm still not sure I completely understand the geography we're dealing with. So, I'd recommend that someone get a map and talk to Dr. Thompson right now—before we all leave—so that we'll all know the exact area we're talking about. Again, we have to make sure *all* of us are on the same path here, and we all work as a team. That's the only way we're going to succeed."

Mayor Burgess interrupted him. "Mr. Demeter, your Chamber office is just down the hallway. Please get a map and bring it back here."

He motioned for Robert to continue. "Finally, and this is most important of all and usually the most difficult of all, we have to find and eliminate the source of the disease or nothing we do will make any difference. Someone earlier mentioned something about a rat's ass. Well, that person, probably without knowing it, targeted what we're looking for. There are other means of transmission that I won't go into now, but I believe it most likely that this outbreak happened as a result of bites from fleas that attach themselves to rats. Given the size of your harbor and its proximity to the area we're talking about, that's my best guess for now. So, and this is going to cost a great deal of money, we'll have to get started on an extermination plan that will target rats, squirrels, and a few other small creatures as well. I can give the specifics to the person you put in charge of this, but we need to wipe out as completely as we can the rat population of Los Angeles. And we need to do it right now."

This time the rumble in the room had the air and tone of agreement. Mayor Burgess stepped back to the lectern and said, "Parting with money doesn't hurt me as bad as it does Charles, but I know I'll feel the sting from this for a long, long time. Because of the work of the Chamber and other groups in this room, we all have to support these efforts even if we have to do it until it hurts. So, with that said, I'm hereby going to authorize from my office the payment needed to chase down and kill the rats."

More applause and light stomping of feet on the floor followed his announcement. Finally, Mayor Burgess motioned everyone to stop. "While we're waiting on the map, everybody listen up. Here's what we're going to do, on my authority. First, Chief Barker, I want you to meet right now with Chief Alexander. For those of you who don't know him, Chief Alexander is our new city Fire Chief. I want the two of you to come up with a plan, within the hour, for getting the quarantine in place. That's on your shoulders. Don't let us down. I don't care how you do it— just do it. Second, because we need to keep all this as quiet as possible, I want Charles Hornbeck to be in charge of keeping everyone informed of progress as we move ahead. I know that is a heavy burden to put on your shoulders, but I'll keep you informed—and then you can keep everyone else up-to-date when need arises. Everyone get that? From here on, if you have questions, contact Charles. I'll make sure he always has the latest news to pass along. Next, I'm appointing Dr. Miller and Dr. Thompson to be in charge of whatever treatment and other medical work that needs to be done. Of course, it goes without saying, I want you two to keep the health departments and other medical agencies informed of progress— and seek their help if you need it. Finally, I couldn't give the name of a rat catcher in this city if my life depended on it, so somebody give me some names before we all head out of here."

He then took in a long breath, exhaled loudly, and said, "Gentlemen, we have much to do. Let's be at it."

When no one moved, he picked up the gavel, banged it on the lectern, and shouted, "What the hell are you waiting for? Get out of here! Get busy! And, if anyone leaks word of this before I say that can be done, so help me God you'll regret it the rest of your life."

As the others quickly stood and moved toward the door, Mayor Burgess motioned for Charles Hornbeck to come up and join us. "Look," Mayor Burgess said, quietly, "I'm not so stupid that I don't know someone is going to spill the beans about what's going on. I'm hoping it will be a while before that happens, but you can bet your bottom dollar it *will* happen at some point. When that happens, I'm going to rely on you three to step forward and convince people not to panic more than they probably already will. Dr. Miller, I'm sure you've faced that before, right?"

Robert nodded that he had.

"Good. Then you'll know what to do when the cat's out of the bag. I just want all of you to be ready is all."

"Don't worry, Sir," I said, trying to reassure him. "If we can get ahead of this before that happens—and I pray that we can—we'll do our best to handle it."

"Then what are you waiting for?" Mayor Burgess asked gruffly. "There's the door."

With that, he turned and shouted to those left in the room, "Where's Demeter? Somebody go find him and get that damn map in here. We've got work to do."

I looked at Charles and Robert and echoed the Mayor's sentiment. "Yes, that we do. We need to get back to the hospital and get started on the isolation wing. Ready?"

"But what about the map?" Charles asked. "You're supposed to mark off the quarantine area."

Looking around, I found a piece of paper on the floor over by the windows. I picked it up and drew a crude map, complete with street names and other landmarks of the Macy Street area I felt should be closed off. When I was finished, I walked over and handed it to Mayor Burgess.

"Here—you don't need me to wait around," I said as I handed him my drawing. "We have plenty of work to do, and we need to start it now. This map shows what needs to be done. If there are any questions about where barriers should be put, have Chief Barker get in touch with me at the hospital."

I didn't wait for him to respond. I just turned and motioned Charles and Robert to follow me out the door. We had no time to waste.

On the drive back to the hospital, Charles, Robert, and I discussed plans for the isolation wing. It went much smoother than I expected, mostly because it was clear Charles wasn't kidding when he said his wallet would be wide open to help with the crisis. This surprised me, but I wasn't going to press him on his motives. All I was interested in was the speed with which we could get plans underway. We disagreed very little with each other, and when we did, it was over only very minor areas. We knew we didn't have the time to get bogged down, so we soon came to full agreement on everything.

We needed to keep the hospital running as normally as possible so as not to draw undue attention to what we were doing. In order to do this and, at the same time fully staff the isolation wing, Charles—again very much to my surprise—suggested I be assigned half a dozen interns and as many of the newly employed nurses as could be moved from their normal responsibilities. That was much more support than I expected, and I was pleased.

If we moved quickly enough, we could bring the interns and nurses together later in the day, swear them to secrecy under penalty of losing their jobs, and give them the information they would need to help treat the patients and to help with the door-to-door searches needed in the Macy Street area.

Reaching over to pat Charles on the shoulder, I said, "Now I want you to take this the right way, but I'm afraid I'm going to have to change my opinion of you. When a crisis is on the line, money isn't a roadblock for you, is it? You better watch out or your reputation will be ruined."

Charles didn't say anything. He just smiled weakly and looked out the window.

Once we were back to the hospital, Charles immediately headed off to track down and give Nurse Adams her marching orders. Robert and I walked straight to my office so I could call Maria to get news from the church. The exhaustion was clear in her voice when she told me Father Brualla had just found four more who were ill and had to be brought to the church. I knew she wasn't going to like it, but I asked her to turn everything over to Father Brualla, so she could come back to the hospital to help with getting the interns and nurses prepared. She balked, as I expected, so I had to promise at least some of the interns and nurses would get over there by early evening to help out.

Then Robert and I went to the morgue to do the best we could to set up a laboratory where we could check sputum, urine, and blood samples. We wouldn't be able to use the hospital's regular lab; we'd have to make do.

We'd have to make do in a lot of areas before this crisis was over.

....

CHAPTER 13

We All Fall Down

October 30
2:47 P.M.

Nurse Adams was hurriedly scribbling on a patient chart as we walked up to her station. When I cleared my throat to gain her attention, she gasped as the chart slipped from her fingers and crashed to the floor.

"I'm sorry," I said, bending down to retrieve the chart. "I didn't mean to frighten you, but I guess we're all a little edgy now."

She frowned. "A *little* edgy? I'm about to go completely off that edge."

"You'll be glad to know reinforcements are here. I know you two met briefly when he arrived. This is Dr. Robert Miller from San Francisco General. He's going to be helping us with this."

"Thank you for staying," Nurse Adams replied. "I have the feeling we're going to need all the help we can get."

"As do I," Robert replied, flatly. "So we better be at it."

Nurse Adams looked back at me and said, "Everything's ready—just as you ordered. We decided the best place for the isolation wing would be the entire south corridor of the first floor, for two reasons. First, we can chain the far doors and have complete control of who gets in and out of there. Obviously, we don't want people accidentally wandering through. The second reason is that those rooms are a little larger than in any other place in the hospital. By doing a little reshuffling of beds, we can take as many as a hundred and fifty patients if need be. I hope that doesn't come to pass, but we'll be ready if it does."

"Excellent," I said. "You've done well. And now, what about the interns and nurses? How do we stand there?"

"I don't know how you convinced him, but Mr. Hornbeck let me choose six interns and seven of the new nurses we've had on rotation. That's a lot more than I thought he'd do."

"Me, too," I said. "That should be fine for now. How soon can we get them together?"

With a pompous air, she replied, "I already called them in, and they're waiting for you. Upstairs in the staff meeting room. They're trapped. Nurse McDonnell won't let them go anywhere. From the minute she got back from the church, she has been a fireball. I swear that woman could run a road gang. Probably better suited for that than nursing."

"You've hit the nail on the head there," Dr. Miller said, laughing.

"Never mind," I interrupted. "Let's get up there."

"I'll take you to them now. I have some questions for Nurse McDonnell about some masks she's ordered. Follow me, doctors."

We took the elevator up to the second floor and continued halfway down the hall to the staff meeting room. Nurse Adams tried to turn the doorknob, but it was locked. She knocked softly, and a few seconds later, Maria cracked open the door just a few inches until she recognized us.

"About time you got here," she quietly scolded me as she opened the door just enough so that we could slip in. She pointed back inside the room and said, "If someone doesn't tell these poor souls pretty soon what's going on, they're going to explode. Plenty of rumors about the hospital's budget are floating around, so most of them think they're here because they're getting the sack or being reassigned. A few look like they're going to throw up."

"Then just wait until we get finished with them," Robert said. "Have buckets and mops handy."

Maria glared at him. "I imagine you've upset a lot of people in your day."

Robert started to respond, but she didn't give him a chance. Turning back to me, she said, "Better calm them fast is all I have to say."

"Don't know if I can do that. Dr. Miller is right. This is a pretty fair case of out of the frying pan and into the fire, but I'll see what I can do."

Maria clapped her hands and commanded everyone to sit as Robert and I made our way to the front of the room. Once we had their attention, I began.

"I think all of you know me. I'm Doctor Thompson. And this is Dr. Robert Miller from San Francisco General. For those of you who haven't yet met her personally, that's Nurse McDonnell back there with Nurse Adams.

You've been selected for a very special and important job. Before we begin, I want to put your minds at ease at least a little. You're not being fired, and you're not being reassigned—at least not to another hospital. So, you can start breathing again."

There were loud sighs of relief, and a nurse on the far left shouted out, "Thank you!"

Nearly everyone started laughing, at least until I broke back in and said, "But, before you celebrate too much and get too comfortable, you've all been reassigned to us temporarily, and what we're about to tackle isn't going to be a walk in the park. You're here because we need your help. We're going to tell you all about it, but I want to stress the importance of keeping what we're going to do as secret as possible for the time being. None of you can talk about any of this with anyone other than those of us right now in this room without first getting permission from one of the three of us."

There were curious stares. "If you're caught talking about this with others, then you *will* be let go. I can promise you that. Mr. Hornbeck has given me full power and authority in this area. Raise your hands if you understand."

The interns and nurses appeared unsettled, but all slowly raised their hands.

"Good. Now let's—"

I looked up to see an intern and a nurse still had hands raised. "Not yet," I said. "We'll have time for questions later, but right now your first job is to listen. Here's what we're going to do."

I stopped again, made sure all eyes were my direction, and asked, "How many of you have heard of . . . *Yersinia Pestis?*"

I spent the next fifteen minutes explaining the situation we were in and some of what we expected them to do for us. Other than my voice, the room was absolutely silent. To say they were shocked didn't begin to cover what I saw in front of me. At one point, Tom Barton, one of the interns I knew fairly well from his rotation in diagnostics, shook his head and laughed softly, appearing to me as if he thought we were just joking with them.

"This is no laughing matter," I scolded him, a little too loudly.

"It isn't what you think, Dr. Thompson," he said, straightening himself in his chair. "Sorry, I was just thinking out loud. Look around. We're all interns, and those are the new nurses. It just dawned on me we're here because we're the expendable ones, right? Not a big problem if some of us are lost. That's what I was thinking. I'd feel a lot better now if you'd tell me I'm wrong."

The same thought must have occurred to others because a low buzz spread through the room.

"It's true," I said, matter-of-factly, which drew more than a few light gasps and sighs from those near the front. "But not in the way you're meaning. While we fight this, here's what you have to understand. We have to keep everything as normal as possible throughout the hospital so word doesn't leak out and a panic doesn't start. Who better to do that than our regular staff? All of you, interns and new nurses alike, are here at County first and foremost to learn. We are, after all, a teaching hospital. So, while you *are* important to the overall workings of this place, we can cover most responsibilities without you. So, Tom's at least partially right. In one sense, you *are* expendable, but only as far as the day-to-day

workings are concerned. *My* first responsibility from here on is your personal safely and welfare. Nothing is going to be more important to me.
You are *not* expendable—just the opposite—because if you become ill
and can't perform your duties, then we could be sunk. I mean . . . sunk!"

I wasn't sure everyone understood or believed what I was trying to
say. I didn't completely believe it myself. Even though earlier in the day I
had seen a side of Charles I hadn't experienced before, I couldn't escape
the feeling he was more than a little indifferent to their plight. The more
I thought about it, he was incredibly quick to volunteer the interns—and
never brought up the possibility of including any of our more experienced doctors or nurses. I knew he didn't want harm to come to anyone,
but I wondered how much sleep he'd lose if anything happened to those
in front of me.

I was so lost in thought Maria flipped a pencil my direction to get me
back to focus. It was time to move on before others came to that conclusion.
"We're going to tell everyone that you are part of a new 'Community Care'
program instituted by the hospital—a program that will take more doctors
and nurses out into the neighborhoods to bring our services to those who
can't or won't, for whatever reasons, come to us. This will allow us to come
and go as we need to. So, if anyone asks what you are doing, this is the line
you are to give: 'I'm part of Community Care now.' It isn't a lie; we *are*
going into the community to help as much as we can with this situation."

Looking first at Barton and then at the others, I continued, trying to
keep my voice as calm and even as possible, "This is the point where I'm
supposed to say if any of you don't want to be a part of this, if you feel
you *can't* be a part of this, then you can be excused. However, you already
know what we're about to tackle, and secrecy is of the utmost importance.
We won't hold it against you if you feel you need to be excused, but if you
decide not to stay to help, you'll be temporaily transferred somewhere to
help make sure no news of this leaks out here. Please believe me when I
say this isn't meant to be a threat. Its just a precaution we must take at this

time. Those who stay with us will receive a special commendation when this is over, and that will follow you throughout the rest of your career. At the same time, when you are ready to move to other positions, Mr. Hornbeck said he'd write special references for all of you."

"That's fine, if we don't all die," Barton said, laughing again.

There were a few nervous laughs as I added, laughing lightly myself, "But look at it this way. If we don't work together to stop this, it might spread to the point we'd all be dead anyway. So, for my money, it is best to pull together now and put up a good fight. I hope you agree."

A tall, redheaded nurse off to the right raised her hand to catch my attention, stood, and said, her voice shaking, "To be perfectly honest, I don't want to be here—but I don't *not* want to be here, if that makes any sense. Somebody has to help, and since we've been chosen, I don't know how any of us could live with ourselves if we left this room now. I'm not being brave. I'm not a brave person. I'm saying this because I've been through this before. I've seen what the plague can do. When I was a little girl, we lived in China for just over a year. My father was a doctor, and while we were there he helped when the sickness came to a village not far from us. By the time it was over, nearly every man, woman, and child in that village was dead. We have to . . . "

Her voice cracked as she sat back down. "She's right," Robert cut in, nodding his head vigorously. "So, if any of you want to be excused, this is the time to speak up because the rest of us need to get working."

I looked into the faces of everyone before me. Some of them might have wanted to jump up and run, but much to my relief nobody did. I also, on purpose, didn't give them long to respond. After just a few seconds, I said, "Good! Now let's get started. First, we have to understand what we're fighting. That's what Dr. Miller is going to share with you now. Dr. Miller is one of the foremost authorities in the world on this subject, so pay attention, so you can help others and not fall ill yourselves. Doctor, the floor is yours."

Stepping forward, he began, "I'm going to make this as straight-forward as I can. But, before we get to identification and treatments, I want you to know a little history of this disease. This is *vitally* important because we're going to be fighting not only the medical side of this disease; we're also going to be wrestling with the fear people have had since the Middle Ages. When the time is right and when we finally do decide to report what's going on here, those same fears—the same ones people had hundreds of years ago—are going to pop up right around us, and we need to know how to handle that as best we can."

As Robert spoke, I scanned the room and was struck by the ironies before me. Maria was now in charge of people who didn't care for her one bit. The interns and nurses were just as trapped in many ways as the people in the Mexican community. And on top of it all, secrecy was taken so far that the lab we'd be using to *save* lives had to be hidden in a place of death—the hospital morgue. I looked over at Maria, and we must have been thinking along similar lines because at the same time we shook our heads and looked to up to the ceiling.

Robert paced slowly back and forth in front of the group. "I'm going to share with you what we *think* we know about plague, but I'll admit right up front there is a lot more we don't know than we do know. Historians pretty much agree the first major European outbreak of the plague occurred during the Middle Ages when about a dozen merchant ships docked at a port in Sicily. After the ships were in port, the story goes that nobody came off, so the locals climbed aboard and were shocked and horrified by what they discovered. Most of the sailors were already dead, and those who weren't were close to it and in terrible agony. They were covered with black boils that oozed blood and pus, and they were so weak they could barely move at all. Those black boils were the reason why the terms 'Black Plague' and 'Black Death' came about. A few people from the town tried to help the sailors, but in the process they became infected themselves, which helped spread the illness. It wasn't long before the few able-bodied sailors who were left were ordered, under penalty of death, to put to sea again. Some of the ships did reach other ports, but each time they docked, the spread continued until the illness eventually reached major cities like Rome, Paris, and London, all of which were along the major trade routes of the time."

At this point, I swear I could have heard a pin drop in the room. All were leaning closer and closer to Robert, and some were taking notes on small tablets they had brought with them. Even Tom Barton moved his chair slightly to the side so that he could get a better view as Robert continued.

"Spread of the disease was one problem, but treatment was the other because nobody had a clue what to do. The traditional practice of physicians back then was a good bloodletting, and they also tried lancing and covering the boils, but it turned out that was one of the worst things they could do because contact with the fluids also dramatically helped the spread. Others believed—and every time there is an outbreak this comes out in one way or another—that this was a curse brought down on mankind because of wicked behavior and loose morals. In other words, many thought people *deserved* the plague because of how they were living their lives—very much like the Sodom and Gomorrah story. So, what did these people do? In many towns and villages the local do-gooders rounded up those who were deemed to be on the road to Hell and helped them get there quickly by killing them. Hangings and burning at the stake were quite popular. Did this stop the plague? No, but it made people think at least *something* was being done to end the horror."

Many of the interns and nurses were shaking their heads and whispering to those around them. It was clear they were getting caught up in the history, but it was equally apparent by how much they were fidgeting in their chairs that they were becoming increasingly uncomfortable as well.

Robert continued, finally drawing over a chair and sitting before everyone. "Almost half the population of Europe died as a result of the

Black Plague. Almost half. Think about that. The death rate in some places got as high as ninety-five percent of those who came down with symptoms because they just didn't know what to do and had no clue of its cause.

"Remember this from your childhoods? 'Ring around the rosies—a pocket full of posies—ashes, ashes—we all fall down.' Some believe the poor children of London, a city decimated by the plague, created that. The 'rosies' and 'posies' were fragrant flowers that were strung around the necks and placed in the pockets of those who were ill because they very soon absolutely reeked. And the 'ashes' here? The bodies of the dead were burned in the streets, their ashes scattered to the winds. 'All fall down' was what everyone thought would happen: they would all die. Not a very happy little rhyme, is it? But it tells exactly what was going through the minds of those who saw the illness all around them.

"That's enough history, many of the same superstitions and misunderstandings crop up when there's an outbreak, and all of you will face that. This is especially true when dealing with foreigners, and we're dealing right now with a community of people who came here from Mexico. I'm not saying they're ignorant. Most of them have come from villages where there was very little education and medical help, so they're going to be more frightened by what is happening than any of you can guess. So, when you treat these people, please keep that in mind. We'll be treating both the illness *and* the fear, a rough combination to overcome. But, we can do it and we *must*.

"I'm going to turn you over to Dr. Thompson. He's going to tell you what to look for in diagnosing plague and what treatments we're going to use. He correctly diagnosed the first cases here, and if it weren't for his quick action, we'd be in a lot worse situation than we're already in. Please give him your complete attention."

Before I began, I asked Maria to come over and stand next to me. I leaned close to her and whispered, "Jump in any time you wish. Let's get this right." She nodded and appeared pleased I asked her to join in. I first went over the characteristics of the three forms of plague—bubonic, pneumonic, and septicemic—and the specific symptoms to look for in each, everything from boils to fever to characteristics of respiration. I next went over how the disease was transmitted, from initial flea bites up through the bubonic stage to person-to-person transmission at the pneumonic form. I spent extra time in this area because I wanted to make sure they understood how easily airborne transmission could take place through sneezes and coughs. Maria jumped in several times to make specific recommendations to the nurses about how they could best help with the examinations. She also reminded everyone—interns and nurses alike—that above all, they needed to work as a team if we hoped to have any success in halting the spread.

I went on to outline the treatments we'd be administering to those we identified with the illness and said additional information would be forthcoming as soon as our medical supplies were gathered. Finally, I explained as best I could how the house-to-house inspections would take place the next morning and that *everyone* who was ill, even those not exhibiting the major plague symptoms, should be brought to the isolation wing at the hospital. It would be better to be safe than sorry, and we'd sort out the plague cases from those who were ill from other causes once we got them into isolation.

Maria then addressed the group and shared with them the need for gloves and masks at all times. She also suggested medical gowns that fit tightly up to the chin. That might have been a little extreme, but I saw no harm in it. I simply nodded my approval and coaxed her on. At one point she stepped over to a large box resting on a chair at the side of the room. She drew forth a mask, held it up for all to see, and said that particular type had been developed at Massachusetts General Hospital specifically to protect medical personnel from becoming infected by *droplet transmission*, which meant by way of fluids expelled during sneezes and coughs. Out of the corner of my eye I noticed Robert had suddenly sat up quite rigidly in his chair when Maria drew the mask from the box. When she was nearly through explaining its use and letting everyone know more were being prepared just for them even as she spoke, he said, "Nurse McDonnell, isn't that the one your father—" She cut him off with an icy stare and a wave of her hand that left absolutely no doubt as to her meaning. Yes, her father had developed the mask, but the last thing in the world she wanted was for others to know anything about her family and personal life. I was starting to understand why, so I also cleared my throat and stared at Dr. Miller. He slouched back in his chair.

Then I asked for questions. There were several, mostly related to the symptoms and diagnosis. A few asked for more information about how the house-to-house inspections were going to be conducted. I did my best to answer them, but for some I could say only we'd know a lot more in the morning after the quarantine of the area had been completed. When the questions ceased, I said they weren't to leave the room until checking in with Maria so she could go over their work schedules and "who would be where" both immediately following our meeting and the next morning.

"Anything else?" I finally asked Robert and Maria. Both shook their heads, so I once again reminded everyone of the need for absolute secrecy and asked them to form a line in front of Maria to receive schedules.

As they did so, Tom Barton, his face almost ashen, spoke up again. "What if *we* get sick? What happens then?"

I started to respond, but Robert cut me off. He smiled broadly, and I could tell he was trying to keep his tone light to help ease the fear and tension within the room. However, his words still came out too much on the side of gallows humor. "Then, as the rhyme says, 'we'll all fall down.' So, take every precaution described by Nurse McDonnell. If you do that, our odds are good we'll make it through this."

No one smiled. No one laughed. All turned back toward Maria and waited for her instructions.

....

CHAPTER 14

Quarantine

October 30
10:23 P.M.

A cool evening breeze sent a steady stream of paper scraps and leaves tumbling down Alhambra Avenue, the northernmost rim of the quarantine area, as Police Chief Charlie Barker stepped from the curb, put his hands on his hips, and shouted, "You stupid idiot! Just what in the hell do you think you're doing? Don't leave any gaps! Get over here and I'll explain it so even you can understand. Now!"

Chief Barker turned to the newly appointed Los Angeles County Fire Chief, Tom Alexander, and said, sighing heavily, "If it was our men, this'd be a piece of cake. But where did these bozos come from? Who sent 'em?"

Chief Alexander laughed, and said, "Mayor Burgess dug them up. They're veterans of the Big War. Before I got here, he made them all guards and 'honorary auxiliary firemen.' I hear he did it to get their votes. They may be veterans, but by the way they look and act, I couldn't swear they were ever on *our* side."

"Very funny," Barker replied as he grabbed Leonard Taylor by the shoulders and shook him roughly. "What rank were *you*? Outhouse Corporal?"

Leonard, a tall, rotund man whose extra pounds were sticking out several places up and down his old Army uniform, backed away and said, "Sorry if I messed up, but all I was told was to put these ropes where I could. That's all I heard. Nobody said anything else to me."

"Listen up," Chief Barker lit into him again. "This section should be done already. All the other sections have most everything in place. I don't know what's the problem here. You men just too dumb to follow directions? I thought that was made clear to everyone. We're supposed to use rope, wire, fire hoses—anything we can find—to cordon off the *whole* Macy Street area. That means, as plain as I can put it, we seal off everything along Alameda, here along Alhambra, then the Southern Pacific tracks, and back along Macy. And that little cutout between Macy and Main to include that church where all them people go, too. It's a square for heaven's sake. This isn't complicated."

Shaking his finger inches from Leonard's nose, he added, "We know the rope ain't going to keep 'em out, but that ain't its purpose. We're going to post men all along it to keep guard. Men with guns. That'll keep 'em in or out, as the case may be. Now get yourself down to the end of the block and explain to the rest of them knuckleheads what's to be done. I'm putting you in charge, and you better not let me down. Now get going."

Leonard turned to the side and muttered softly as he started walking away, "I was a sergeant."

"What'd you say, Mister?" Chief Barker asked as he moved toward him. "Lippin' off to me, are you?"

"I said I was a sergeant. That's what I was. And I was a damn good one."

Screwing up his face and replying as condescendingly as he could, Chief Barker replied, "Well, Sergeant Chucklehead, you get yourself right down there and get 'em straightened out. That's an order."

Leonard saluted him crisply, turned, and slowly walked away, shaking his head all the way down the block.

"See what we're working with?" Chief Barker said to Chief Alexander, making sure he was loud enough Leonard could still hear him. "A bunch of good-for-nothing morons. What'd we do to deserve this?"

Chief Alexander replied, "They're doing the best they can. Ease up on them some. After all, they weren't rounded up until about three hours ago. I'm impressed they got the other streets taken care of so quickly. Alameda here curves so much back and forth it's taking twice the time."

"We don't have time to molly-coddle 'em. The docs said this 'malignant pneumonia' thing can spread like wildfire, and if that happens, we're all cooked. No, we're supposed to have the quarantine in place by midnight at the latest, and that's just over an hour and a half away. No time to waste. If I have to chew some hindquarters to get the job done, I will."

"You're worried, aren't you?" Chief Alexander asked, his voice softening. "Personally, I think those doctors are just gettin' us all riled up for nothing."

Chief Barker looked down at the street, and responded, this time his voice almost a whisper. "No, I've been through this once, and that's enough for anybody. This is my home, and I'll be damned if I'm going to let a bunch of Mexs poison it. I was there in O-Four, in San Francisco, when this same thing happened. It happened in the China part of town. Those people stick to themselves, so they didn't say anything when they started droppin' like flies. Hundreds of them were dead as doornails before we found out. When we finally heard about it, we quarantined them, too, and it's a damn good thing we did. Over two thousand of 'em croaked, and if we hadn't penned 'em in and put a stop to everything, the docs there said the whole city might have been wiped out."

"I didn't know that," Chief Alexander replied. "How'd you keep them all together there? How'd it work?"

"Wasn't easy. We got soldiers from the base there, not a bunch of goof-offs like these. They were armed to the teeth and ordered to shoot to kill if anyone tried jumpin' out of the quarantine area. We let that be known to everyone in Little China, and we didn't have too much trouble after that."

"Did you have to shoot anybody?"

Chief Barker looked right at Chief Alexander and smiled broadly. "Not so as anyone could tell."

Chief Alexander shook his head, and said, "What if someone tries getting out of this area? What are we going to do?"

"That's up to Smoky, but for my money, if they try to run, we shoot 'em like rabid dogs. After all, they're just Mexicans who shouldn't even be here in the first place. All they do is bring disease and crime. Have you ever met a decent Mexican? One who wasn't dirty as a rag and just as lazy? They brought this on themselves. This malignant pneumonia came from some fleabag village south of the border, right? I'll get in touch with the mayor soon as we're done here and see what he wants us to do."

"Like dogs?" Chief Alexander asked, raising his eyebrows.

"Just like dogs," Chief Barker replied.

....

Charles Hornbeck saw Stuart Bunning leaning against a local landmark, an exceptionally large and full avocado tree, where they had agreed to meet near the intersection of Alhambra and the Southern Pacific railroad tracks. He rushed up to him, shook his hand firmly, and said, "Got your message and got here fast as I could. Everything's going according to schedule, so why'd you want me here? What's so important?"

Stuart didn't answer his question, at least not directly. "Take a look. There is Stage One, and it's coming along just fine. We'll know more about the rest soon enough I suppose."

"Stage One?" Charles said, his voice indicating his curiosity. "What are you talking about?"

"That's why I called you here. You couldn't make it to the emergency meeting tonight. We tried getting in touch with you, but your secretary said you were busy and couldn't be reached. The Council felt we had to act fast, so we met and came up with the rest of the plan."

"What 'rest'? What are you talking about? What's going on?"

"Just look up and down the street. The quarantine's already almost done," Stuart said, pointing in front of him and waving his hand from side to side. "Get everyone penned in. That's just Stage One."

"I thought that was *all* we were going to do for now. What else did the Council decide?"

Stuart smiled. "After the quarantine starts, at the stroke of midnight, and all the sick are taken to the hospital in the morning, we move right to Stage Two."

Charles asked, "Which is what? We can't do anything else too fast. That wouldn't be smart. Eventually, when the news about the plague finally comes out, the homes and land in there will be worthless. 'Plague City.' Once everybody knows about it, we'll be able to pick up everything for cents on the dollar. Maybe even free—just to take the land off their hands for *safety* reasons if our lawyers can convince the current landlords and owners that they might somehow be responsible for all this and could be taken to court. Good plan, I say. All we have to do is wait. *That* would be a great Stage Two. I remember everybody agreeing on this. I don't see how we could hurry it up now."

"You're right that's still what we're shooting for at the end. But we decided tonight a way the plan doesn't have to take nearly as long if we're smart about it. We *can* hurry this up, and the majority of the council was in favor of that."

"What do you mean? What'd the Council decide?"

"Oh, you haven't heard anything yet. Get this. You know Old Man Bryson? Has that string of warehouses down at the harbor. He came up with a plan at the meeting that is pure genius. He said, and I can just about quote him here, 'Why not make sure there's no way for the Mexs to come back here—to make the area absolutely useless to everyone. That is, to everyone but *us*.'"

"What did he mean by that? What's he talking about?"

Stuart smiled again, picked up a small rock, and threw it in a high arc across the street. The rock skittered noisily down the tin roof of a small shed directly across from them. When it finally fell back to the ground, he turned to Charles and said just one word: "Bulldozers."

"Bulldozers?"

"To start with, everything we can on the streets just inside both Alhambra and Alameda, and then we'll work our way farther in. Steam shovels next. Knock it all down and, if possible, burn it up. Houses, shacks, lean-to's, sheds, whatever we can drive them out of now."

Charles removed his hat and ran his hands nervously through his hair. "What in the name of blue blazes are you talking about? Are you out of your minds? We can't do that."

"Relax. It's for the Mexs' own good, see. After all, we have to destroy where the rats are hidin' out, right? And to do that we'd have to get rid of where they live, which is probably under the houses and other structures. Leastways that's what the docs said. And especially Shack Town over there in the field that runs down to the tracks. It needs to be torched—all of it. Hate to wreck their homes, but what if we don't nip this in the bud? What if more and more rats show up and this spreads everywhere? What would the rest of Los Angeles—heck, the rest of the country—think of us if we didn't do everything in our power right now?"

Charles shook his head slowly. "And by doing *everyone* a favor by leveling this area, we're doing our civic duty *and* will be first standing in line to grab the land. And empty land will be easier to buy, right? And this'll make it so we can buy everything quicker, right? That's what you're telling me?"

"Exactly. This will be a great investment for the future for the Council, and that means *us*. Stage Two. That was a genius plan Old Man Bryson had, wasn't it?"

"I don't know. I can live with my reputation as a miser, but . . . burning their homes and all their possessions—all for a land grab? This is just wrong."

"We'll be heroes. Saviors. The men who saved Los Angeles. We'll all get statues one of these days. Who knows?"

Charles, growing more upset by the minute, grabbed Stuart by the wrist and spun him around. "This isn't at all what we talked about. And keep something else very important in mind. Those who are sick can't stay in the hospital forever. These people have to have someplace to go once this is over, and I thought we all decided they could come back here until we buy everything. Now where will they go?"

"That's also in the new plan. Two birds with one stone. We'll get the land, and they'll be forced to go back to Mexico or somewhere else. Frankly, I don't care where they go—just as long as they go. The Council will make a big splash out of providing funds for these poor unfortunates to return to loved ones and their wonderful villages they left behind. And, in the meantime, if they stay longer in your hospital, the Council decided they'd cover that cost, too. See, we really will be heroes all the way around."

"What you mean is we'll be *rich* heroes. Isn't that right? But I don't think everyone's going to understand this when the bulldozers get rolling. Aren't you just a little worried we'll be seen as money-grubbing monsters?"

"Once everyone else in the city hears about the terrible and contagious malignant pneumonia here, do you for one minute think anyone is going to stop and think about us or our motives? Not on your tintype, Mister. All they'll think about is themselves. And with a little help from the newspapers—a careful word here, a story there—we can let everyone know what we did saved lives. How could we be faulted for that?"

Charles watched two men stretching an old fire hose between two trees across from them, and said, "I'm sorry, but I just don't like this. It's one thing to buy when nobody else will because of the plague. That might be taking advantage of the situation some, but it's good business and I could live with that. But, it's another thing entirely to put families on the streets without warning and destroy what few possessions they have."

"But, think of the profit. Put your mind to that. You know we've talked about the need for expansion of the downtown area for a long time, but there just isn't any way to spread out north or west. This direction, south and east, is the *only* way we can grow, and now's the chance we've been waiting for. We have to move in while we can. It may take a while, but this will be prime real estate—a gold mine." Stuart paused before going on, this time his voice even more serious. "There's also something you better not forget. The Council voted on this tonight. It was the will of the group. If you buck this, you might find yourself outside the gate."

Charles turned rigid. "You didn't have to mention that. I don't need to hear threats. If it's what they decided, I'll go along. All I said was I didn't like it—that I think the original plan was a better way. The end result will be mostly the same, so I'll just bite my tongue and ride along. I'm too far into this now to do anything else anyway."

"That's more like it. We'd all like to be more charitable and helpful in situations like this, but there are times when we just have to be, well, *practical*—for the interests of everyone involved. These people will be happier back where they came from. And all of this won't hurt us none, either. You just relax and take care of everything at the hospital. That is your job right now, and everyone in the Council is counting on you. By the way, everything *is* ready now, right?"

Charles nodded. "What time is it?" he asked, without looking at Stuart.

"Just under an hour before the fireworks begin. I think I'll stick around and watch a little. Join me?"

"No, I better get back to the hospital. I left a lot of orders to be carried out, and I should check everything one more time before morning. You enjoy the show for me."

"Oh, you can bet I will," Stuart said, beaming. "Let those fireworks begin!"

Charles turned and walked slowly back to his car.

....

Chief Barker eased his new police vehicle, a specially designed Ford truck with a small wire-screened "jail" attached at the very back, to the curb where Mayor Burgess was standing with Major Jack Burke. Major Burke was an ex-Army Colonel who had made a name for himself as a "get-the-job-done" officer during the war. He had been assigned by Mayor Burgess to take charge of keeping order within the ranks of the veterans—just sworn in as guards—who were helping establish the quarantine boundary along Macy Street.

"Your Honor," Barker yelled out his window. "You asked me to come get you when we finished everything over to Alameda and Alhambra. That's done as best we can for now. We're ready as we're ever goin' to be."

"Very good," Mayor Burgess replied, stepping toward the vehicle. "Now I want you to drive me around the perimeter. The two of us need to make sure there aren't any holes anywhere and men are stationed as instructed. We want no slip-ups."

"Then get in. We'll drive up Alameda, around and across the river, then back down here. Shouldn't take us too long if one of those damn trains doesn't crab the works."

Looking at his watch, Mayor Burgess said, "We're down to less than an hour. Let's get going."

As they drove slowly up Alameda and then across Alhambra toward the tracks and the river, the first thing they noticed was that, as ordered, police officers, firemen, and veterans, most bursting with pride in their old uniforms, were stationed at fairly regular intervals. Most had rifles slung over their shoulders. Each group also had barrels full of wood they were instructed to fire up at midnight to provide enough light to see clearly all up and down the quarantine boundary—just in case there were *violators*.

Burgess and Barker also made sure there were no gaps in the barrier strung along the way. The fire department had run out of extra hoses quickly, and even rope was soon in short supply. However, Michael

Warrenton, a prominent rancher in the Valley and one of the leading members of the Greater Los Angeles Economic Progression Council, had come to the rescue and provided enough barbed wire to complete the job. Thanks to his donation, everything appeared to be in order.

Chief Barker noticed the barbed wire being strung to a pole right at the railroad tracks and said, "Nasty stuff—but mighty effective. Probably should have used just that all the way around. That'll get the Mexs' attention."

Mayor Burgess nodded and looked down into the field just to the south of where Alhambra and the railroad tracks intersected. "Those lights over there. That's Shack Town or whatever they call it, isn't it? I've never seen it before. Horrible. Just horrible. How do people live like that? There isn't a regular house anywhere in there. Looks like just a bunch of lean-to's and boards stacked here and there that a good, stiff breeze would knock down. The whole place is probably infested."

Chief Barker groaned and replied, "Bunch of rat-traps is what it is. They stole all the boards they've cobbled together to make them shacks. And that tin used for roofing? Stole it, too, from the railroad yard and farms all over the Valley. They come in like locusts and steal everyone blind."

"You know this for a fact?" Mayor Burgess asked, raising an eyebrow.

"Your Honor, everyone knows it. Just the plain truth is all. Where else would they have gotten it from?"

Mayor Burgess didn't respond. Instead, he ordered, "Turn here. Let's head down to Macy Street and check the southern edge as fast as we can. I see the light of a train coming our way. It's pretty far off, but if you drive fast enough, we can get down to Macy and cross the tracks there before we get trapped. Think you can do it?"

"I can with this," Chief Barker replied, proudly, flipping on a switch next to the steering wheel. The loudest siren Mayor Burgess had ever heard blared out from under the hood. "Everyone who ain't deaf will get out of the way of us now, and the massive cow catcher on the front bumper will knock the rest to the side. Here we go. Hang on to your hat!"

When they reached the Macy Street intersection, without slowing down Barker jerked the steering wheel hard to the right. With tires screaming, they reached the tracks no more than ten seconds before the train crossed. Mayor Burgess, too startled to utter a sound, braced himself against the front window support and closed his eyes. The front tires bounced high as they met the tracks, and Mayor Burgess's first thought was the train had rammed them. He opened his eyes, and the wall of air following the train's path hit him squarely in the face. As the car's tires came back to earth, he shouted, still unsure of their safety, "Sweet Moses! Look out! We could have been killed! Are you out of your mind!"

"Nothin' to it!" Chief Barker shouted back, proudly, swinging the car back to the middle of the road. "Had it made all along."

"I left my stomach back there! That was too close!"

"Nah. Plenty of time. You can ease up now. We're all right."

"Maybe you are, but that took five years off my life!"

Chief Barker laughed loudly. "Any time you want to get somewhere fast, just let me know. I'm your man. And besides, your office paid for this wagon, so you're entitled to it whenever you want."

"I'll take that under advisement. For now, please slow this thing down so we can check out the cordon along here. And while you're at it, see that man with the white straw hat up the road. Pull over there next to him a minute. I want to talk to him."

"Yes, Sir. Will do."

The man with the straw hat was Reno Bartolo, a retired member of the City Council and a Colonel during the war. Mayor Burgess had put him in complete charge of the Macy Street boundary, and now Bartolo was shouting orders as Barker eased the vehicle to a stop.

"Colonel!" Mayor Burgess called out. "A moment please."

"Your Honor, I have only a moment. Time's running close now.

We've still some areas to seal off up ahead. I've ordered men stationed every fifty feet all along Macy because this is where we'll have a lot of Mexs crossing through, hoofin' it to and from jobs. I've also been waiting for instructions about what to do with the *uncooperatives*. I need to know now. What are your orders on that?"

Chief Barker didn't wait for Mayor Burgess to reply. Instead, he cut in, "There will be *no uncooperatives*. I want that understood. Your men aren't carrying them guns for their health. If need be, fire away. That's the only way we can handle this right."

Bartolo looked at the Mayor, who just exhaled loudly and said, "Do what needs to be done, but try not to get to the point where you have to shoot anybody. Just remember this: nobody in after midnight, and nobody out. No exceptions—except for the doctors and nurses. They can come and go as they please, under my direct orders."

"Yes, Sir," Bartolo shot back. "Understood. Now I better make sure the last of the wire is in place. If you need me, I'll be around the perimeter all night checking on everything. Just ask for me. Somebody'll know where I am."

"Thanks, Colonel," Mayor Burgess said. "You're doing your city a great service."

Bartolo didn't turn around. He just waved behind him and started walking ahead until something out of the corner of his eye caught his attention.

It was at that exact moment five men on their way home from work at the docks walked up through the tall grass and shrubs across Macy Street. They stopped dead in their tracks when they saw the men and barbed wire barricade before them. The oldest of the group, Juan Carlos Munoz, turned to the others and said, his voice almost desperate, "*¿Qué es esto? ¿Quiénes son estos hombres?*"

Juan Carlos' younger brother, Esteban, whose English was good and getting better every day because of his work at the docks, stepped ahead of the others and crossed over to the barbed wire. He tugged at it gently while looking around, as if waiting for an explanation from someone. Three men, two armed with rifles and the third with a pistol, immediately surrounded him.

"Halt! Let go of the wire!" the man with the pistol shouted, taking aim directly at the middle of Esteban's chest. "You stay right there. Don't move!"

Juan Carlos and the others started running toward Esteban, but the two men with rifles quickly swung around their direction and also commanded they stop. They did, but not before Juan Carlos screamed he'd kill the first one to put a hand on his brother. "*Usted le hizo daño a me hermano. ¡Mueres!*"

Off to their left, Chief Barker leaned toward Mayor Burgess and said, loud enough for everyone around to hear, "Well, well—looks like the real definition of a 'Mexican Standoff,' doesn't it? Why don't we just shoot a couple now. Would send a powerful message to the rest, wouldn't it?"

"Quiet!" Mayor Burgess ordered. "The first encounters are going to be the most difficult. Don't make them any worse than they need to be!"

Bartolo, whose Spanish was passable, stepped toward Esteban and did his best to tell him no one meant him any harm.

"I speak English," Esteban shot back. "Please, tell me. What is going on to us? We want to go to our homes."

Bartolo held up his hand and replied, "Please, give me a minute." Then, turning to Esteban's brother and the others, he added, trying to diffuse the situation as best he could, "*Por favor, esto va a ir bien.*" And then again in English, "Please, this will be fine."

While walking back over to Mayor Burgess, Bartolo asked, softly, "Well, want to make these the first? I was told the ones we're not letting back in are to be taken to that high school over on Tucker and kept there until we can figure out what else to do with 'em. Still about fifteen minutes to the curfew. Your call here, Smoky."

"I say let my men handle 'em," Chief Barker growled, clenching his teeth and pounding his right hand to his left palm over and over for all to see.

Mayor Burgess glared at him and snapped his fingers. Turning to his right, he studied Esteban carefully before looking at the others. "No. I think I have a better idea."

Pausing only a moment, he pointed toward Esteban, lowered his voice and said, calmly, "Young man—come here."

When Esteban didn't move, he repeated, even more gently this time, "Come here, please. No one will harm you."

After first looking toward his brother, he stepped slowly toward Mayor Burgess. "Señor, we didn't do anything wrong. We live here. We just want to go home."

"And you will, "Mayor Burgess replied. "But I have a favor to ask of you—and a job to offer. You do the favor first. The job will follow, and you'll be paid well."

Esteban blinked rapidly, folded his arms across his chest, and said, his voice now cracking slightly, "What is it? What do you wish me to do?"

"I'm going to ask you to help prepare your people for the help we're going to be giving them. There has been an outbreak of a terrible illness in your neighborhood, and we're bringing in doctors and nurses to help everyone get well again. To do this, we must make sure no one leaves the neighborhood or gets back in—starting right now. Then, at first light tomorrow, the doctors and nurses will come and help those who are ill. As I said, we can't let anyone leave or get in to make sure the illness doesn't spread and harm more people. This is why you see all of these men and the barricades we've put up around your homes. Do you understand what I've said to you so far?"

Esteban shifted his weight lightly from one foot to the next and looked at his brother before turning again to face Mayor Burgess. "What is this illness? Is it what killed *Señor* Lujan? Francisca?"

"Yes. It is a type of pneumonia, a lung illness. It spreads very quickly from one person to another. It must be stopped because if we don't treat those who are sick, they will probably die, too. That is all I can tell you for now. Trust me. We *must* do this—now."

"And you are not going to let us back to our homes? What are we to do?"

"*You* and your friends there *will* go home because I have a very important job I want you to do. Now, please tell the others. Do it as fast as you can. We're out of time, and you'll be the last ones let inside."

Esteban relayed the information as quickly as he could, but Juan Carlos and the others appeared quite frightened and confused. Mayor Burgess smiled at them weakly, then called Esteban back to him again.

"Sorry, wish I could give you more time to explain to them, but I can't. We're blocking off the neighborhood at Alameda, Alhambra, the railroad tracks, and here along Macy Street and down around the church. Here's the job I have for you, and I'd be grateful if you could also explain this to your friends there. I want *you* to go up and down the homes along Alameda. Ask one of the others to take the homes along Alhambra. Send another down into the field along the tracks, and the last two can work inside the wire here along Macy Street. I know most are probably in their beds now, but please stop at several homes on each street, wake the people up, and let them know what's going on so that they won't be so frightened. Tell them help will be coming tomorrow morning."

Removing his money clip from his vest, Mayor Burgess drew out five five-dollar bills. He handed one to Esteban before saying, "That's for you—for your help. The rest of these are for your friends. Give them each one. Tell them they will be doing a great service to the community—and the city."

"Why are you asking us to do this?" Estaban asked while rolling the bill between his thumb and forefinger. "Why us?"

"I'll be blunt—because none of us here speak your language very well.

You, on the other hand, can spread the word very fast. We can't. It's that simple. Plus, we just learned of the illness, which seems to be only in your neighborhood right now, so we want to let everyone know as quickly as possible what will be happening. Can you do this for us?"

"I'll ask my brother and the others," Esteban replied.

"Explain everything quickly. There isn't much time."

There were audible gasps and sighs while Esteban relayed the mayor's words. By the tone of their voices and expressions on their faces, it was clear the others were anxious and wanted more information, but Esteban did his best to calm them. Finally, he handed each a five-dollar bill. When he did so, the group became absolutely silent. Juan Carlos grabbed the bills from the others, including his brother, and started walking toward the mayor. Esteban grabbed his arm, swung him around, retrieved the bills and handed them again to the other men. He shook his head and told his brother they were keeping the money. Juan Carlos didn't reply. He just looked off in the distance, pulled a cigarette from his pocket, and lit it, inhaling deeply.

Esteban walked back to the Mayor and said, "We will do this for you. But we have a question first. What of the others of us who are also now on their way from the harbor? What will become of them? I ask because we have another brother who stayed to work later."

"Thank you," Mayor Burgess said, relief in his voice. He reached to shake Esteban's hand, but Esteban waved him off.

"No need for thanking me. I do this for my family—and for the others."

"And you are good men for doing so," Mayor Burgess replied.

"And of the others—and my brother? What of them?"

"Oh, yes—them. Right now we're setting up beds at a high school and several churches nearby. Those who aren't back by midnight will be taken there, where they'll be fed and taken care of. Don't worry. They'll be fine, and we'll figure out a way to let their families know where they are."

"And this has to be done?"

"Yes" Mayor Burgess replied. "This *must* be done, or many, many more will become ill. I know you want to protect your families. We all do. This is why we are doing this."

"I'm going to trust you," Esteban said, taking a step back. "Our families mean everything to us. We will do this for our families. We'll tell as many as we can tonight."

"Then bless you, young man. You're doing an act of mercy. I won't forget it."

Suddenly, three shots, one right after the other, rang out in the distance. Just after the third, a rifle report could be heard farther up Macy Street. Mayor Burgess flinched as Chief Barker shouted, "Trouble already!"

Mayor Burgess, quickly regaining his composure, said, "That's *not* trouble. It's the signal."

"Signal of what?" Chief Barker asked, his voice still full of excitement.

Bartolo stepped toward the Mayor and said, "The signal that it's midnight. The quarantine is now in effect. Your Honor, you'll have to excuse me. I've work to do. Now it begins."

"Yes, it does," Mayor Burgess replied, drawing his pipe from his pocket and sticking it roughly in his mouth. After lighting it and taking a few quick puffs, he turned again to Esteban. "Are you ready now—and your friends?" Esteban nodded. "Good."

Then, pointing to the guards at the barbed wire fence, he commanded, "Let these men through. They're working for us."

The last to cross the wire was Juan Carlos. As he did so, Mayor Burgess called after him, "And Godspeed to you. Godspeed."

Juan Carlos glared at him and spit loudly on the ground.

....

CHAPTER 15

"Inspections – No Exceptions"

October 31 (Halloween)
7:23 A.M.

"It's about time you got here," I teased Maria as she walked toward my car. "Are you sleeping your whole life away these days?"

I had told her the night before we'd meet by the Emergency entrance at precisely 7:15 A.M. and head straight away to the church, so we could give final instructions to the interns and nurses before the door-to-door inspections began.

I had expected her to look tired. Instead, her steps were lively as she approached me. She wore a crisp, newly laundered nurse's outfit and pressed hat. It was strictly against hospital policy, but she had ditched the standard, flat nursing shoes for a pair of two-toned oxfords of the latest style. I didn't say anything. Shoes were the least of our troubles.

She looked at her watch and said, drolly, "Eight minutes. Exactly eight minutes."

"But you're still late," I said, opening the door for her. "Jump in—we need to make tracks."

As she sat down, she looked around the interior and asked, "Where's your shadow? I thought surely he'd be here—and that he would be so excited he'd be eight minutes early."

"Dr. Miller? I'm leaving him here to take charge of the final arrangements for the isolation ward. He requested it."

"I bet he did. He's so full of himself he'll probably have everyone bowing to him and by the time we get back."

I eased away from the curb and headed down toward Macy Street.

Very few vehicles were on the road, so we made rapid progress. However, as was now becoming the rule, we were once again held up by a train at the tracks by the Los Angeles River.

"Here we go again," I said, pounding my palms on the steering wheel. Turning to Maria, I asked, "So, what's new? We've got this time to kill, so I thought I'd ask. Anything exciting in your life these days?"

Maria looked at me blankly, frowned, and replied, "Nothing. Not a thing. And you?"

We both burst out laughing. We then sat in silence a few moments before she said, "Thirty-two, thirty-three, thirty-four . . ."

"What are you jabbering about?" I asked.

"Just counting the train cars. You're such a lively conversationalist I've nothing much better to do."

"I'm sorry," I said, reaching over to touch her shoulder. "It's just—"

"I know," she cut in. "Me, too. What are we going to do, really? Do you truly think we can get ahead of this today?"

"I have to believe it. I keep thinking about what Dr. Perry said about the outbreak in San Francisco. Over two thousand people died because they didn't provide treatment right away. Well, that's not going to happen here. We can't let it."

Maria looked out the window. "I know we've gone over treatments, isolation, and prevention of spread, but I have this sick feeling we've for-gotten something—*important*. Even having Dr. Miller here to help out doesn't make me feel that much better, and he *is* good. I just know there's more we should be doing, but I can't think of it right now. And you?"

I laughed softly. "I feel the same, but, after all, this is our first Black Plague together. We can't know everything just yet."

She turned to me, shook her head, and laughed again.

I said, "I think if we follow our plan, we'll know much more by tonight and can take stock and rethink everything then. Let's just do the best we can now and trust we'll come out on top."

"And one more thing," I said, purposely not looking at her. "I don't want you getting sick. Don't take any chances—not a one."

As the caboose finally rumbled past, Maria squeezed my hand, tightly, and said, "Lean over here a minute."

"What? My tie crooked?" I replied. "Never could tie these dang things."

"Just lean a little farther."

I did so and was shocked when she kissed me on the cheek. I also flinched slightly, causing my elbow to hit the horn button. A quick "oooogah" shot out from under the hood.

"Why, Doctor—you're turning red as a beet. Never been kissed before, eh?"

For one of the few times in my life, I was speechless. Except for the times when "Miss Wonderful" would glance over at me and let out a muffled laugh, we drove the rest of the way in silence.

....

The only way into the community from Macy Street was to pass through a makeshift guard shack about two blocks north of the church. Four armed men wearing faded and ill-fitting army uniforms formed a line in front of us as I eased to a stop.

"Your purpose here?" the oldest of the guards asked. His shirt was missing its bottom three buttons, which allowed his ample stomach to jiggle up and down as he spoke. Maria must have seen this, too, because she stifled a laugh.

"I'm Dr. Thompson. This is Nurse McDonnell. We're in charge of the medical personnel today. We're on our way to the church to get started."

The guard first peered intently around the interior before walking slowly around the car, kicking the tires and pushing up and down on the rear fender.

"What's he think we're doing? Smuggling in rats?" Maria asked, exasperated. "Good grief! Let us in already."

The guard heard her and walked slowly around to her window. She smiled coyly at him and dramatically crossed her legs, raising her skirt slightly.

He cleared his throat, stepped back from the car, and shouted, "Let 'em through! They're okay."

"You *are* absolutely horrible," I scolded her as I pulled ahead.

"We've already been through that before," she replied, laughing again. "But I got us through quickly, didn't I? He'd have been taking your car apart and inspecting everything in sight."

I started to speak, but she interrupted me. "You're turning red again."

"No doubt," I replied.

Before she could say anything else, and just as we turned the corner, we saw it at the same time: a large crowd assembled in front of the church.

"I was afraid this was going to happen," Maria said, shaking her head. "You're going to need me today, and this time I don't mind it'll be for my interpreting. I just hope we can calm them."

The crowd was so large there was no way I could get close to the church, so I parked about half a block away. "This is probably better anyway," I said, stopping the motor. "We'll walk the rest of the way and see if we can hear what they're talking about, although I have a feeling I already know."

After only a few steps, Maria grabbed my arm to stop me as she intently tried making out what a woman in the crowd was screaming at Father Brualla, who was standing on the top step of the church.

"We better get there quickly," she said, still holding my arm but this time urging me to follow her.

"What is it?" I asked, while trying to keep up with her.

Maria glanced back and replied, disbelief in her voice, "They think they've been rounded up so they can be sent back to Mexico. They're scared to death."

There must have been close to two hundred people spread out in a horseshoe shape around the front steps of the church and spilling back to the plaza across the road. Many were women holding infants and doing their best to keep their other children close at hand. Others were men holding lunch pails and a variety of tools, obviously there because they had tried to get to work and had been turned back at the quarantine boundary. At the very back, dozens upon dozens of youngsters milled back and forth, whispering to each other and occasionally laughing. It finally occurred to me they should have been on their way to school but were denied exit from the community.

When we reached the outer edge of the crowd, I could see our interns and nurses huddled together behind some bushes to the left of the entrance of the church. They looked nearly as frightened as those standing before Father Brualla. Maria took my hand and pulled me behind her as she said over and over, *"Lo siento, lo siento."* Once we were through, we quickly climbed the steps until we stood right next to Father Brualla. When the crowd saw us, they started booing and shouting words that didn't need translation. By the expressions on their faces and the tone in their voices, the meaning was quite clear to me.

"Bless you!" Father Brualla shouted above the roar of the crowd, turning to hug Maria and at the same time pat me on the shoulder. "I don't know what to say to them. They're—"

Maria interrupted, "Frightened and scared out of their wits. I heard some of it. Father, we'll do our best, but please stay right here. Don't move. When we're finished, a prayer might be in order."

She moved forward a step and waved her arms above her head as she urged the crowd to quiet down. They did so, save for one of the workers standing near the back who shouted, *"¡Ustedes son unos demonios!"* I knew part of that meant "devil," and I had a pretty fair idea who he was talking about.

I turned to Maria. "I'll speak in short bursts and stop so you can translate. Please try to keep close to what I'm saying, but if you feel you need to add something, fine. Just let me know what else you tell them, okay?"

She nodded, so I began. "I am Dr. Thompson from Los Angeles County Hospital, and this is Nurse Maria McDonnell. We're going to do our best right now to let you know what is going on."

I looked over at Maria and said, "Let's start with that."

When she had finished, I continued, "I know you are all frightened, but please listen to me closely. What I have to say is very important. First, *nobody* is being sent back to Mexico, at least not now. Please trust me about this. That is *not* why this is happening."

Maria translated, and this time a loud rumble spread through the crowd. It was clear many were greatly relieved—to the point that some even started to leave and go back to their homes.

"Wait!" I shouted. "There's more!"

"We've got to keep them here," Maria said, the urgency clear in her voice. "I'll tell them what you just said. Maria then called out, "*¡Espere! ¡Hay Más!*"

All but two of those who were leaving stopped and turned around. The other two kept moving and never looked back.

Once I had the attention of most, I continued, pausing at times when I felt necessary so that Maria could continue translating.

"An illness has come to your community. It is a type of pneumonia, a lung illness, that is very serious. It spreads quickly, and people who have it become very ill. If they are not treated, many may die. This is what happened to the Lajun and Samarano families. We're here to help everyone and to keep this illness from getting to others."

I had to pause at this point because the crowd became quite loud again. While most knew of the deaths, it was clear no one knew there was a connection. Suddenly, the questions started coming in waves.

"What are they saying?" I asked both Maria and Father Brualla. "What is it?"

Above the noise of the crowd, Father Brualla said, "Most want to know if this is the Influenza again. We were more fortunate than most when it came, but they know what it would mean if it returned."

I turned to Maria and said, "Please tell them it isn't. They need to understand that so that we can get their attention again."

She spoke for several minutes as the crowd grew quieter and quieter. I caught only a word and phrase here and there, but whatever she said had a calming effect on most everyone. Finally, she motioned for me to speak again.

"To protect you and wipe out this illness—and because all the cases so far have been from here—it was necessary to quarantine the area. We had to do this quickly, so that is why we've closed off the streets. Starting in about an hour—and for as long as it takes—we are sending doctors and nurses to all of your homes to check on everyone there. If we find people who are ill, they will be taken to Los Angeles County Hospital for treatment."

Voices suddenly rose up again. Clearly they believed being taken to County Hospital was not a good idea by any means. Several more shouts rang out, but Maria just turned to me and said, "Trust me—you don't want me to translate that. You'd better figure out a way, and fast, of convincing them this is necessary."

"Please, listen to me!" I yelled as loudly as I could. "I want to explain."

When it became apparent they weren't interested in listening to me again, Father Brualla called out to them. He spoke briefly, finally turning to me and saying, "Try again."

I looked out at the faces before me and saw a blend of fear, distrust, and even hate. I said the only thing I could think of to say. "If I were you, I wouldn't trust me either. Not at all. You're being forced to stay here in your community. You can't leave, and many of your loved ones are outside and aren't being let back in to you. And you weren't told why any of this is happening. I understand why you're upset, and I'd feel the same way if I were in your place."

I stopped here and said to Maria, "Please say that—as close to the way I did as possible."

As she finished, Father Brualla spoke next—for several minutes. At one point, Maria leaned over and whispered to me, "He's telling them he trusts you and is asking them to do the same. He's saying you are honorable and would not tell them something if it weren't true. He said if they don't trust you, then that's the same as saying they don't trust him. He's sticking his neck out for you."

At the same time I appreciated what he was doing, I also started feeling a wave of guilt coming over me. "Pneumonia." That is what I was asking them to believe. It was, in a sense, pneumonia that presented the most immediate danger to those who were ill, but I was telling them only a half-truth, at best. This was Black Plague, plain and simple, but I couldn't tell them that. And here was Father Brualla telling them to believe everything I was saying. At that moment, I felt very small.

"You can continue now," he said, urging me forward. "They are waiting."

I turned to the crowd and said, "Thank you. I'm here to help."

I explained as simply and directly as I could that it wouldn't be bad if someone needed to be taken to the hospital. I described the isolation ward and told of the reasons for it. I assured them the cost of treatment was not going to be their concern because County Hospital and others in Los Angeles agreed to help by taking care of all medical expenses. After that, I decided I needed to talk in general terms about the treatments we'd be providing, including the importance of lowering fever and doing our best to prevent breathing problems. I explained that this could not be done effectively in their own homes, and that was the reason for the hospital's involvement.

I had already mentioned the subject before, but I stated again, emphatically, that the new Immigration Act was not something they needed to be concerned about right now. I asked them to believe me when I said being taken to the hospital was not a trick to get them on a train or bus back to Mexico. I was sure there were many who wouldn't believe me, but Maria and Father Brualla translated my words in such a way that at least there were no more shouts about the subject.

At that point, I had one last area to cover before the door-to-door inspections could begin. As clearly as I could, I went over what would happen when the doctors and nurses came to their homes. "Please stay in your homes today. It is important all family members be there to be examined. After today, and until we stop the illness, please don't get together in groups, so there won't be more chances for this to spread. And finally, I don't want anyone to worry about food or water. Los Angeles Catholic Charities will be bringing to each home enough food and water for a week. We'll start with that, and if you need more, we'll see that it is brought in."

I was surprised there wasn't more of a reaction to the news about the food. Instead, all eyes were still focused on me. I knew it was risky, but I asked if anyone had any questions. Very slowly, a few hands started popping up. As the questions were asked, Maria explained them to me. I honestly couldn't answer most of them. Some wanted to know what would happen to their jobs if they couldn't get to work. Others wanted me to tell them again this wasn't the Influenza—a reassurance I *could* give them. Still others wanted to know what would happen to family members who were not being allowed back inside the quarantine area. Father Brualla knew more about that than I did, so he explained how schools and other churches just outside the community had stepped forward and would be providing food and shelter for them. Two women standing together about half way back in the group asked at the same time, almost in chorus, when the quarantine would be lifted. All I could say was it would happen as soon as we had stopped the spread of the illness, which clearly didn't impress them much. A young man standing right next to them asked if they could all still come to the church for Mass. When I said that would not be possible, there were shocked looks and sad expressions all around. I followed up by saying that Father Brualla would be coming around from house to house to help out as needed and to pass along regular updates about the situation. That seemed to satisfy.

When the questions had ended, I started to ask them to leave at once and go directly back to their homes. However, before I could finish, one more question rang out from the back, from a man wearing little more than rags and with a large pick slung over his shoulder. His voice was loud, strong. In broken English, he asked, "I no go to hospital? What happen?"

Maria shouted back at him, a little too loudly, "Then you won't get treated, and you'll die. That's what. So, you can be stubborn and stupid and die—or you can come to the hospital. It's as simple as that."

The man moved his pick slowly to his other shoulder, stared intently back at Maria, and simply nodded. Then, he turned and walked away. Maria followed up by saying something to the crowd, which brought forth more than a few laughs and smiles.

"What'd she say?" I asked Father Brualla.

He smiled broadly. "She told the others that man asked if he needed to go bathe and shave in case he was to be taken to the hospital. She said she told him that those standing close to him would probably appreciate it if he did that right now—that we'd all appreciate it if he didn't wait."

"She didn't!"

"Oh yes—she did."

I just shook my head. Maria looked over at me and said, "What?"

"Nothing," I said, looking back at Father Brualla. "Nothing at all."

Then, addressing the crowd one last time, I urged them to get home quickly to receive the doctors and nurses. There were no more questions. The people turned and started walking away.

....

The interns and nurses started walking toward us as soon as the crowd began to disperse. As I expected, Tom Barton stepped forward, acting as spokesman for the group. "Somehow, I get the feeling we're not wanted around here." A few nervous laughs followed, but most stood rigid, waiting for me to reply.

"I'm glad you heard what they had to say. We're not going to be their favorite people, and they're still pretty frightened. However, we're their last hope, and they'll come to that realization soon enough, especially as more in the neighborhood become ill."

Before I could continue, I noticed that off to the right Ed Armbruster and four other men were walking toward us. Pointing to those with him, Ed said, "Well, Doc, I called in a few favors. These are all ambulance drivers from other hospitals in the area. Mr. Hornbeck also cleared it with their bosses. They'll be helping out today. And best yet, they brought their own vehicles, so we're all set to go. Just tell us what you want us to do."

"Perfect!" I said to Ed and his fellow drivers. "You'll be vital to the success of this day, and I want you to know how much we appreciate what you're doing. Thank you for coming."

They joined the interns and nurses. "I've got something to say, and I'd like all of you to hear it."

Tom interrupted and said, "Dr. Thompson, take a look back there. There's more of us. We were told we were to bring them along. Nurse Adams said they'd be our translators. So, here they are."

In all the excitement, I hadn't even noticed two men and four women standing at the back.

One of them, a woman I guessed near to fifty and wearing a plain, brown skirt and white blouse, stepped forward. "I'm Chita Concepción. Nurse Adams picked us, but we don't really know why we're here, other than all our families came from Mexico years ago, and we all speak Spanish. All of us either cook or clean at the hospital, and Mr. Hornbeck said we had to be here to keep our jobs. We've also been told people here are mighty sick, and we better not catch it. We don't want to be here. What are we supposed to do?"

"I'm glad to see all of you as well and want to thank you for coming," I said. "You have a very important job today." Looking around one last time, I added, "I think that's going to be all of us for now. At least I hope so. We're getting to be a pretty large group. We'll look like an army!"

I expected a few smiles, but there were none. All eyes were focused on me, waiting for me to continue. We had to be about our business, so I started right in.

"Ambulance drivers and translators move in closer to the doctors and nurses. You need to hear the first part of what I'm going to say. After that, Nurse McDonnell will take the drivers and translators over to the other side of the church and tell you something about the illness and share with you the safety precautions we expect you to follow that will keep you from becoming ill. But right now, here's what we're going to do today— and possibly tomorrow or longer.

"I want to emphasize that we are to canvas the entire quarantine area. We check every house. Keep this motto in your minds: 'Inspections—no exceptions.' We have to check *everyone*, or risk that the illness will continue to spread will climb. There are some who didn't get back to their homes before the quarantine went into effect, so some of the homes will be empty. However, we need to make sure nobody is inside. If you can't get anyone to come to the door, check the door handles yourselves. We're been authorized by the police to go right in if possible. If no one answers and the door is locked, I want you do what I explained before. Paint a large, red "X" on the curb in front of the house so that it can be checked later. When you are in a home and find people who are ill, before you leave for the next house paint a red 'I' on the curb. Then send for the drivers to take the ill to the hospital. Later we need to come back to those homes and make sure no one else there became ill."

Another of the interns, Jack Andrews, raised a hand. "I think I'm becoming a pretty fair doctor, and I listened closely to everything you said to us yesterday. However, I've never actually diagnosed this, this malignant pneumonia before, so I'm just going to be honest and say I'm worried about missing some cases. If we're unable to make a reasonably positive diagnosis, are we to send for you?"

"I'm glad you asked that," I said, looking around the group again. "It isn't your job today to make a positive diagnosis. Your job is simply to find people who are ill and mark them to be taken to the hospital. This malignant pneumonia manifests itself in the different ways I shared yesterday, so even I could be fooled. Even if they have just the sniffles or a cough, off they go. After we get them to isolation and observe them, we'll then be able to make a more definitive diagnosis. You can leave that to Dr. Miller and the others. Identify those who are ill with *anything*, and then send for Ed or one of the other drivers. Does everyone understand?"

They nodded or glanced at each other, so I continued, "And now about our translators."

As I said that, the translators all walked toward the front and stopped just a few feet from me. They were a disparate group, to be sure. Two of the men were wearing the white uniforms required of those who cooked in the hospital kitchen. Two others had on loose fitting overalls—no shirts underneath—and were holding mops and pails. The last of their group, a woman about twenty, also had a mop in her hand. Ocie Lee held a broom in hers. Maria leaned over to me and whispered, "They look so scared I bet they'll need those mops and buckets for themselves before the day's through."

"Maybe they will," I replied, flatly.

"You translators," I began, "I can't express just how important you will be for us today. Our doctors and nurses won't be able to communicate well with those in the neighborhood. I do *not* want you to go into the homes with them, unless it is absolutely necessary. I want you to stand in the street outside the homes the doctors and nurses go in. If they need you, they'll call out. If they find someone ill inside who needs to be taken to the hospital, then you might say a few comforting words to them or answer a question or two while they are being put in the ambulance. But, as Nurse Adams will explain to you in a few moments, keep your distance—and stay safe."

I turned my attention back to the interns and nurses. "You can ask the translators to come inside if you feel that is absolutely necessary, but Nurse McDonnell spent a good part of last night writing out for you the important questions you will need to ask—in Spanish. She wrote the questions so that you should be able to see how to pronounce the words. You may not understand everything said back to you, but I think you'll have a pretty good idea if they are saying 'yes' or 'no' to you. Before you leave, get a list of the questions from her."

"And one last thing," I said, taking a step forward. "I'm sorry, but some of you will have to do double-duty today. That is, after we're finished here in the neighborhood, we'll need two groups to go to the places we've kept people who were outside the area when the quarantine started to check everyone there. That will mean a long day for some of you. Nurse McDonnell also has maps for that and will be giving them to those we've chosen for this task. I'm sorry, but it must be done. Now, any questions?"

"Plenty!" Tom shouted, smiling. This time there was plenty of laughter, but it was clearly the nervous variety.

Maria looked at her watch, then to me, and said, "They're as ready as they'll ever be. Turn them loose."

"Let's go to work," I said, clapping my hands. "For now, Nurse McDonnell and I will stay here at the church, which we've set up to be our headquarters. If you need us, send someone running. You drivers and interpreters, go with Nurse McDonnell over to the other side of the church. What she has to say won't take long. For the rest of you, you know what you have to do. Good luck—and stay safe."

Just as everyone started moving, I looked across the street and saw Charles Hornbeck leaning against the door of the neighborhood barbershop. He waved.

"What in the . . . " I said to myself as I started crossing the street. When I was within earshot, I asked him, "What are you doing here?"

He stepped forward and shook my hand, firmly. "Just wanted to make sure we're doing everything possible for these poor people." He lowered his voice. "I don't know—are we doing enough? What else could we be doing?"

He seemed sincere, but I couldn't resist the temptation to say. "Frankly, Charles, I'm surprised to see you. Aren't these 'just Mexicans,' as you described them the other day? Why the sudden change of heart? What's gotten in to you? If you're not careful, you're going to wreck your reputation."

He didn't answer my question. Instead, he replied, "I need to get back to the hospital. I just wanted to make sure we were . . ."

His whole demeanor had changed. I didn't see "Bottom Line Hornbeck" in front of me. Instead, I saw a man who was clearly wrestling with himself about something.

"Look," I said, "Nurse McDonnell and I will see this done right. Don't worry. You've done plenty already. You should be proud of that."

He smiled weakly, thanked me, shook my hand again, and headed toward his car.

....

CHAPTER 16

The Cries

October 31
8:38 A.M.

Tomas Cardoza opened the front door to his home, rushed in, closed the curtains at his front window, and called for his wife, Carmen. Even though some men had stopped by just after midnight, woke him from a sound sleep, and told him he wouldn't be able to leave the neighborhood until further notice, he had still gotten up early and tried to get to his job. He was the maintenance supervisor at the trolley depot in downtown Los Angeles, a position of great importance to the city given the number of breakdowns that occurred daily. He knew he had to try getting there. But on this morning, as he approached Macy Street, two guards with rifles had ordered him to go back home immediately. Just after they had done so, Tomas heard loud shouts coming from the direction of the church and decided to see what was going on.

Tomas had joined the large crowd assembled at the church and listened to Father Brualla and Dr. Thompson describe a serious illness that had found its way into the neighborhood. His ears perked up immediately when he heard them say house-to-house inspections were going to begin and those who were found to be ill would be taken to Los Angeles County Hospital for treatment. Once the inspections were mentioned, he eased out the back of the crowd, trying not to draw attention to himself, and started walking toward his home. Rather than rushing, he took his time as he tried to decide what should be done before anyone showed up at his door.

His two-year-old daughter, Felicita, was ill. He did not believe it was serious, but she did have a light cough and her nose was constantly running. He had just heard Dr. Thompson say everyone showing *any* symptoms of being ill would be taken away at once. Tomas didn't want Felicita taken away, but that wasn't the only reason he didn't want the inspectors in his home. Tomas had come to California from Mexico City just over a year before to look for work. He was a skilled mechanic, so it was not difficult for him to find employment. He chose the job with the city over two other opportunities because his boss promised to help him secure the legal documents required for him to stay in the country. Through his hard work and dedication, he rose quickly through the ranks and was chosen to be the maintenance supervisor when the previous one moved his family back to their hometown of Chicago. Then, once Tomas had saved up enough money to put a down payment on a small home at 916 Augusta Avenue, he sent for his Carmen and Felicita. They had arrived only the previous week.

However, even though Tomas was in the country legally, Carmen and Felicita were not due to the requirements in the recently created Immigration Act, which he heard was being strictly enforced throughout the city. His mind was racing as he considered the possibility that not only would his daughter be taken to the hospital, but his wife might be sent back to her parents' home in Mexico City.

Carmen stepped into the front parlor and said, "I told you so. Those men said no one would be allowed out." She smiled. "Not even my very important husband who makes sure everyone gets to their work."

Without responding, Tomas drew open the curtain a few inches and looked out. "Come see this," he said. "It has already started."

"What has?"

For the next few minutes Tomas relayed what he had heard at the church. No sooner had he finished when Carmen, who had also been looking through the front window as her husband spoke, stepped back and shouted, "Oh, no! Look!"

Tomas slid the curtain open a few more inches so that both had a clear view of the events taking place at Felipe and Galena Pérez' home directly across the street. Felipe and their seven-year-old son, Lorenzo, were being led down their front steps by a nurse. A doctor was still on the porch, and it appeared he was trying to explain something to Galena just as the nurse helped Felipe and Lorenzo into the back of an ambulance parked at the curb. The second the ambulance door closed, Galena rushed down the steps and over to the ambulance, where she started pounding her fists on its roof. She was crying loudly as she called out, "Felipe! Lorenzo!"

Carmen reached around her husband and jerked the curtain shut. "Our Felicita! What do we do?"

Tomas saw the tears welling in her eyes as he replied, "She has just a child's cold, not the illness that was talked about. Maybe we should hide her until they go away—behind the secret wall in the closet."

One of the previous owners of the home had built a special wall within the deep closet in their bedroom. This wall was almost three feet from the back of the closet, and the area behind it was large enough for at least three grown men to sit comfortably. Very small hinges on the left edge allowed it to be opened easily. Several large nails spaced evenly across the middle, convenient for hanging clothes and hiding the knowledge of what lie behind.

"She would be frightened. They would hear her. She closed herself in there one day when we were playing a hiding game and screamed until I found her and let her out. I don't think she would go back there."

Tomas nodded. "Yes, but she would not worry if you were in there with her."

"Me with her? Why?"

"Because they shouldn't see you, either. You do not have the papers yet, and I'm afraid they might send you away from me. I was too long without you before. I won't let that happen again."

He could tell by her expression she had not thought of herself up to that point. Looking toward the rear of their home, she said, calmly, "I'll get Felicita. Please open the closet."

....

Dr. Tom Barton, flanked by his nurse, Constance Mercer, and their interpreter, Chita Concepcion, had been given the task of checking the homes on the west side of Augusta Avenue. No one appeared to be around at the house on the corner and the door and windows were locked, so Nurse Mercer painted a large "X" on the curb in front of it so that it would be checked again later. At the home next up the street, all members of the Cortez family were well.

"Maybe we'll get lucky and no one will be sick on this street," Nurse Mercer said as they walked toward the Cardozas' home.

"I wish you hadn't said that," Chita responded, shaking her head. "That probably jinxed us. There'll probably be someone ill every place we go now."

Dr. Barton turned, smiled, and said, "Why, Chita, you're not superstitious, are you?"

"You bet your stethoscope I am," she replied while crossing herself three times in rapid succession.

Tom said to Nurse Mercer, "And I've noticed you aren't stepping on any cracks along the sidewalk. You, too?"

She smiled back and said, "Just not taking any chances. I don't mind saying I'm scared, all the way down to the heels of my shoes."

Chita added, "I'd rather be any place but here."

Dr. Barton put out his arms and stopped them both. "Look, I'm not wild about this myself, but we have to do this, plain and simple. And we don't have time to look for four leaf clovers or wish on stars, so let's buck up and get this done as fast as we can so we can get out of here."

"I'm for that," Chita said. "Let's get going." Nurse Mercer nodded her head and pointed toward the Cardoza home. "And don't forget—gloves and masks."

Tomas had watched them come up the sidewalk and opened the door just as they stepped onto his porch.

Dr. Barton bowed slightly and said, "This is Nurse Mercer, and that's Mrs. Concepcion. I'm Dr. Barton from Los Angeles General Hospital. I'm sure you've heard by now about the pneumonia in the neighborhood. Today we're checking every home to make sure those who are ill receive treatment. May we please come in?"

"No one here is ill," Tomas said, closing the door slightly. "You would waste time."

"I'm sorry, Sir," Dr. Barton replied, "but we'll have to be the judge of that. We really do need to come inside. These are the mayor's orders. If we don't check, the police will be sent. Do you understand?"

Tomas said, his voice cracking slightly, "Then if you must, I cannot stop you." He opened the door all the way and motioned for them to come in. Having discovered Tomas' English was good, Dr. Barton told Chita she could remain on the porch. With a heavy sigh of relief, she leaned back against the porch railing.

Once inside, Dr. Barton and Nurse Mercer sat on a small couch just to the left of the window. Tomas remained standing.

"We have a few questions to ask first," Dr. Barton said. "Nurse Mercer will write down your answers. First, what is your name, and what are the names of others who live here with you?"

Tomas didn't respond, so Dr. Barton leaned forward slightly and said, this time more gently, "Please, what is your name? Don't be afraid. We're here only to help. That is the truth."

Clearly agitated, Tomas walked over next to them and stared out the window. "Why did you take them?" he said, pointing across to the Perez home.

Turning to look outside, Dr. Barton responded, "That wasn't me. Another doctor is on that side of the street. If people were taken to the hospital, it was because he felt they needed help. That's why we are here."

Still looking out the window, Tomas said, "My name is Tomas Cardoza. And I am not ill."

As soon as Nurse Mercer had written his name on a tablet, she asked, "And what are the names of the others who live here with you?"

Tomas walked to the other side of the room and sat down in a wooden rocking chair. "I am the only one here."

Dr. Barton looked over to the corner of the room where saw a doll and a dozen colorful wooden blocks scattered about. "Whose are those?" he said, pointing to the toys.

Tomas was slow to respond. When he finally did speak, he said, not looking at their faces, "For my niece. She comes over once in a while." Then, standing again, he moved quickly to the door of the bedroom on the left side of the house, opened it, and said, "See. No one is here."

As he opened the door, Nurse Mercer saw a beautiful, flowered robe hanging from the bedpost. She leaned over to Dr. Barton and whispered, "Take a look."

When Dr. Barton stood and started toward the bedroom, Tomas moved in front of him and said, his eyes pleading, "Please leave. I beg you. Go."

Sitting back on the couch, Dr. Barton folded his hands, cleared his throat, and said, "Mr. Cardoza, I'm going to be blunt. If people who have this illness are not treated, they will probably die. If I knew of anyone who was ill with anything right now, I'd make sure a doctor examined her. Especially if these were people I loved and cared for, I wouldn't take any chances because if they died, I'd never be able to live with myself. I'd feel it was my fault, and I know I'd never get over it. Do you understand?"

"It is so serious?" Tomas said, this time looking right at Dr. Barton and Nurse Mercer.

"I assure you it is," Nurse Mercer said emphatically.

Tomas started into the bedroom, stopped, and turned back.

"Where are they?" Dr. Barton asked. "Please, we must check everyone."

Turning again, Tomas walked to the closet and knocked on the inside wall. Suddenly, the wall swung out, and Mrs. Cardoza and her daughter came out. Seeing Dr. Barton and Nurse Mercer, she screamed, "No! No!" Then, stepping in front of her daughter and pulling the sides of her dress out the side to shield Felicita, she pleaded, "Please do not take her! She has but a cold. That is all." Facing her husband, the anger building in her voice, she shouted, "How could you?"

She started raising her hand as if to strike Tomas, but she let it fall limply to her side and began sobbing.

Dr. Barton stepped forward and tried to comfort her. "You are right. It is probably just a cold, but we will have to examine her. Please have her sit on the bed."

While Mrs. Cardoza continued crying, Tomas picked up his daughter, who was also crying, and sat her on the edge of the bed. Terrified, Felicita clutched at her father's arm as Nurse Mercer stepped toward her. Tomas sat on the bed and drew his daughter in his lap, holding her firm. "Please," he said, "examine her now. I will keep her here."

Dr. Barton bent down and pressed his stethoscope to her chest. Even though she was crying loudly and coughing every few breaths, he felt satisfied he had heard nothing out of the ordinary. The sinuses appeared inflamed. Her pulse rate was elevated, but that was expected given the circumstances. Felicita's forehead was cool, and her lymph nodes were not enlarged.

Stepping back and placing the stethoscope in his bag, Dr. Barton said to Mrs. Cardoza, "I believe you are right. This looks like a cold to me."

Mrs. Cardoza stopped crying instantly, beaming and saying, first to her husband and then to Dr. Barton, "I knew this! Now she will not have to go to the hospital!"

Her jubilation didn't last long. Dr. Barton turned to Tomas and said,

"We will still have to take her—to make sure the symptoms don't change. But don't worry. . ."

That was all he could get out before Mrs. Cardoza began wailing at the top of her lungs. "Not my Felicita! Please, God, no!"

She reached for Felicita, but Tomas stepped in front of her, picked up his daughter, and handed her to Nurse Mercer.

"No! No!" Mrs. Cardoza continued to scream as Felicita cried loudly and reached out her arms for her mother.

"Go now, Doctor!" Tomas commanded, urging him toward the door.

Mrs. Cardoza cut in, "I go where Felicita goes! I must!"

She broke free from her husband and lunged toward Nurse Mercer, who turned just in time to keep her grip on the little girl. At that moment, Chita, who had been listening from the porch, opened the door and came inside. She stepped over to Mrs. Cardoza, and hugged her while saying, "I, too, am a mother. This is not easy, but it must be done. I would let the doctors take my daughter to be sure she is not sick." Chita started crying and added, "You must do the same."

Mrs. Cardoza hugged her tighter, placing her head on her shoulder and she continued crying. Tomas motioned for Dr. Barton and Nurse Mercer to head for the front door. Once they were down the steps and to the ambulance, Nurse Mercer gently handed Felicita to Ed Armbruster, who helped her to a cot. Just as Ed closed the rear door, Chita and Mrs. Cardoza appeared on the porch. Not seeing her daughter anywhere, Mrs. Cardoza ran down the steps while calling her name, "Felicita! Felicita!"

Mrs. Pérez raced across the street and embraced her tightly. "I know," she said, bursting into tears. "They took my Felipe and little Lorenzo. What are we to do?"

As the two women held each other, Chita walked over to Dr. Barton and said, "You and Nurse Mercer should go. There are many more houses on this side. I'll be along soon. I want to stay with them a little while."

"I understand," Dr. Barton replied. "I don't know what you can say to them. I don't know what any of us can say at a time like this that will do any good."

"But I have to try," she said, tears sliding down her cheeks. "I think of my own children. I think. . ." Her voice trailed off as she started walking back toward them.

Dr. Barton motioned for Nurse Mercer to follow him up the side-walk to the next home.

....

CHAPTER 17

To the Ground

October 31
8:16 P.M.

With an exaggerated wave, Chief Barker directed Ed Armbruster through the Macy Street quarantine gate and watched as he steered his ambulance toward the hospital.

Clapping his hands together, he said to Chief Alexander, "That's the last of 'em. Now we can get to work. How many'd the docs take out today? Wish they'd take the whole damn lot of 'em."

Chief Alexander replied, "Last I heard it was over a hundred. Ambulances took them straight to the hospital. Many homes are empty now."

Chief Barker removed a small flask from his inside vest pocket, took a quick draw from it, and offered the same to Chief Alexander, who declined. "Here in public? Are you out of your mind? You're supposed to be upholding Prohibition."

He didn't respond. Instead, Chief Barker lit his cigar, looked across the street, and said, "Don't worry about 'em being empty. Sick people were in them homes, right? Gives us the right to do what we need to do, and you know what *that* is."

"Yes. Got to get the rats out of there. This should be a night to remember."

"You got that right. One nobody'll ever forget if I have my way."

"You sure we have permission to do this?" Chief Alexander asked, bluntly. "I mean, to charge right in there."

"Smoky told me to do what it takes, and that's what I intend to do.

He put me in charge, so I'm takin' charge. He might be too skittish to do it himself, but I don't think he'll be mad, neither, once it's done. And I sure won't lose any sleep. Should have run these bums out of here a long time ago. This will light a fire under 'em."

"Light a fire under 'em," Chief Alexander repeated, shaking his head.

"Exactly. And I'll get the matches."

"So, where do we start? What's first?"

Chief Barker rolled his cigar back and forth in his mouth before replying, "We burn everything under the places that have that big "I" painted in front of 'em. That's where the sick were. The docs said we have to kill all the rats, mice, squirrels, and anything else that can hold fleas. Even dogs and cats if they're under there. We'll start with Clara, Avila, Date Street—and then work our way up and across Augusta and Bauchet. After that, we'll move toward the tracks."

Chief Alexander interrupted him and said, "I'll have my men standing close by. When you're talking fire, you're in *my* territory."

"Well, just don't have 'em standing too close. Let's just let the fire do its job."

"You're just going to use torches under there, right? And everyone's been told to be careful, yes?" We don't want their houses catching fire while we take care of what's below."

Chief Barker exhaled a long string of smoke, blew on the end of his cigar until it burned bright, and said, "That'd be a shame, wouldn't it?"

"I don't know . . . " Chief Alexander said, his voice trailing off. "If we're not really careful, the whole neighborhood might go up. I know the Mayor doesn't want that, and I want to keep my job. I'm still new, and I like it here in Los Angeles."

"You'd like it a whole lot better if these Mexs were gone. You don't know 'em like I do."

"That may be. I don't know. But, tell everybody to go slow and easy, especially at first, and see what happens. To me, that's the smart play."

"Just make sure your men don't get hurt. I'll take care of the rest." Chief Barker just smiled and called over his men.

....

While Chief Barker readied his men, Chief Alexander gathered all the firemen together half a block away. When they had all circled around him, he asked, quietly, "Do any of you know Chief Barker? I mean *really* know him?"

The firemen were still getting used to their new Chief and didn't know how much they could tell him about anything. No one said a word.

"None of you know him? Come on, somebody must. I need to know."

Darrin Kimball, a veteran of seventeen years with the department and one of its senior members, finally spoke up. "We're not sure why you're asking, Sir, but I might have something to say."

"Then speak up," the Chief said. "It'll stay right here."

"Most folks think he's a brick or two shy of a load. I'll just say it seems like he enjoys his job a little too much. A lot of his prisoners show up in court in pretty rough shape—and they didn't start out that way."

Jack Butler, one of the newer men, added, "Got caught speeding downtown once. They took me to the station for it. See this tooth here? Before they found out I was a fireman, the Chief had one of his men take care of it with a nightstick. For speeding. Speeding!" Then Jack opened his mouth to show a lower front tooth that had broken in half. Several other men added their own stories about Chief Barker, none of them flattering.

"Thanks, men," Chief Alexander said, shaking his head. "I had a feeling, but I wasn't sure. We're supposed to clear out everything under the houses where the docs found sick people today. Rakes, shovels, and a torch or two would probably do, but Barker is hell-bent on burning under there to kill anything that moves. Controlled fires—with torches— wouldn't be bad, but I don't think that's what he has in mind. I'm afraid he's match-happy."

"Then we better be right there with the hoses to the ready," Darrin responded, pointing to their trucks. *Right* there."

"Exactly my thoughts," Chief Alexander said. "Let's shadow 'em as best we can and try to get the work done *ourselves*. Let's not have this whole area in flames. Kimball—I'm putting you in charge here. Pair up the men and get everything ready. While you're doing that, I better go find the Mayor."

"Good idea, Sir," Kimball replied.

Not a single man disagreed.

....

Before Darrin Kimball and two of his men, Bernard Dill and John O'Leary, could make their way half way down Bauchet Street, they saw flames shooting out from under a house toward the end of the block.

"It's started!" Kimball shouted. "O'Leary, you come with me! Dill, run back and get one of our trucks!"

By the time Kimball and O'Leary reached the house, smoke was coming out the front door. Four policemen, three City officers. and one from the Valley, were standing across the street and intently watching the fire spread.

Kimball pushed the officer closest to him hard enough on the shoulder that he stumbled and fell to the ground.

"Watch it, Buddy. Who do you think you are?" the officer said, righting himself.

Kimball pointed to the insignia on his helmet and replied, "L.A. County Fire Department, that's who—and I'm in charge here." Then, turning to O'Leary, he ordered, "Go close that door. The fire's drafting. It doesn't look like the upper is burning yet. We've got to shut off the air, or it'll all go up like a straw hat. I'll keep these firebugs out of your way."

Officer Charles Cross stepped toward Kimball and growled, "Now you just wait a minute. We didn't know it would spread like that—that fast. We're just doing what we were told."

"You were told wrong," Kimball shot back. "You need to let our men take care of this."

"We take orders from Chief Barker and nobody else. If you have a problem, take it up with him."

At that moment, with lights flashing and bell clanging, the fire truck roared down the street toward them. Dill was driving, and as soon as he skidded to a stop, he yelled for the two men on the back to unroll the hose and get to pumping water under the house.

Officer Cross stepped back toward Kimball and said, "What you're doing ain't right. We're not done here."

"Oh, yes you are. You've done enough," Kimball said. "We'll take it from here, and you can take that back to your Chief."

Before Officer Cross could respond, O'Leary ran up to Kimball and said, pointing behind them, "Look over there— that's Clara Street. Flames shootin' high."

"What in the . . . This has to stop! O'Leary, run between those houses over there and see what's going on. See if any of our men are there yet. We'll finish up here fast as we can and come over."

"There's more!" O'Leary shouted, looking this time in the direction of the railroad tracks, where plumes of thick smoke drifted skyward.

"One at a time," Kimball replied. He turned around just as his men extinguished the last of the flames under the house.

Officer Cross then stepped directly in front of him. He kicked the dirt, smiled, and said to his men, "I think we can go now."

As they started walking away, he turned one last time toward Kimball and said, grinning, "Have a nice night."

Over their heads in the distance, more smoke curled upward.

....

The area called "Shack Town" ran from Alhambra Avenue down along the Southern Pacific railroad tracks just west of the Los Angeles River. It consisted of nearly seventy-five acres dotted with tents of all shapes and sizes and homes crudely assembled with railroad tie floors and scrap boards and lumber pieced together for walls and roofs. At any given time, as many as three hundred lived there. Most of its inhabitants were new to the country and hadn't yet been able to save enough money to secure more permanent housing in the nearby neighborhood. Still others had not been able to find work and were still seeking jobs.

There was a special camaraderie among those who lived in the neighborhood built on shared circumstances and cemented by kindness: the sharing of food, shelter, and clothing. Its residents saw Shack Town as a place of *beginnings*, a place to hole up while fighting to achieve their dreams. At the same time, they prayed that it would not be where their dreams ended. Secreted in a grove of oak and hackberry trees where the railroad tracks made a sharp bend, nearly two dozen unmarked graves, most of them holding infants, reminded them that time in Shack Town should be kept short as possible.

Major Jack Burke, still in charge of the guards around the quarantine area; Stuart Bunning, present to represent the interests of the Greater Los Angeles Economic Progression Council; and Chief Barker peered intently down into Shack Town from their vantage point atop a small knoll at the eastern-most edge of the perimeter.

Chief Barker pointed ahead and said, "Major, that's where we need you to send your men. To this upper section where most of them shacks are. I'm thinkin' that's where the rats are hidin'. Most likely anyway. Your men got to get everybody out of there—pronto. We'll send in the bulldozers and knock them eyesores down and mash rats while we're at it. Then we'll burn 'em. Got to be done."

Major Burke turned to him and said, "You sure about this? I'm on the fence here. Some won't like what we're doing. Stuart, what do you think?"

"The Council approves. The Chief is right. Got to be done."

Major Burke asked both men, "And what about Chief Alexander? If he shows up, he'll have a conniption if he sees fires."

"Don't worry 'bout a thing," Chief Barker replied. "I've taken care of that. Why do you think we're usin' fire at the homes where they found sickness? All them do-gooder firemen will be puttin' out fires there and won't see us. This strip of land will be cleaned out before they blink. It'll be cuttin' off the head of the snake. With the people in them shacks gone and everything cleared, there won't be nothin' for nobody to come back to. They'll have to go somewhere else—like back to Mexico."

"What about the Mayor?"

"I've said this a dozen times tonight. Smoky told me to get the job done, and he's backed by the Council."

"Okay," Major Burke said with a shaky voice. "Then I guess we'll get to it."

Calling over the bulldozer operators, who were all clustered by the Chief's car, he ordered, "Just the upper section, men. Concentrate on anything made out of wood—lean-to's, shacks—but leave the tents alone. Give us fifteen minutes before you get rolling. First, I'm going to get my men to shoo everyone out of there. Then it'll be your turn."

Carl Stevens, a mountain of a man and the senior member of the crew, asked, "What if they won't leave? What then?"

Chief Barker cut in quickly, giving Stevens a cold stare. "Then *accidents* might happen."

"I'm not killin' anybody tonight," Stevens shot back. "Somebody better be through each structure before I move toward it to make sure it's empty. Otherwise, I go home right now." The other operators nodded their support.

Chief Barker gritted his teeth and started to reply but thought better of it. Turning toward Major Burke, he said, angrily, "You heard 'em. Get your men down there right now and clear 'em all out so these, these *gentlemen* can get to work. We're wasting time."

He walked quickly to his car, reached in, drew out his rifle, and came back through the middle of the group. Once through, he paused, turned, and said, "Major, get your men movin'. Let's go!"

As Chief Barker stomped off down the hill, Major Burke and Stevens looked at each other for a moment, neither saying a word. Finally, Major Burke said, "Let's be careful here. You're right—I'm not here to kill anyone, either."

Stuart Bunning, who to this point had decided to stay out of the discussion, finally stepped forward and said, pointing down toward Chief Barker, "But I wouldn't swear about him."

Major Burke replied, "I'll send a couple men to keep him company. Might be helpful."

"It might at that," Stevens said, while motioning his men to their machines. "And forget about that fifteen minutes. We'll give it twenty, thirty—as long as it takes to get the people out of there. Those are *my* orders."

Major Burke nodded his approval. "Take *all* the time you want."

....

On the other side of the neighborhood, three-quarters of the way down Rosa Bell Avenue, Chief Alexander and three of his men had just extinguished the last of the flames under one of the newer shotgun homes in the area. Felipe and Rose Montez had just moved in two months before after finally securing jobs that provided them enough money to cover the rent and keep food on the table for their two children. It was the first place they ever lived they felt they could call *home*. While the firemen had been able to save the home, thick smoke was still seeping out through the cracks around the front windows.

Felipe took his wife's hand and started leading her up the sidewalk toward the front door. One of the fireman quickly blocked their way and shook his head to indicate they were to go no farther.

Felipe, turned around to face Chief Alexander and asked, his eyes wet, "Where we go? Is our *casa*. Must here."

The Chief motioned for Felipe to return to the street while he said to his men, "Be careful, but go open the door and windows. Let's see what we can do for them. I doubt they can go back in tonight, but let's try to air it out as best we can. Get the openings at the back, too. You know what to do. Let's go!"

The Chief did his best to make Felipe understand what they were doing. He wasn't sure he had been very successful, but Felipe finally nodded to him before urging his wife and children to sit in the front yard next to a large cottonwood tree growing there. Once seated, none of them said a word. They just stared intently at their home.

Chief Alexander knew his men always kept sandwiches on their trucks, so he decided to see what he could find for the Montez family. As he got to the back of the truck, he noticed something in the shadows behind the axe holder. Leaning closer, he saw it was a little boy he guessed to be about four years old. He was clutching close to his chest a pitiful looking gray cat, limp, and missing large clumps of its hair. The evening wasn't cold, but the boy was shivering. He also had rips in his trousers at both knees and wasn't wearing a shirt or shoes. The boy didn't put up a struggle as Chief Alexander picked him up and carried him to the side of the truck where blankets were kept in a box attached above the wheel well. He wrapped him in a blanket, picked him back up and held him close, but then didn't know what to do with him. The boy put his arm around him and drew himself even closer, whimpering and coughing repeatedly as he did so.

Mrs. Montez had been watching and called out to Chief Alexander. The Chief didn't understand her words, but the motions of her arms indicated she wanted the boy brought to her. He took the boy over, sat him at her feet, and smiled and nodded. Chief Alexander turned back toward the truck and had only gone a few steps when he felt something clutch at his left leg. It was the boy again. Mrs. Montez came over and tried to corral him, but every time she got close, the boy edged around the Chief's leg just enough to keep out of her reach. Mrs. Montez shrugged, shook her head, and went back to her own children.

"Now what am I going to do with you?" Chief Alexander said, patting the boy on the head before picking him up again. "Where do you live? Oh, that's right—you don't understand me, do you? Well, I guess I'll just have to ask somebody else."

However, looking up and down the street, he realized there was no one around to ask. Except for police, guards, and his fire crews, the streets were empty. As they had been ordered, the local residents were still inside their homes. Those who had been burned out or chased away had gone immediately to the church seeking shelter. Other than a mangy dog limping up the street, there was no other movement in that direction.

Turning to the boy again, he said, gently, "I'm going to take you with me, to the church anyway." He saw one of his men coming around the side of the house and called over to him. "Frank, look what I found. I'm going to drive him over to the church and then be right back to pick you up. You should be done by then. It won't take long."

"Got it, Chief," Frank replied. "We'll be here."

As Captain Alexander drove to the church, he noticed the boy had a terrible cough that seemed at times to make it difficult for him to catch his breath. "You take it easy, young man," he said. "We'll get you some food—and then somebody'll find your parents. You'll be all right."

Father Brualla, standing on the top step of the church, was arguing loudly with a policeman down at the curb when Chief Alexander eased his truck to a stop. The Chief eased from the truck, taking the boy and his cat with him, and started up the steps. "Father," he said, "I found him not far from here, but I don't know who he belongs to. Thought I better bring him to you. He's lost—and pretty scared."

"As are many of us this night," Father Brualla said, loudly, staring angrily at the policeman. Chief Alexander placed the boy in Father Brualla's arms and started turning away, but the boy started crying and held tightly to his coat sleeve.

"I have to go," the Chief said to the boy, squeezing his hand. "The Father will take good care of you. Don't you worry none."

The boy coughed again so long and hard he lost his grip on the sleeve and his cat, which started sliding down his chest. Father Brualla drew his arms tightly around both and started toward the door.

"Take good care of him, Father."

"And what about them?" Father Brualla replied, his voice cracking, as he pointed off in the distance where fires blazed and a thick cloud of smoke hung over the neighborhood.

"I'm sorry, Father. We're doing the best we can."

"To do *what*?" Father Brualla shouted back, this time his tone angry, bitter.

Chief Alexander was ready to reply, but caught sight of flames that suddenly shot high into the air a block to the north.

He turned and walked slowly back to the truck.

....

Elena Mendoza was worried.

She relied on the income from cooking and cleaning for a wealthy family close to downtown on College Street to provide food, clothing, and the rent on a tiny bungalow for herself, her two children, and her mother. Each morning Elena left just before 5:00 A.M. and made her way across the dry bed of the Los Angeles River and up the embankment to Alhambra Avenue. From there she began the two and a half mile walk to the home of the Sawyers, a family she had served as nanny, maid, and cook for nearly a year.

However, on this morning she was an hour ahead of schedule, the result of being jolted from a restless sleep near three-thirty by the sounds of people shouting and running up the street outside her open window. Peering outside, she had seen several fires off in the distance but decided they were probably just marking boundaries of the quarantine area. She knew she wasn't supposed to leave the area, but also knew she had to try to get to work as hers was the only source of income for her family.

Her mother appeared in the doorway. She had heard Elena's coughing throughout the night, and now seeing her pale face, urged her to go back to sleep. "*No te preocupes*," she had reassured Elena, promising to watch over the children and get them off to school.

Elena had replied, her yawn interrupted by a raspy cough, "*Yo no trabajo. No comemos.*" If she did not work, the family would not eat.

Coughing repeatedly and rubbing her aching chest, Elena dressed, grabbed two slices of bread and half an apple, and exited quietly out the back as her mother stood there, arms folded, shaking her head.

Elena was halfway through the thick brush and a stand of young oak trees on the worn path up the hillside toward Alameda when she saw them. There, before her, were half a dozen men, each wearing a badge, carrying a rifle slung over a shoulder, laughing and pointing across the river toward the field known as "Shack Town." Suddenly, an explosion rang out so powerfully that Elena felt the vibration under her shoes. For an instant, she considered going back home. But, her mother was there with the children—and they needed money—badly.

"One of the shacks!" the man closest to Elena shouted. "Blown to smithereens. Let's go look."

"We're not supposed to leave," another protested.

"We're only going to be gone a minute. Who's gonna know?"

Several others nodded their approval and then headed down the path toward the river. Elena, her heart pounding, darted quickly to her right and sprawled herself on the rocky ground behind the trees. She held her breath and placed her hands tightly over her mouth as she fought to stifle a cough. She didn't move or make a sound until the men were well past her. Once she was sure she couldn't be heard, she dropped her hands and began a series of wracking coughs that made her temples throb. Finally regaining composure, she stood, brushed the dirt and leaves from her blouse, and looked up the hill to make sure no one else was there. After looking back toward her home one last time, she slowly made her way up the hill.

....

CHAPTER 18

To Catch a Rat

November 1
6:06 A.M.

After barely four hours of restless sleep for both of us, Robert and I threw on clothes and wolfed down a breakfast of toast and jam and a half pot of lukewarm coffee. We grabbed our medical bags and hats, rushed to my car, and drove as fast as we could back to the hospital. This time we missed being held up by a train by a matter of seconds.

Maria and Tom Barton, who had now become something of a spokesman for the interns and nurses, were waiting for us in my office when we walked in. They looked absolutely exhausted, like neither had taken much of a break during the night. Tom nodded to us. Maria just waved and slouched back in my chair.

"Make yourself at home," I said, smiling and pointing to my desk.

She squinted and replied, "Don't worry—I did." Picking up a tablet on the desk, she continued, "I just got off the telephone with someone at Los Angeles Catholic Charities. Woke her up. She wasn't too happy at first, but she came around. Bless them—they've decided to help more than I hoped for."

"How's that?" I asked.

"In just a few hours they're going to start delivering to each home in the quarantine area enough food for about ten days. They're also going to rush delivery of bottled milk and tins of coffee. On top of that, I got them to put together supplies so that parents can have their children gargle several times a day with a mixture of hot water, salt, and lime juice. I'm not swearing it will work wonders, but I did a little more digging and found out that seemed to help protect the little ones when they fought this in China a few years back."

"In my past experiences, I've seen that as well, with different citrus added in," Robert said. "It does seem to work. Good job getting that. Your work is excellent, as usual."

She glared at him as I asked, "How are we doing here in the ward? Can you give us a quick update, please?"

Before responding to me, she turned to Tom and ordered him down to the morgue to get the morning report. As soon as he had gone, she said, "Please close the door."

Robert pushed it shut, and we both pulled up a chair next to the desk. She looked again at the tablet and continued, "We had four more die last night. I have their names here. All were from the same block on Clara Street. My judgment is they were all pneumonic but, as you and I discussed before, I went ahead and ordered immediate autopsies to make sure."

"I know it sounds bad to say 'Just four?'—but I expected more than that," I replied.

"Me, too," Robert said. "This may be just the tip of the iceberg though, so we better brace ourselves."

Maria nodded. "I believe you're right. We brought in a hundred and fourteen last night with a wide variety of symptoms. Fifteen cases are definitely pneumonic. Ten or fifteen more are *probable*. With the rest, it's too soon to tell, but they all have one symptom or another that should keep them here: headache, cough, wheezing, pains here and there."

Robert whistled softly and said, "One hundred fourteen. There's room for all of them? Have they all been separated by symptoms as I ordered?"

"We followed your orders to the letter," Maria replied, flipping the tablet back on the desk. "I know you two will want to make your rounds now, but I want you to see someone first—at the very end of the corridor. He's been asking for you, Dr. Thompson. While we head down there, I'll show you what we've done."

She stood up and headed toward the door before either of us could respond, at the same time motioning us to follow along. When we reached the entrance of the isolation wing, four guards were stationed there, two on each side of the hallway. Maria waved to them and said, "Coming through, boys." A large sign had been attached to the wall: "Contagious Pneumonia—Authorized Personnel Only."

"You'll notice all the doors have sheets of paper tacked on them—yellow, blue, or red. The yellow indicates people with undetermined illnesses so that we can watch them to see how they progress. We've kept these closest to the lobby because right now they seem to hold the smallest risk. The blue rooms up ahead we kept mid-way down the hallway. These are for probable cases, those showing at least some symptoms of fever, weakness, pain in the chest region, confusion, cough, and so on. We've started initial treatments on them. Finally, if you'll look toward the end of the hall, you'll see the 'Red Rooms.' We put them last, so there wouldn't be as much traffic around them. These patients have been diagnosed as pneumonic. As I'm sure you've noticed, there's a small table outside each room where gloves and masks are kept. Nobody gets in *any* of the rooms without wearing them."

A few feet before the last "Red Room" on the right, Maria asked us to stop for a minute. "For these patients, we've started an intravenous drip of Mercurochrome solution, along with aspirin and quinine for fever reduction. Then, ice compresses to the chest to help control heart rate, respiration, and pain. When the pain has been severe, we've also, as you instructed, started a course of morphine. When they're able, which isn't often, we're urging fluids, especially coffee—the stronger the better."

"You've done exceptionally well," I said, reaching over to squeeze her arm. "I'm proud of you, Maria. Thank you."

"No need to thank me," she said. "It's what I'm paid for." Then, turning toward the small table outside the room, she said, "Masks and gloves, doctors." Finally, she added, reaching for the door, "But this isn't what *he* was getting paid for."

There were three beds in the room along the far wall. There, in the middle bed, was Ed Armbruster. He had been with us since the beginning, driving the Lujans to the hospital and later organized the ambulances to help with evacuations. When he saw me, he tried to sit up but was too weak to get his back more than a few inches from the mattress. He fell back, heavily, which caused the tube from the Mercurochrome solution bottle to sway back and forth near his right arm.

"I'm so sorry, Ed," I said, taking his wrist to check his pulse. "We'll do *everything* we can."

"I know you will, Doc," he replied, his voice weak, raspy. "Please, just don't let me die."

Robert came over to the bed and said, gently, while examining his eyes, "You're already on the best treatment we have, and we'll be taking care of you round the clock. Don't you worry. Try to drink as much as you can, little sips at a time, and keep resting. We'll take care of the rest."

"He's right," I said. "We've an army of people here to help out. We'll have them keep a special eye on you, right Nurse McDonnell?"

Maria smiled weakly and nodded her head. I said, "We'll come back in a couple of hours and check on you again. In the meantime, see if you can get some sleep, Ed."

I turned and started to leave but stopped and looked at Ed again. "That first day—we didn't know . . . "

Ed managed to raise his head slightly off the pillow and said, his voice cracking, "Just don't let me die. Please."

I walked back to the bed, took his hand, squeezed it, and said, "We need you too much around here. You'll have everything we can do. I promise you that."

"Thanks, Doc. Thanks," he said closing his eyes and turning away.

....

We weren't half a dozen steps out of the room when Nurse Adams came running up, pausing only an instant to catch her breath before saying, "Father Brualla is on the telephone. You better talk to him. More cases have shown up."

Robert, Maria, and I all looked at each other before Robert finally said, "Maria and I will do the rounds. Go. See what else we're up against."

"Thanks. I'll get word back to you as soon as I know something definite." Turning to Nurse Adams, I said, "Have the call transferred to my office. I don't think I should stand at your station and talk to him there. I'll hurry."

The phone was already ringing when I got to my office. Without identifying myself, I asked, "What is it, Father? How bad?"

"Send an ambulance quick," he replied. "Four more came to the church this morning—all very, very sick. I don't know how they made it all the way over here. They were hiding in the cemetery all night."

"I'll send an ambulance over right now to get them." Then, thinking about what he had just said, I asked, "Why were they hiding in the cemetery, Father?"

Dead silence. I asked again, and this time he said, the frustration apparent in his voice, "Have you not heard about last night? About the destruction, the neighborhood, their homes . . . "

"Destruction? What are you talking about?"

"I still can't believe it. I can't believe it happened. Fires everywhere. Homes lost—destroyed. Many hurt, some very badly — burned, overcome by smoke, roughed up by guards. Many have no place to go."

"Slow down, Father," I said. "Tell me again. What happened, and who did it? Why?"

"I do not know. Police, maybe. Or the guards from the quarantine gates. I'm not sure. What I know is something better be done or there will be bloodshed tonight. People came to me all through the night. They are so full of rage nothing I say will stop them. They have decided if anyone tries to come in tonight, they will fight back so this will not happen again. Knives, axes, and some have guns. If this isn't stopped, it will end badly." His voice trailed off, choked with emotion.

"I still don't understand. Why did this happen?"

When he was able to speak again, he said one word, loudly, "Rats!"

"They were trying to destroy rats?" I asked. "Then why—"

"They were also trying to destroy much more. Much more."

There was a loud click as he hung up. I stared at the phone as I placed it back on the desk. All I could think of to say was one word: "Rats!"

....

After my talk with Father Brualla, I ordered an ambulance sent to the church. Then I sat in my office several minutes as I tried to decide what to do next. I stood up, walked over to the window, and looked out in the direction of the Los Angeles River. I couldn't see it, but I could tell a train was going by there, its horn growing more and more faint until all was quiet. When I turned around, Maria was in the doorway.

"I see it in your face," she said, folding her arms. "You couldn't hide an emotion if your life depended on it. What is it?"

I repeated as best I could my conversation with Father Brualla, but I still didn't know exactly what was going on. When I finished, she rolled her eyes and blew out a breath.

"For someone who's supposed to be a great diagnostician, you're sure barking up the wrong tree here. You really don't see what's going on?"

"No, I guess I don't. And *you* do?"

"A blind man could see this," she said, sitting again in my chair. "Don't you get it? Do you really think that would have happened if the illness was downtown or in one of the rich neighborhoods across town? You can't be that naïve."

Looking back out the window, I replied, "But we're fighting the illness . . . "

"That's right—we are. *We* are fighting the illness. Others are fighting a different war, one that has been going on for a long, long time. I've known about it all my life. You're just seeing it now, and it isn't pretty, is it?"

"'They're only Mexicans,'" I said flatly, quietly.

"What did you say!" Maria shouted, standing up and kicking my chair back toward the wall.

"No!" I shouted back. "I didn't say that. No, I mean it isn't what *I* . . . That's just what I heard someone say to me a few days ago. Those aren't words I'd ever say. I was just repeating—"

Her eyes still glaring at me, she cut me off. "Wake up, Doctor. Take a look around."

"But we're doing all we can," I protested.

"I'm not talking about here at the hospital," she shot back. "What did you just say—'they're *only* Mexicans,' right? And then think about what happened last night and why this is being kept such a secret. Think about that."

"We're keeping it quiet because we don't want a panic on our hands. We've already talked about that."

"It isn't just the disease that people are afraid of. This goes much deeper than that, and you know it."

"But what else can *we* do?" I asked, tapping my index finger on the desk.

"That's for you to decide," she said, closing her eyes and leaning back in the chair. I looked at her closely. She was tired, dead tired—and I realized that was so in more ways than one. I recalled her once saying "They're not my people," but as I looked at her now, I was starting to understand what she had meant. They really weren't *her* people. But underneath all the bravado, salty language, and sarcasm, she truly believed everyone should be looked at the same—as people who were to be treated with the same dignity and respect. It was clear to me now that was in her heart. But it was also becoming more and more clear just how many others didn't share the same feelings—and to what degree.

When she opened her eyes, a single tear slid down her cheek. I pulled my handkerchief from my pocket, walked over, and wiped it away.

I said, finally, "I'm going to see Mr. Hornbeck and ask him to get in touch with the Mayor right away. Somebody needs to step in here. We can't let anything happen tonight."

"And I know what I need to do, too," she said, matter-of-factly.

We both left the room.

....

Charles' secretary showed me right in. He was seated at his desk and fiddling again with his radio. He didn't look up as I pulled up a chair.

"Morning, Mr. Hornbeck. "I'd like to talk to you about something that happened last night."

"I already know about it," he said, handing me a screwdriver. "Do you think you can fix this? Do you know anything about these infernal contraptions?"

I placed the screwdriver gently on the desk and said, "I talked to Father Brualla this morning. He told me what happened, but I'm here because of what he said might take place tonight. I hope you'll consider calling the Mayor. The last thing we need right now is violence."

When he didn't respond and continued studying the back of his radio, I knew I'd have to come up with a reason he'd consider important. "If there's a fight and it gets bloody, I know word of it is going to get out, and people all over the city will find out what's going on. If that happens, it won't be good for anyone. And there's one more thing to consider. If fighting erupts, some in the neighborhood are no doubt going to try to get out of there, and some might make it. If they do and if they're ill, we're looking at a spread that somebody gets blamed for—and it might just be us."

That caught his attention, and he finally looked at me. "I was thinking of something very similar myself. I do admit it all seems very unfortunate, like it didn't need to happen like that."

"Then what can we do to keep the same from happening tonight?"

He clasped his hands together, smiled at me, and said, "I'm already working on it. I'll see what I can do."

Just then his secretary knocked gently and opened the door. "Mr. Hornbeck, a Nurse McDonnell is here with someone she says both of you should meet. Should I send them in?"

"Who? What do they want? Did they say? I'm very busy right now."

The second I heard her name I snapped up straight in my chair and thought, "Oh, no—what's she up to now?" Turning to Charles, I said, "Nurse McDonnell is the one I put in charge in the isolation ward. Maybe she has an important update for us."

Charles looked at his watch, then back at me. "Guess we can give them a couple of minutes, but that's all. Show 'em in."

Maria stepped in first, smiled, and said, her voice sweet, gentle, "Thank you, Mr. Hornbeck and Dr. Thompson. I found this gentleman looking for Dr. Thompson and thought I better bring him up here right away. I hope I wasn't wrong in this, but he said he is going to get to work as soon as he talks to you."

She winked at me before turning and motioning someone to follow her in. I had never seen the likes of what appeared next. The man was enormous, and not just in his height. He must have been near to seven feet tall and close to a good three hundred and fifty pounds. He had on faded overalls that appeared to be a conglomeration of several pair stitched crudely together to allow for his girth. There were several holes in the material over his chest, and long, dark hair protruded, reminding me of weeds growing up through a sidewalk. I looked at his hands, and his fingers were as large as hot dogs. When he smiled at me, I saw he was missing his front teeth, top and bottom. This could only be noticed when he smiled because he also had a thick, bushy moustache that almost completely covered his mouth. When he saw us, he quickly removed a tattered straw hat and bowed slightly. As he did so, a toxic blend of body odor and sulfur drifted toward me, causing me to take an awkward step back.

"This is Mr. Micholovich," she continued. "He's the exterminator the Mayor hired to take care of our little problem. Says he needs to ask Dr. Thompson some questions before he can do the job. I knew Dr. Thompson was here, and I thought, Sir, that you'd also like to hear this. I hope I wasn't wrong."

I rolled my eyes and shook my head slightly at Maria, making sure Charles didn't see me. "Thank you, Nurse McDonnell," I said as formally as I could. "You did right."

"Thank you, Doctor. Then I'll excuse myself and go back to work. I'll let all of you get to visiting."

Just before she got to the door, she turned and winked again. I squinted and stared back.

Then, turning my attention to Mr. Micholovich, I said, "You have no idea how happy we are you're here."

He extended his massive hand, and as I shook it, my hand seemed to completely disappear in his. "People usually are," he said while spitting tobacco juice in a small can he held in his left hand. "If you've got critters and crawlers, I'm the one you want. Just call me 'Slim.' That's what I go by."

"Mr. Mic . . . I mean 'Slim,'" I said, "What can I, *we* do for you?"

Slim smiled and looked around at the chairs, realizing none were large enough for him to squeeze in. Turning back to me, his expression brightening, he said, "Mayor Burgess sent me to see you. When he told me about puttin' my attention to rats and squirrels, I know'd what was goin' on here. Seen it before overseas when I was in the army. He made me promise I'd never say a word to nobody. I understand why, and I won't. Wanted you to know that first off."

He was frank and to the point, which was refreshing considering all the secrecy we'd been hiding behind. "Then why did you want to see me? How can I help you?"

He stared at the floor a few seconds before turning to look out the window. "Mayor told me 'bout what them amateurs did last night. Darn shame. But, big area to cover. Sewers, wooded areas, farms, shanties everywhere to the east. Mayor said you'd be able to tell me where to start and how far to throw the traps. Need to know that first or nothin' I do will make a hill of beans."

"I see your point, Slim. Give me a moment and I'll draw you a rough map of where I think we should concentrate first, where we've already had the most *problems*. Then I want you to look at it and tell me where you think we need to branch out based on what you know of the city. Mr. Hornbeck, have you a piece of paper and pencil I can use?"

While I drew a map of the neighborhood and the boundaries of the quarantine area, Slim walked over to the window and sat heavily against the radiator underneath. Charles likely echoed what the Mayor had told him earlier, expressing how important it was to work around the clock if necessary to accomplish the task. He asked Slim what he'd try initially.

"Well, Sir, I already know from Mr. Mayor that most of them houses are raised up on blocks and rocks. That'll make it some easier. I aim to use my petroleum spray on everything above and then a sulfur mix for below. Rats and just about everything else hates both, so that'll drive most out from there. For them that don't move, I make me a special rat poison that I'll scatter everywhere both under and *inside* homes. Have to make sure no kids eat it, though. One bite'd make 'em dead as a bag of hammers. Got my own recipe. Make it thick like syrup, add a little honey, and stir through it good ol' arsenic. Looks so good I'd eat some myself if I didn't know it'd make me see spots and keel over."

Slim started laughing, heartily, his overalls bouncing up and down with his belly. I looked up from my drawing and caught Charles' eye. "Flabbergasted" was the only way to describe his expression.

Slim continued, "Now for them empty buildings, I got a hydrocyanic gas. It's cyanide, more to less. Can't use it if people are there. Bodies'd be stacked up like cord wood. Use that when I can, though. If the place is nice and tight, I also like hookin' up a hose to my truck and pipin' in exhaust. Nothin' drives 'em out or kills 'em faster. Amazin', really."

Here he paused, walked over to look at my map, and said, "I can kill them rats and squirrels, but you got a bigger problem to come if he don't take my advice."

"And what's that?" Charles asked, standing from his chair.

"Mr. Mayor said he was hirin' me, but he also said he was of a mind to spread it out that he'd give a bounty of a dollar a rat for anyone who could get 'em. You ask me, that's a poor thought. Some what don't know what they're doin' gonna catch this if they grab a handful. I seen that happen before, too."

"Wise advice," I said, looking up briefly. "Mr. Hornbeck, I'd also urge you to call Mayor Burgess and have that idea nixed. Slim's right. We don't want just anyone helping out."

"Don't want no amateurs in my way, like them guys last night. Don't want 'em running around where I use the gas."

He walked back to the window and looked outside. This time I noticed he was dragging his right leg slightly.

"One more to give thought to," he said without looking back at us. "Got near to two hundred traps, but for a job like this, that ain't enough. Mr. Mayor said he'd *try* to get more, but there ain't no *tryin'* goin' to help. Got to have 'em."

"Consider it done," Charles said, firmly. "I know some businessmen who can get items here quickly. I'll call them right after you leave."

Slim nodded several times. "'Preciate it. Need more to a thousand. More if you can get 'em. And fast as you can get 'em."

I finished the map and called him over. "This is the main area to cover for now. If you'll notice—"

He put his hand over mine to stop me and said, "That's the river there, ain't it?"

"It is. It's the boundary to the east, right there at the railroad tracks."

Slim shifted his weight and said, "Bad. Very bad. If they're comin' from there, could be comin' from either direction. This gonna' take some time looks like to me."

I shook my head. "We don't have the time. This is spreading fast, and we have to stop it now. Do *everything* you can. When can you start?"

"First got to get some men together. Will need a fair number."

Charles interrupted him and explained he could have as many of the guards as he required.

"Good. Let's round 'em up soon as you can so I can tell 'em what I'm needin' 'em for. We can spread some poison and put down some traps yet today, but the big work's comin' tomorrow morning between three and four when rats are out lookin' for food and places to hunker down. Good time for us because we can lay bait while they're out, and if we can see 'em scurry 'round, we can follow and find their other homes. Best to work at this before sunup 'cause they ain't much for runnin' during the day."

"Do what you can as soon as you can," I repeated, urging him to look one last time at the map to tell us where he'd suggest we extend the search.

"Just leave that to me," he said, stuffing the map in his pocket. "Been doin' this a long time. Know what to do."

"Then we wish you the best of luck," Charles said while motioning to the door. "Don't let us keep you."

He tipped his straw hat first to me and then to Charles. He smiled broadly and walked toward the door. Stopping there, he turned back to face us and said, "Luck won't have nothin' to do with it. My poison will."

He opened the door, stepped heavily into the outer office, and closed the door behind him.

"What do you make of him?" Charles asked, snickering.

"Obviously loves his work. I just hope he doesn't poison half the city in the process."

Charles smiled again and said, "Well, if anybody could do that, I'm betting *Slim* could."

We both laughed, the laugh of men who knew time and options were running short.

"I know you've telephone calls to make," I said, moving toward the door. "I'll be off. I'll make sure Nurse Adams knows where I'll be at all times if you need to get in touch with me."

"Thanks, Matthew," he said.

"There's still so much to do," I replied.

He nodded and waved to me as I left the room.

....

CHAPTER 19

¡No más!

November 1
6:37 P.M.

Chief Barker and Stuart Bunning, who had been chosen by the Council to be the official liaison with the police, had just turned from Alameda onto Macy Street when Stuart pointed ahead and said, "What in the world is that?"

About a block more down the street, just outside the Macy Street entrance to the quarantine area, a large crowd, most of them guards and policemen, were backing up slowly toward the other side of the road as if they were being forced that direction.

"Was afraid of this," Chief Barker said, pushing the brake slowly and easing to a stop. "It's what we get for pussy footin' around with these people. Should have stayed all night last night and finished the job when we had the run of the place. We better stop this right now."

When they reached the outer reaches of the group, which was still inching backward, Chief Barker saw Officer Charles Cross, walked up to him, and asked, "Cross, what is this? What's going on?"

Officer Cross pointed ahead and shouted, to be heard above the commotion around them, "They were laying for us. When we got here, there were hundreds of 'em armed to the teeth. I would have just shot at two or three, and I bet you then they would have backed down. But before I could do anything, the guards started back. Bunch of cowards. Cowards!"

Stuart asked, "Who was waiting? What are you talking about?"

As more and more saw Chief Barker inching his way forward, the crowd began to open a path for him to make his way to the front. Stuart and Officer Cross followed at his heels.

When the last of the crowd stepped aside and let Chief Barker through, he was caught completely off guard by what he saw in front of him. "Can't believe it," he said, turning to look at Stuart. "Didn't think they had an ounce of fight in the whole lot."

Those of the neighborhood had created their own quarantine line just a few feet inside the one which had been imposed upon them. Nearly a hundred men were standing shoulder to shoulder, clustered in rows at the quarantine entrance, and well over a hundred more in an evenly-spaced line up and down Macy Street where they were positioned facing the guards. Most were armed with axes, railroad spike hammers, pitch-forks, sharpened broomsticks, or torches. However, three at the very front held shotguns pointed straight ahead of them. When they had cocked the hammers of their weapons, the crowd before them had slowly started easing back.

When Chief Barker saw the shotguns, he called out, "Officers, guns to the ready! Move back this way!"

At that moment, Father Brualla stepped around those with the guns and gently pushed the barrels down until the three were pointing to the ground. Then, stepping in front of them, he shouted over to Chief Baker, "This is not a time for violence! I will do all I can to prevent this! But, you must hear us tonight! No more! *¡No más!* There will not be another like last night!"

"Get out of the way, Father!" Chief Barker yelled back to him. "Those men are breaking the law, and I'm going to arrest them right now. And then we're comin' in. We've declared most of this, this *neighborhood,* a 'public nuisance,' so that gives us the lawful right to do what we will. Nothin' you can do about it now. Move aside."

"I do not think so," Joseph Arroyo, a tower of a man who worked as a gang foreman for the Southern Pacific, said, stepping forward with his pitchfork held toward Chief Barker. Pointing behind him and up and down the street, he added, "Who has the advantage now? Some of us may be hurt, some may die, but your losses will be greater. You will *not* get in this night."

One of the men with a shotgun raised his weapon and pulled the trigger for one barrel. The discharge was so sudden, so loud, almost everyone on both sides, including Chief Barker, immediately ducked and stepped back, raising arms to shield themselves.

The men behind him erupted in cheers and held their own weapons high into the air. Father Brualla ran to the middle of the street, waved his arms and broke in, "No violence! Please! We must talk. We must all understand—"

A voice behind him cut him off. It was Nurse Maria McDonnell, who was making her way through the crowd toward him. "Now everyone just wait a damn minute!" she shouted. "I've something to say, and you're all going to hear it!"

Standing next to Father Brualla, she started to speak, but the crowd across from her suddenly started shifting as a small group made its way through to the front: Mayor Burgess, Charles Hornbeck, and two other police officers.

"What's going on here?" Mayor Burgess asked. "What was that shot? Who's responsible for this?"

"Take a guess," Maria called over to him as sarcastically as she could.

"And who are you, young lady?" the Mayor asked, stepping forward. "What have you to do with all of this?"

"She's one of them," Chief Barker said, sneering. "Look at her—one of *them*."

"She's one of *mine*," Charles cut in, stepping forward and glaring at Chief Barker. Turning to Maria, he said, "Nurse McDonnell, what's going on here? What can you tell us?"

Maria stepped in front of Father Brualla, pointed up and down the street, and began. "It's pretty simple. These people are frightened, and can you blame them? They don't know what has happened to their relatives and friends who were taken from here to the hospital—whether they're safe or dying or have already died. They were promised they'd be told, and there's been no news of any kind for any of them. They don't know what's happened to those who were turned away and not allowed in when the quarantine started. Many husbands, brothers, sisters were coming home from work only to be stopped. They want to know if they're okay and where they are now. I've told them some were taken to schools and churches close by, but what of the others?

"And last night. What could I tell them about that? Homes were torn down and burned. Take a deep breath. You can still smell the smoke. And some homes were looted! Yes, *looted*, and not by others in the neighborhood. Their dogs, cats—and even chickens, goats, and donkeys—all taken out to the fields and shot. They want to know why. And the illness—they want to know everything we're doing to stop it, but nobody has come back here to tell them anything. They haven't been allowed news of any kind. No newspapers have been brought in and nothing has been picked up on radio. Mr. Hornbeck, Mr. Mayor, look around me. Look at their faces. *This* is what is going on."

Father Brualla put his arm around Maria's shoulder. "This is all we want. We want to know what is happening to us. Is that too much to ask?"

"She's right," Charles whispered to Mayor Burgess. "Everything she said."

Maria shouted, looking this time directly at Chief Barker, "One more thing! There can be no more fires near their homes. There can't be. Mr. Mayor, the exterminator you hired has already started spraying *every- thing* with petroleum. Just one fire and the whole neighborhood could be up in flames, and with the breeze we have tonight, it could spread all across the city!"

All eyes were on Mayor Burgess. He looked at those standing behind Maria, seeing the fear and anger in their faces. Next, he looked at those standing next to him and saw anger and fear of a different type. The similarity, and the contrast, shook him. Finally, he cleared his throat and spoke. "There was miscommunication last night. We can do better. We will explain more to everyone about this malignant pneumonia or virulent pneumonia that we're facing here. But for the time being, for the safety of everyone in this neighborhood and the rest of Los Angeles, steps must be taken."

A few boos rang out, and others holding tools with long, wooden handles struck them repeatedly on the ground.

"Hear me out," he implored, clapping his hands to regain their attention. "These steps must be taken for the safety and welfare of all. First, everyday activities that would take people out of their homes should cease for the time being. Everyone must stay home. No gatherings of any type, like *this* one, so this pneumonia can't spread. Your children must be kept home from school until further notice. Finally, the exterminators are going to have to come into every home and building, so please let them in and cooperate fully with them. We all have to work together on this."

Maria responded, "That seems reasonable to me, under the circumstances, but what about news of those who were taken to the hospital or denied entrance back here to the neighborhood? Something has to be done about this."

"I agree," Mayor Burgess replied. "We'll start working on that right away. You have my word on it. We'll find a way to have the information sent in."

Looking at Father Brualla, he asked, "Father, if we can get news to your church every morning, do you think you could help make sure it gets out to everyone?"

Father Brualla studied him closely before replying. "I will do my best."

"Good," Mayor Burgess said, nodding. "This is a start. We'll try to be better about letting everyone know where we stand with our efforts. I'll try to get regular updates sent as well."

Pausing only for an instant, he continued, "Now about tonight. There will be no fires." He looked sternly at Chief Barker. "I promise you that. But we do have to get in there and do our best to stop the spread of the illness. That will mean more homes disinfected, more traps and poisons put out, and more vacant buildings taken down so that rats don't nest in there. This has to be done, but I've asked Chief Alexander of our Los Angeles County Fire Department and his men to station themselves at every intersection to help make sure we're more organized in our efforts. If anyone has any questions or concerns while this is taking place, the firemen can be approached. They've agreed to help in this manner."

Father Brualla said, "If what you say comes to be, it is a good beginning—but only a beginning. I have understood you, but many here do not understand the language as well. I would like a few moments to speak to everyone—to explain to them what it is you have said."

"I understand," Mayor Burgess responded. "Yes, but do so as quickly as you can."

After Mayor Burgess spoke, Chief Barker, who was caught completely off guard by the Mayor's order that the fire department step in to take the lead on this night, held his holster close to his thigh and climbed awkwardly onto a wooden fruit crate so that everyone could see and hear him. Just as he started to speak, he lost his balance and fell forward, crashing violently to the street. His head hit the curb with such force that blood immediately gushed along the gutter.

There was a moment of panic on both sides of the street as everyone tried to decide if the fall had been an accident or if someone had been the cause of it. Nurse McDonnell quickly rushed forward, knelt down, and turned Chief Barker over so she could inspect the wound. Officer Cross quickly ran up, drawing his gun as he approached.

Father Brualla saw him, held up his right hand, and screamed, "No! He fell himself! No one hurt him!".

The men with the shotguns raised them again as they saw Officer Cross approach Father Brualla and Maria. Officer Cross saw the resolve in their eyes and stopped short, quickly lowering his pistol.

"Help us!" Father Brualla said, motioning for him to kneel down as well. "He is hurt badly. Someone call for an ambulance."

Staring first at the blood, which was still gushing along the street, and then at Nurse McDonnell, Officer Cross said, quietly, "Can't. He ordered all ambulances away from here. Said they weren't to be used tonight."

"Then go get some men!" Nurse McDonnell ordered. "We need to get him to a car and to the hospital—fast. There's not much we can do here in the street."

Mayor Burgess and Charles Hornbeck also knelt down next to Nurse McDonnell. "Anything we can do, Maria?" Charles asked, gently.

"His skull has cracked open. This isn't good. Someone find a telephone and have a surgeon standing by. We must get him in quickly."

Father Brualla leaned over and said, "You go with them. I will speak to everyone. I will do my best to make them understand—I pray it will be better."

"It better be," Maria shot back, looking directly at Mayor Burgess. "Otherwise, all this commotion will draw attention, and I don't think anyone, especially the city officials, want much said about what's *really* going on here. *Somebody* might tell. This *is* the 'Paradise of the West.' And we all want it kept that way. Tonight will be very peaceful, won't it, your Honor?"

Mayor Burgess' mouth dropped open an instant before he responded, sharply, "Young lady, this better not be a threat, because if it is—"

"Don't be ridiculous," Maria replied, smiling.

Her intent wasn't lost on Charles, who immediately ordered her to stay with and attend to Chief Barker all the way to the hospital.

Maria grabbed Father Brualla's hand, squeezed it, and said, "I'll be back very soon."

Father Brualla smiled and said to her, "But these aren't your people, remember?"

"That's right," she replied, dryly, as two men rushed over with a stretcher.

....

CHAPTER 20

Like Ghosts

November 2
6:21 A.M.

Nurse Adams furiously waved and ran toward me the second she saw me enter the hallway. Holding her side with her breaths coming in short bursts, she was finally able to say, "I was going to send the police looking for you. We're in trouble. Bad trouble."

As she caught her breath, I asked, "What's going on? Were more brought in this morning?"

At last able to speak normally, she replied, "We've five new patients. Three definitely pneumonic, but you better look at the other two right away."

Out of the corner of her eye, she caught sight of Tom Barton exiting one of the red rooms at the end of the corridor. She motioned for him to join us. "He'll explain. He's the one who found it, and thank goodness he did."

"Good morning, Tom—" was all I could get out before he handed me two charts and said, "Take a look at these. I'm no expert by any means, but from what you've taught us, I think I'm right."

"About what?" I asked, scanning the charts. Then, at the very bottom of the reports, I saw it—and was stunned: "Suspected *Bubonic*."

Still studying the charts, I waved my hand and urged both to start walking ahead of me. "Tell me—what drew you to the diagnosis?" I asked as we made our way down the hallway.

"Boils under their arms and at the groin. One also has a large boil at the base of the neck. Plus, the lung sounds are still fairly normal, especially when compared to those who are pneumonic. I wasn't completely sure, but I felt strongly enough about it that I put them in a separate room and wasn't going to let anyone else in until you took a look."

"That's good. Thank you, Tom. Come with me. If these *are* bubonic, it would indicate another outbreak, and the source could be from just about anywhere, inside or outside that neighborhood. Maggie, I'll meet with you later so we can go through the overnight reports."

Tom and I put on gloves and masks and entered the room. I stopped short, frozen. There, in the bed before me, was Father Brualla. Chief Alexander was in the bed off to his right. Both appeared to be sleeping.

"Oh, no!" I said, more loudly than I should have.

"Their pain was significant, so I started both on morphine," Tom whispered, stepping to the side. "And aspirin for fever. I didn't want to do more until you got here."

I slowly stepped toward Father Brualla, took his wrist, and checked the pulse rate. I next checked under his arms and felt three large boils on the left side and two on the right. I looked at Tom and nodded. As I did so, Father Brualla opened his eyes and smiled weakly.

"Matthew, don't bother with me," he said, pulling his covers closer to his neck. "I'm cold, but I will be fine. Go help those who need you. The Lord will protect me."

At that moment, Chief Alexander rolled toward me and said, "I'm cold, too. So cold. Can't stop shivering. Can I have more . . . blankets? Could sure use some."

"I'll order them right away," I said. "Chief, I'm very sorry about this, but don't worry. Let me take a look at you, and then we'll talk more."

I discarded my gloves, put on a new pair, and stepped toward Chief Alexander to examine him. The symptoms were the same, except he had a large boil on his neck and small boils every few inches running from the shoulder down to the groin. "Other than cold," I asked while listening to his lungs, "how are you feeling?"

Chief Alexander closed his eyes and replied, "My head hurts so bad, like I've been hit with a board. Hurts so bad my eyes aren't focusing good."

"We can give you something for that, too," I said, making a note on his chart. "And you, Father? Headache?"

"Just tired is all," he responded. "I've had not much sleep lately."

"You need your rest—and lots of it," I said, stepping back so they could see me. "But, I need to ask you some questions."

Then, choosing my words carefully, I continued, "You aren't ill like the others. You have something different—something only you two have now. That's why I need more information."

"Then we don't have the illness?" Chief Alexander asked, his voice rising as he closed his eyes again for a moment. "Then what do we have?"

Father Brualla rolled toward him and said, slowly raising a hand and pointing up, "We are in good hands. Both from Him and here, too. Do not worry. We must have faith."

Again being careful, I replied, "Father is right. You're in the best hands for this right now. And, we'll know more soon. There is very little chance you caught this from each other. I know you've both been all over the neighborhood, but try to remember exactly where you've seen each other the past few days. Think hard."

When neither responded, I asked again, "Please, think. You must have seen each other. At least I hope so."

Chief Alexander raised himself slightly and said, "I've seen Father Brualla several times. Kind of hard to miss that collar."

"Where were you then?" I encouraged him to go on.

"Just around," he moaned. "Mostly when he was coming out of homes. Once, I think—maybe twice—rounding one street and heading over to the next."

"And at those times, were you ever in the same yard or home together?"

"No. Definitely not in a home together. But I'm not sure about in a yard at the same time. Everything has happened so fast."

"And how about you, Father?" I asked. "Do you recall being with Chief Alexander? Anywhere at all?"

"I don't think so. I recall seeing him—hard to miss that big, red hat."

Chief Alexander smiled weakly and said, "We both stand out some."

"You did the night of the fires," Father Brualla said, his voice low, sad. "All through the neighborhood."

"Please," I said, trying to gain their attention again. "Think again. Where were you together?"

I was about to give up when Chief Alexander tapped the bed rail twice. "There was one time," he said, wincing and rubbing at his left arm.

"And?" I asked, hopefully.

"Probably nothing." Exhaling loudly, he continued, "Those blankets here yet? I'm freezing."

"They'll be here soon," I said. "Now back to what you said before. Let me be the judge of whether it's important or not. Tell me."

Looking over at Father Brualla, he said, "You remember—the little boy with the cat. I brought him to the church. That's the closest we got to each other, I think. Remember?"

Father Brualla nodded. "That is right. That night. I took him from your arms. He was cold, too. He cried all night—because his poor little cat died in his arms."

I interrupted him, sharply, "Father, where is this boy now?"

"He was so frightened I kept him with me. I put him on a cot in my room."

"And the cat—what did you do with the cat?" I asked, moving closer to the bed.

"I was going to bury it behind the church, but he would not let it go. I wrapped the poor creature in old cloth and put it in a box by the cot."

"And it's still there?" I asked, my voice growing louder.

"I do not know. I became dizzy and fell at the altar. Then I was brought here. I hope someone is with the boy."

"I'm going right away. Thank you, Father, Chief. Dr. Barton will start you on some medications now. Try to rest as much as you can and drink some water every time you wake. Small sips are fine. I'll be back later today to check on you. Doctor Barton here will take *very* good care of you. Now, please, try to get some sleep."

"Thank you, Matthew," Father Brualla said while making the sign of the cross. "Go with God."

"But what do we have?" Chief Alexander pleaded as I started stepping back. "I want to know. What is it?"

"We'll call it a different form of pneumonia. We're lucky you were brought here right away. By starting treatments early, you may not end up like the others. Now try to get some rest."

I looked at Tom and nodded toward the door.

Once in the hallway, Tom turned to me and rubbed his forehead, "I don't like admitting this, but I'm confused. You told us the bubonic form can't be passed from person to person, so why'd you keep pressing them on where they were together?"

"To get to an animal, in this case the cat," I said. "That's what I was looking for. Somewhere, they had to have had some type of common contact. Unless I'm wrong, the cat's the link. Rats aren't the only animals that can harbor fleas. Cats work just fine. So do dogs and squirrels. I need to get back to the church and examine the boy. If he's in the bubonic stage, we're on the right trail. Now that the cat's dead, the fleas will be looking for somewhere else to go, if they haven't already. We need to seal off the church and get the exterminator there.

"Tom, I'm going to take Dr. Miller and Nurse McDonnell with me, so I'm leaving you in complete charge. Let's start them on the same treatment we've done for the others, but let's increase by double the dosages of the Mercurochrome drip and the aspirin. If we can keep it from becoming pneumonic, they've got a fighting chance."

"I understand, Sir," he replied, boldly. "You can count on me."

"I know I can, Tom. I'm proud of you."

He flipped a chart shut, smiled, and headed back down the hallway.

....

Maria was sitting in my office when I got there. As soon as she saw me, she said, "I just got back. Slipped home to change and to get a bite to eat. It's been another long night. Seven more dead—and several others barely hanging on. We're doing the best we can, but it's not enough. We're losing too many too fast."

I must have looked as stricken as I felt because she stopped speaking for a moment and concern filled her eyes. "Nurse Adams told me where you were. I'm so sorry about Father Brualla. He's a good man. I know that now."

"Yes, he is," I said, walking over to the window and staring out at the traffic moving slowly by below. "I just wish I could live up to the faith he has in me."

Maria spoke, softly. "This reminds me again of something my father always says. Good things happen to bad people, and bad things happen to good people. We can't do anything about that, so we just treat the illness and keep going. That's all we can do."

"Yes, and that doesn't help much when it involves someone you really care for."

She walked over to the window and took my hand. I wanted to say more, but it seemed I always ended up tongue-tied or just plain mute when Maria and I had private moments, and I hated that. She could be a pain and the dictionary definition of "contrary" at times, but she was also more and more entering my thoughts when we were apart. I never knew what she was going to say, in any circumstance, and the unpredictability was part of her charm for me. I had never known anyone like her before.

Finally turning to face her, I said, "Maria, I . . . I want to tell you. That is, I want you to know . . ."

She looked deeply into my eyes, squeezed my hand again, and saved me. "So it's bubonic. I didn't expect this now at all. What do we do?"

I brushed back a strand of hair that had fallen out of her hat. After another awkward pause, I told her what I had discovered about the link between Father Brualla and Chief Alexander. "So," I finally said, "we've yet another drive to make to see the boy and find out what's become of the cat. If we're *lucky*, we'll be able to find out where they came from and end this before another outbreak happens."

"And what if we're not lucky?" she asked, moving back to sit in the chair at the side of my desk.

"Honestly, I don't know. Certainly a lot more dead. A *lot* more. Maybe Robert will have a suggestion based on what he's experienced before with this. But, first things first. We need to be off to the church. Before we go, though, we need to talk about something."

"Oh, really? Something you'd like to say to me now that you've finally found your tongue again?"

"Maybe later. First, though, I actually want your advice—and Robert's, too. Where do you suppose he is?" I looked at my watch. "He went straight down to the lab when we got here, but he should be back up here by now."

"Likely telling someone how wonderful he is," she said.

"You really should let that go," I said. "I'm not taking sides here, but you two should just go to neutral corners and consider the past the past."

She lowered her head and looked to the floor as I continued. "Wherever he is, we need him here, now. Before we go inside the church, I want us outfitted in something more than gloves and mask now that we're looking at Bubonic again. We could very well end up in the same area as the fleas, and I don't want any risk that we could get bitten. I keep thinking about one of those suits that divers wear, the ones with a globe around the head and a hose to pump in air. We need the land equivalent of that. I'm not going to put you—us—in harm's way."

Maria tapped a pencil rapidly on the desk and said, "I think I can help with that. Robert will also probably have his own ideas, but here's what I can offer. Back during the Influenza, my father came up with a type of examining suit for doctors visiting patients' homes. It was very primitive, but it did the job."

"What was it?" I asked, pulling up a chair next to her. "Go on."

"Some of the homes they went into then were less than sanitary—bed bugs, fleas, mites. So, they took pillow cases, cut holes large enough to see through, and covered those holes with a flexible clear material—a type of celluloid film I think—and taped it in place. They slipped on surgical gowns and taped them tightly shut just above the feet. The pillow cases went over their heads next and were taped at the neck. Thick socks and shoes completed it. The pillowcase material was thin enough they could still breathe through it, but nothing could get inside. The doctors looked like ghosts, and they did scare the wits out of some of their patients, but the suit worked well. If we could get some celluloid and some good tape, I could have a couple made in a matter of minutes."

The suit sounded like exactly what we needed, so I said, "Perfect. We're not going to wait any more for Robert. I'll only take a minute, but I want to go see Nurse Adams and see the reports from last night. We have celluloid sheeting in the lab to wrap tissue samples and store organs for dissection. I'll call down and have them get some ready for you. Then, see if you can find some tape and make your suits. If you get stalled anywhere, use my name and Mr. Hornbeck's."

I looked at my watch. "Let's meet back here in thirty minutes, and have two of those suits ready. I'll find Robert in the meantime and fill him in. Thirty minutes—and then we better be off."

"I'll be ready," she replied, standing. I walked over to open the door for her, and she brushed closely against me as she slid by. I stopped her for a moment.

"I don't want anything to happen to you," I said, turning her to face me. "Maybe you should stay here."

"Then who would take care of you?"

"Maybe I do need someone around for that," I replied, putting my arms around her and hugging her gently.

She said nothing, just stepping back and smiled.

....

The Southern Pacific Railroad did it again. We were stuck a full fifteen minutes at the tracks while load after load of coal rumbled past. As the frustration set in, Robert got out of the car and walked back and forth along the drainage ditch off to our right. Sitting in the front seat, Maria had tilted her head back and closed her eyes. I took the opportunity to inspect the two suits Maria had assembled, making sure there would be no gaps where fleas could slip through.

Robert finally came back to the car, propped his hands against my window, and said, "Wake her up. Something else we need to talk about."

"I heard you," she said, yawning and turning her head toward us.

"Good," Robert said. "This isn't going to be a popular decision, and it might take all three of us to sell it. As soon as we examine the boy and find the cat, we're going to have to get everyone out of the church and seal it up so the exterminator can do his job and kill anything else in there that could host fleas. That'll mean no church for the area, likely for several days. I know how important the church is. Some are going to be mighty upset."

"You're right," Maria said. "That won't be popular at all, especially now that Father Brualla isn't there. Father sent for help before being brought to the hospital. I hope the new priest understands and can help us with this."

"He'd better," Robert responded. "I'd hate to call in those guards to force everybody out of there. This neighborhood doesn't need any more of that."

The caboose finally went by, and as soon as we were moving again, it took just a few minutes to get to the Macy Street quarantine gate. A young guard had us pull over until we could explain who we were and what we were doing. Finally, he waved us through and motioned for the others up ahead to let us pass. As we drove the rest of the way to the church, I was struck by how empty and sad the neighborhood looked. There were homes burnt to the ground on every street, many more than I expected to see. Others had the large red "I" on the curb out front indicating the illness had struck those inside. For three blocks I didn't see a person or animal anywhere. "It's like a ghost town," I said more to myself than to the others. Maria heard me and said, softly, "It didn't have to be this way." No one said anything.

When I stopped the car, I said, "I'll go knock and ask the new priest to step outside to meet with us. After we tell him why we're here, Maria and I will suit up and go in. Robert, if we had another suit, you'd be coming with us, but you can help most by staying out here to examine the ambulatory we send out. Okay? Now, let's do this."

The door opened just as I was ready to knock, startling both of us. "And who are you?" a short, round, balding man asked, taking a step back from me. I guessed him to be just barely over thirty. His English was excellent.

"I'm Doctor Thompson. There in my car are Dr. Miller and Nurse McDonnell. We have—"

Cutting me off, he said, sharply, "I have heard of you. You are a friend of Father Brualla, yes?"

"Yes. We've known each other a long time."

"And how is Father Brualla?" he asked, placing his foot so the doorway was blocked. I noticed him doing this but didn't say anything. I could hardly blame him given the events of late.

"I examined him earlier this morning. We've started treatment, and he was resting when I left."

"He is strong, both in his heart and his faith. I will pray for him."

"As will I," I said. "And your name, Father?"

"Father Mendez. The Diocese has sent me until Father Brualla is able to return. What can I do for you?"

For the next several minutes I explained as best I could what had transpired over the past several days. I could tell he already knew most of it because of the way he kept looking off into the neighborhood while nodding his head. I decided not to tell him that Father Brualla had a different illness than the others because I didn't want to risk word getting out and causing even more fear than was already sweeping through the area. Instead, I chose to focus on how I believed Father Brualla became ill.

"Father Mendez, I'd appreciate it very much if you could step down to my car so that we can ask you a few questions."

"Would you rather come inside?" he asked, finally appearing to trust us enough to make the offer.

"No, but thank you just the same. It would be better if we spoke first. Please, Father, will you visit with us a few minutes?"

Maria and Robert stepped from the car, and I made the introductions. Robert didn't waste any time, asking, "Father Brualla brought a young boy into the church the other night and took him to his room. The boy was holding a small cat that we understand has since died. Is the boy still in there, and if so, how's he doing?"

"I arrived just a few hours ago. I found an older couple, Mr. and Mrs. Valdez, and a young boy here. All seem to be fine."

"And the cat?" Robert asked. "Has it been buried?"

"I saw no cat. You may ask the boy about it if you wish."

Maria then spoke up. "Father, we don't want anyone to be frightened, but Dr. Thompson and I are going to put on special suits that will help keep us from becoming ill while we make our examinations."

She pointed at him and said, her voice as gentle as I'd ever heard it, "You have your cassock—and we have our own special clothing that helps us with our work. However, *ours* looks like it could scare a saint."

Stepping forward and taking her hand, Father Mendez said, "I've scared my share in my day."

Robert cut in, "Father, are there any other pets inside that you are aware of? Other cats, dogs? Have you seen any rats or mice since you've been here or evidence they might be around?"

"I have not, but this does not mean they are not there. Why do you ask?"

Robert wasn't as diplomatic as Maria had been. "Because that's why they are going to wear those suits. It's a precaution we must take. Then, after they look around, We're going to have to get everyone else out and close up the church. We'll have to do this right away."

Maria glared at Robert and said, "Glad you gave him the news gently. Awfully kind of you."

"What's this?" Father Mendez asked, looking first at me then to Maria. "Why?"

By the look in his eyes, I knew I had to say something quickly. "Fleas from animals are a cause of the spread of the illness. I'm very sorry, Father, but Dr. Miller is right. We have to close the church until the exterminator can make sure there are no fleas. I wish I could tell you how long this will take, but I can't."

"And where am I to go? What am I to do?"

Maria calmly said, "There's an empty home a few blocks away. A large one. I saw it the other night. Later on I'll help tell everyone they can find you there."

"I don't know what to say," he said, looking back at the church. "This must be done?"

Maria nodded. "I'm sorry, Father, but it must."

"We should see the boy," I said, placing my hand on Father Mendez' shoulder. "Nurse McDonnell and I are going to put on our suits. We'll need a few minutes, and then we'd appreciate it if you could take us to see him."

Robert helped button us in, placed the cases over our heads, and then taped all up and down the rows of buttons to form a tight seal. When he was finished with that, he added multiple layers of tape around our ankles and neck. The final touch was a gooey line of camphor he spread across the tape. He'd explained earlier that the camphor's consistency and pungent odor seemed to keep insects at bay. Maria was right: we *did* look like ghosts. I was just glad no one else was around to see us.

Even with the eye holes cut rather large, it was still difficult to see and walk without bumping into objects. On top of that, every time I breathed through my mask, the eye openings fogged up slightly.

"He is over here," Father Mendez said, pointing to a cot just outside the entrance to the rectory. He's been sleeping well over an hour. Would you like me to wake him?"

"Yes, Father," I said. "And please tell him we're here to help and not to be frightened by our suits. He probably still will be, but at least prepare him as much as you can."

Father Mendez bent down next to the cot and gently shook him until he opened his eyes and rolled to the side. Out of the corner of his eye he saw us and started rising up, just as I had expected. Father Mendez held his arm, drew him close, and whispered something to him that we couldn't hear. Still frightened, the boy sat up, crossed his legs on the cot, and leaned back on his hands.

"He is ready now," Father Mendez said, motioning us to step forward.

Maria went first. She spotted a chair off to her right, pulled it carefully over next to the cot, and sat down. I started to follow, but she waved me back.

For the next several minutes, she spoke to him in Spanish, stopping at one point to let the boy touch her suit and examine the eye holes. Then they both laughed heartily. Father Mendez joined in, the first time I had seen him off his guard since we had arrived. Maria somehow managed to get the boy to lie down so she could examine him. She checked his pulse, held two fingers before his nose to feel and then count respirations, and finally felt around his neck, arms, and the area near the groin. When she finished, she patted him gently on the back and said something that again had him and Father Mendez laughing. However, this time the laughter didn't last long. She asked several other questions. The boy answered some but simply shook his head for others. Maria then said something to Father Mendez, stood up, and waved goodbye to the boy.

"What did he say?" I asked as she walked toward me.

"A mouthful," she replied. "Let's get outside and out of these. We don't need to check for other animals. We're going to have to close this up and get the exterminator anyway. We can't waste time. Let's go. I want Robert to hear this, too."

We weren't three steps out the door when Maria started tugging at the case. Unable to remove it, she called down to Robert, "I need help. Get this thing off me. I can't stand it."

Robert unwound the tape on both our suits, and in a matter of minutes we were set free again. Maria pointed to the bottom of the church steps and said, "You've got to hear this."

"What did he say?" I repeated. "I couldn't make out a thing."

"First off, this isn't the boy we were looking for."

Robert and I started standing up at the same time, but Maria said, "Easy does it. Sit back down. Wait for the rest."

She told us the boy she had been speaking to had been with his parents the night the field by the railroad tracks had been burned and bulldozed. In all the confusion, they had become separated. He knew where the church was located and came there for shelter, figuring his parents would finally find him there. He knew of the boy we had come to see. He said that boy seemed quite ill and kept complaining that his head and neck hurt.

"The mother of that boy showed up this morning and took him away. He may have been one brought to the hospital this morning. This other boy told me where that family lives, so if he isn't at the hospital, we can pick them up later. I don't want to sound cold, but I didn't ask as much about him as I did about the cat."

"And the cat?" Robert asked.

"I'm getting to that," she scolded. "The boy inside, Felix, knew right where the other got the cat. It's where they all get their pets and hide out from their parents when they don't want to work or go to school. As soon as we're ready, Father Mendez is going to bring him out, and he's going to show us the place."

Maria was beaming. Turning to me again, she said, "At the start, all you wanted was my Spanish. Remember? Well, maybe it has helped a little."

"A little," I said, smiling. "But, before we celebrate too much, we have a lot to check."

She didn't have a chance to respond because the door opened, and Father Mendez and Felix walked down toward us. Father Mendez and Robert got in the back while Maria sat next to me, pulling Felix up on her lap. We drove to Bauchet Street, where Felix directed us to angle over toward the tracks. He said something to Maria, who translated for me.

"His family had a tent down there by that grove of trees. That's where he was separated from his parents when the fires broke out and everyone scattered."

Felix stood up, held tightly to the window frame in front of him, and excitedly pointed ahead. "*¡Ahi está! La gran caja.*"

Maria urged me to slow down and slowly cross the open field toward what appeared to be an old, faded orange boxcar behind a thick stand of tall lilac bushes.

"Pull up there but not too close," Maria said. "*I'm* not going inside, so guess who has to put the suit back on again so he can look inside? Felix says there's a flap at the back over a small opening where they crawl in. That is, where the cats and he and his friends always did. Just be sure you don't rip anything getting in there."

Robert asked, "Want me to go in with you?"

"No," I said. "I think I'll be able to find out what we need. Probably dark in there, though. Anyone have any matches? I need to make a torch of some kind."

Nobody did. Felix tugged at Maria's sleeve, as if asking why no one was getting out of the car. She said something to him, and he immediately reached for the door handle and started to jump out. Maria corralled him and pulled him back just in time. Felix's eyes lit up as he said, pointing ahead, "*Tenemos una vela—y los fósforos.*"

Maria thanked him, turned to me, and said, "Looks like you'll find everything you need in that can over by the tree. A candle and matches. The boys keep them there. Just be careful."

Robert followed close behind as I stepped out of the car. It took a little longer this time for me to get into my suit because I hadn't taken my time tearing away the tape when I removed it at the church. My haste had caused some tears, which had to be carefully patched. When I was properly suited and the layer of camphor was spread, I waved to everyone and started for the can. Just as Felix had said, inside was a candle and a small box of matches.

It was clear the boxcar had been abandoned years ago because it had settled evenly a good two to three inches in the soft dirt. I walked around it and saw the opening at the back, in the lower left corner, was covered by a thick sheet of rubber attached only at the top. As such, it served as a flap, one through which animals and children could come and go as they pleased. As I lit the candle, I thought again of the warning Maria had given: "Just be sure you don't rip anything getting in there." That stuck in my thoughts because the moment I bent down to crawl inside I could smell a powerful stench, something akin to rotting meat, even through my mask and the case over my head. I held my breath, raised the flap, pushed the candle ahead of me, and started inside.

I heard them before I saw them. Rats. Dozens of them, jumping and furiously climbing over each other in the hay spread out across the floor the very second they became aware of the light from the candle. I started to back out, but my suit caught on a nail at the top of the flap. I knew a rip could mean contamination, so I eased forward again just as a rat darted up my outstretched arm. I felt its sharp claws through the material as it jumped off just before it reached my shoulder. Instinctively, I flinched. The suit didn't rip open, but I was held fast. Raising my left arm, being careful not to let the candle go out, I lifted the material off the head of the nail. As I did so, I lowered myself closer to the ground to avoid other nails and felt several rats scurry up over my head. My heart pounded as I threw myself back out as fast as I could move, losing my balance and flopping in the soft dirt outside. When I caught my breath, I realized I had dropped the candle inside. I quickly righted myself, my mind still racing, and realized I needed to make sure the candle hadn't ignited any of the hay. A fire would make everything inside try to break free, and if that happened, there was no telling how far they would all spread—and the plague with them.

Slowly lifting up the flap again, I stuck my head inside and, much to my relief, saw the candle wasn't still burning. However, the rats were becoming more and more agitated, squeaking loudly and jumping high against the wall at the back corner. I knew I had to act fast. I tried lighting the candle again, but the match broke. My hands shaking, I removed the last match from the box and struck it slowly and steadily until it flashed. I lit the candle and crawled deliberately forward until I could see all around the interior. Two more rats scampered toward me, but this time I pushed the candle forward and yelled as loudly as my dry mouth would allow, "Woah! Back! Back now!" They halted, one running to my left, and the other to my right. As my eyes followed the one moving left, I saw the source of the horrible smell: four dead cats. Three had been partially eaten and the other appeared to have died only recently. Just as I was about to inch closer to get a better look, a dozen or so rats started toward me. Again waving the candle and shouting, I scooted back out, threw the candle to the side, and held the flap firmly against the ground.

Off to my right, several old boards were stacked on top of each other in the dirt in front of one of the lilac bushes. I ran over, grabbed as many as I could carry, and began stacking them in front of the flap. When I had made a solid base, I propped the smaller pieces upright against the upper part of the flap and placed stones against them to hold them in place. I looked around and there didn't appear to be any other holes where the rats could escape, and now none would be coming through the flap. I could hear them scurrying and squeaking. Stepping back a few feet, I studied my handiwork. Even as frightened as I was, an old expression came to mind. They were now, I hoped, "trapped like rats."

A few feet from the car I grabbed the case over my head and ripped it off in one motion.

"Now you truly do look like a ghost," Maria said, stepping out of the car and moving toward me. "You're white as one. White as a sheet."

"You would be, too, if you'd seen what I just did. This is it. There's no doubt in my mind this is where the boy got his cat. Several dead cats in there and plenty of live rats to keep them company. Rats everywhere. I sealed it up the best I could, but we need to get Mr. Micholovich over here right away so he can take care of this. This has got to be every exterminator's dream—or nightmare."

Robert took a few steps toward the boxcar, stopped, turned, and asked, "You sure it's sealed tight enough."

Holding out my case, I said, "Feel free to look for yourself if you want to."

"No thanks," he said, waving me back. "I'll take your word for it. We better get the exterminator here before it gets dark and they try to get out to forage. If this place is the cause of the new cases, we've no time to lose."

"Help me get the tape off so I can get out of this suit. I don't ever want to be in one of these again. I'll tell you the rest while we drive back. Just get me out of this thing!"

As Maria and Robert ripped off the tape, I took one last look back at the boxcar. I'd never forget it—no matter how hard I tried.

....

CHAPTER 21

Death House

November 3
7:05 A.M.

The previous day had been a series of small victories and large defeats, all of which left us more tired and frustrated than ever. After discovering and then sealing the boxcar, Maria and I managed to track down Mr. Micholovich, who promptly destroyed the rats, fleas, and any other creatures inside. We were certain that would end the spread of bubonic cases and were, as a result, feeling pretty good about ourselves.

However, back at the hospital, the deaths mounted. No matter which treatment regimens we provided, one patient after another fell until by the time midnight struck, the death toll sat at eleven. Among the dead was the little boy rescued by Chief Alexander and cared for by Father Brualla. Eleven—in one day—and a dozen others were critically ill.

A few days before, Maria had called her father to see if he could help speed up delivery of a new serum that many in the medical community thought would halt the progression of the disease even in patients who were already deep into the pneumonic state. The only available serum was kept at a laboratory on the East Coast. Because each passing hour meant more deaths, it was decided delivery would be made by airplane rather than by rail, thus saving at least two days—and possibly even three. The serum was largely untested, but at this point we were hoping for a miracle and decided we'd try anything. Our treatments certainly didn't have a high success rate. We were doing our best, but it wasn't good enough by any measure. Only two in ten who became pneumonic survived, and we couldn't even swear our care was the main reason for recovery. We had many right at the edge of death.

After we left Mr. Micholovich the previous afternoon, Maria made another telephone call to see if she could be provided any news about the delivery of the serum, only to find out the news was bad. Two army lieutenants taking turns piloting an Army Air Service Fokker T-2 transport airplane had taken off from a field just outside New York City. From there, they field hopped to Cleveland and then to Chicago and Omaha. According to reports, all was going well until the leg of the journey between Omaha and Salt Lake City. Strong storms met them as they attempted a landing at the small field at Salt Lake City. There, they crashed upon landing. The pilots and serum were unharmed, but the same could not be said of the airplane. A broken propeller, cracked wheel support, and damage to the tail would keep them grounded until parts could be rounded up and repairs made. No one knew how long this would take. Maria had received this report only minutes before two sisters died in the same room. Both pieces of news taken together caused our spirits to fall to a new low.

Just after midnight I ordered Maria to go home for some rest. Robert and I left shortly thereafter. Once at my home, we ate several drumsticks and some biscuits Nurse Adams had sent with us, washing all down with reheated coffee. Neither of us spoke. We were too tired and too frustrated. Finally, without so much as a "Goodnight," Robert headed straight for the couch while I retired to my bedroom. I set an alarm, but we didn't need it. Fitful sleep saw to that. We were both up, dressed, and headed for the door just as the hour turned six. We drove to the hospital in silence until at one point we thought we heard the propeller of an airplane. "Could it be the serum?" Robert asked, looking out the car window toward the sky.

Squinting up at the sky, I replied, "Don't think so. Not the way our luck's been running."

He finally looked over at me and said, so quietly I could barely hear him, "Neither do I." We traveled the rest of the way in silence.

Once at the hospital, we made our rounds and checked in with Charles Hornbeck to share with him the events of the previous day, including the newest death count. Then we headed for my office to meet up again with Maria. As we walked in, she was sipping coffee and reading a newspaper.

"You two won't believe this," she said, tapping a finger against the paper. "Sit down and listen. Whoever spilled this better watch his head today. This is *exactly* what the Mayor didn't want to have happen."

We knew she wasn't going to quit until she had shared the information, so we didn't put up a fight. I motioned for Robert to take the chair on the left while I sat in the one to the right.

"This is from a St. Louis newspaper Nurse Edward's brother brought with him on the train last night. She gave it to me as soon as she got here this morning. Listen to this headline: 'Plague Grows in Los Angeles; Death Toll 28.' They're short on the number, which is probably good for us, but, gentlemen, the cat is definitely out of the bag."

"I can't believe it!" I said, falling back in my chair. "Who do you think talked?"

Robert asked, "Maria, what else does it say? Please read on."

She shook the paper, cleared her throat, and began, "'Seven more deaths were reported in Los Angeles today as the result of the pneumonic plague. A total quarantine has been posted around the affected area, the Mexican district where the 'Black Death' originated and has been confined. Yesterday, as soon as the California city's epidemic was known, leading health officials across the country immediately instituted a watch over their own Mexican districts. At this point, it is not feared the illness will spread to people of other communities before it is brought under control.'"

When she finished reading, Maria slammed the paper to the desk and said something loudly in Spanish that, by the look on her face, I was glad I couldn't understand.

"You see what they're doing, don't you?" she said. "They're saying this is just a Mexican disease, that Mexicans caused it and that as long as it stays in their communities, nobody else needs to worry. Everyone will be just fine if they stay away from the dirty Mexicans."

There was no way to get a word in, so I crossed my arms and hoped she'd soon start winding down.

"What this means," she said, picking up the paper again and rapping it on the desk, "is that we better do our best to stop this outbreak because if we don't, the quarantine will just be kept in place until more and more people become ill and die. We can't let that happen."

She paused, and I saw my moment to step in. "First of all, nothing has been said in any of the newspapers anywhere around here, so most still don't know what's going on. However, now that this has happened, Mayor Burgess will have to do something fast before a full-scale panic is on us. We need to give this paper to Mr. Hornbeck and have him call the Mayor. I just hope something can be done right away, so people who might be infected don't try to flee the city."

"You couldn't be more right about that," Robert added. "Fighting the disease is bad enough, but when panic sets in, we could be looking at a spread that could rival what happened in the Middle Ages. We have cars and trains today, so transmission could be lightning fast."

Maria flipped the newspaper to a table by the door and spread several drawings on the desk. "I don't want to just sit here and watch everyone die. We were very lucky yesterday to find the boxcar. Maybe we did stop another outbreak, but we're still losing the fight right in front of us. We're going to have to do something ourselves. We aren't going to get more help, especially after stories like that one. This is *our* fight now, and it's up to us to finish it."

She pointed to the drawings and continued, "I have an idea. I've got something to show you that may help. There's something very strange about how the plague has spread. Back during the Influenza, my father showed me how to chart spread paths. So, the night after the house-to-house inspections, I drew a map of the neighborhood and started marking where each confirmed case came from. After that, each day I started adding locations of new cases and deaths. Take a look at this."

Maria pointed to a neatly penciled outline of the Macy Street area, complete with most of the streets drawn inside. There was one red star about half way down Clara Street and small blue circles scattered throughout the neighborhood.

Pointing to the red star, I turned to Robert and said, "This is where we started—the Lajun home. We found the first cases there, a father and his daughter."

Robert nodded and asked, "Then the blue circles—they're the ones that followed?"

"They represent what I don't understand yet," Maria replied. "Hernandez, Soto, Martinez, Armando, Jimenez and the others. Yes, they're the cases that followed.

"As best I can tell, these people had absolutely no contact with the Lajuns. If that's the case, how were they infected? This just doesn't make any sense. However, I keep thinking about something else my father said, 'It's important to know where Adam was, but it's Cain and where he went that really is the most important information of all.' In other words, we're pretty certain Mr. Lajun is Adam, the first victim, but who is Cain who traveled out and caused all these blue dots? We need to get back out there to the neighborhood. I want to start with the Lajun home. The wife didn't catch it, and I have a lot of questions for her. Then we'll go to the next circle and keep going and try to figure this out. Are you coming with me?"

I studied the map carefully, making note of where the blue circles were in relation to the Lajun home. None were close by. "The way your circles are placed makes this look like a shotgun blast. No, it doesn't really make any sense," I said, shaking my head. "But you're right. We better find out *why* it doesn't, especially now that we may have more bubonic cases on our hands."

I started turning back to Maria, but suddenly my eye caught something that wasn't there on the map. "Wait a minute. The home next door—that's the Samarano home, isn't it? There's no circle there. Mrs. Samarano took care of the Lajun daughter and then became ill and died. So what if . . . ?"

Maria sighed heavily. "I can't believe I forgot that. Since they were next-door neighbors, I guess I must have just lumped the two families together in my head. I can't believe I did that."

Robert said, "Let's get back out there and ask a few questions and see if we can find Cain. It's never easy to trace, but we have to understand the spread, or we'll just end up spinning our wheels while more suffer, especially now that it appears we won't be getting any more help. We know— at least we *think* we know—the origin, the Adam in this case, but where did *he* contract it? We've got a lot of holes to fill in to make sure we have a chance at getting this under control. I'm with you. And Matthew—you should come along as well."

"I'm going with you," Maria said, her voice indicating there wouldn't be any argument. "They'll talk to me. After what's happened to them recently, I doubt anyone will talk to you."

"You're probably right," I said. "I'll run this newspaper up to Mr. Hornbeck, and I won't let him trap me into a debate. I'm just going to tell him he'd better contact the Mayor and then I'll get right out of his office. After that, I'll go find Barton and tell him to take charge again while we're away. I wasn't sure I liked him at first, but he's the one intern all the others seem to listen to."

Maria groaned and said, pointing to Robert, "He's just like someone else I know who's *completely* full of himself."

"Doesn't matter as long as he's good," Robert replied.

I expected a snappy retort of some type from Maria, but instead she looked at me blankly and said, "I'll gather up my maps and wait at your car. Don't take too long."

"Are you giving the orders now?" Robert asked, smiling again.

"Somebody better," she replied. "Somebody whose head will fit through the doorway."

As she walked away, Robert turned to me. "Ouch! I guess she meant me, right?"

"Like as not, she meant *both* of us."

Robert playfully slapped his forehead, looked at me, and said, "You really don't get it, do you?"

"Get what?"

"She didn't mean you. She's head over heels. You're just too blind to see it."

"You're just playing with me," I replied. "Her? Me?"

"Go see Hornbeck—go find Barton," he said, shaking his head again. "You're hopeless. Go! Go! I'll wait at the car."

Still shaking his head, he was halfway down the hallway before I could say anything.

....

The same young guard stopped us at the quarantine gate. This time he was more talkative.

"Hi, Doc. Sure is strange today."

"What is?" I asked, leaning my head out the window.

"The neighborhood. We haven't seen anything move in there since early last evening. The exterminators came again and the police drove through every half hour or so, but other than them, nothing. It's eerie— like a ghost town."

"You shouldn't be surprised at all," Maria leaned over and said to him, her voice filling with anger. "If they step outside their homes, we haul them away to the hospital. We've shot all their pets. Many of them have been robbed and had their homes ransacked. Their family members and neighbors are getting sick and are dying, and they aren't sure why. And you wonder why you don't see anybody? What are you—a moron?"

The guard's mouth actually dropped open. He took two steps back, pointed ahead, and said, "Through!"

"That was real nice," Robert said from the back seat. "Classy."

Maria swung around, but I cut her off, saying, "At the Lajun home— what was the wife's name?"

"Carlita, I think," she said, glaring at Robert. "Yes, I'm sure that was it. I want to start with her."

There was a large, red "I" painted on both the curb and the front door at 700 Clara Street. The front windows were open and curtains were rustling with the early morning breeze, but I didn't see any movement inside.

"How do you want to do this?" I asked Maria. "Do you want both of us to come with you? Just one of us? What do you think is best?"

"I think both of you can come in, but don't say anything unless you're asked something."

"Then why should we come along?" Robert asked, clearly perturbed. "I might just know a little about how to track this, you know. I've been down this road before, remember?"

Maria replied, "I need you because they're all scared to death of doctors. Most of the time they think you're right up there with the Devil himself. So, by comparison, I'm going to look pretty good to them—and they're going to want to talk to me—so they don't have to talk to you."

"So, you're using us," I said, laughing softly. "Basically, we're just props."

"Yes, I am," she shot back. "You're necessary evils."

Looking at Robert, I said, "Well, let's go in. We might as well make ourselves useful."

"Just don't say anything," Maria repeated again, staring at Robert. "Nothing at all. Now, gloves and masks, doctors. Put them on. We don't know what we'll find in there."

Maria knocked loudly on the door while Robert and I stood several paces back and to the side. It wasn't long before the door opened and Mrs. Lajun, looking very tired and expressionless, stood before us. Maria made the introductions, and Mrs. Lajun invited her in. Maria then pointed to us, Mrs. Lajun nodded her head, and we were allowed inside as well. As we entered, Maria whispered to me, "I should have left you outside."

We were taken into the front parlor where half a dozen worn wooden chairs were in a tight row in front of the side window. Mrs. Lajun motioned for each of us to sit there.

"I speak the English," she said, softly. "Would coffee for you?"

"That is very kind of you but, no, thank you," Maria replied. "We have just a few questions we'd like to ask you, and then we will leave."

"I have only my son now," she said, brushing back her thin, gray hair. "Not here. Do not know where. He outside when we, we . . . closed in. Not see since that night. Have no one else. You stay you want to. I do not mind."

"I'm so sorry," Maria said. "This has been a tragedy for so many. I'm so, so sorry."

Scooting her chair until she was right next to Mrs. Lajun, Maria continued, "The illness has harmed many, and we are trying to stop it before it hurts others." She pointed back at Robert and me before adding, "You can help us with this. We believe your husband, Jesús, was the first to be ill, that the others became ill after. I brought with me this drawing. The blue marks show where others lived who got the sickness. I'd like you to look at it, please, and tell me if you remember Jesús being with any of them here in your home or outside in the neighborhood after he was feeling sick. This is very important. Please, look at this."

She handed the drawing to Mrs. Lajun, but she let it fall to the floor, immediately covering her face with her hands and sobbing until her shoulders shook. Maria knelt before her, took her hands and pulled them back until she could see her face. Mrs. Lajun closed her eyes, turned to the side, and sobbed even harder. Maria squeezed her hands and said, "Carlita, it is all right. I understand." She looked again at us, her expression clearly indicating she wanted us to stay seated and do nothing.

Mrs. Lajun finally pulled her hands from Maria's grasp and wiped her eyes as she slowly regained her composure. Finally, still breathing heavily, she asked Maria to return to her chair. When Maria was seated and facing her again, she said, "After we closed in, all say my Jesús a bad man, that he bring sickness. He Devil and he die for it, and me next."

She wiped her eyes again, took a deep breath, and said, her voice growing very calm, "But Jesús not first sick. I not say because my brothers."

Robert and I looked at each other as Maria asked, seeming to sense our thoughts, "What do you mean? What about your brothers?"

Staring out the window, Mrs. Lajun continued, "My brothers sick. Then Jesús. My Jesús no Devil."

"The Devil has nothing to do with this," Maria said, softly. "Illness is part of life. There is nothing evil in it. People who are ill are not devils. They are just ill. Just ill."

Maria moved her chair closer again and asked, "Tell me about your brothers. When did they become sick? How long before Jesús?"

"I no care what happen but cared for brothers. They come from Hermosillo. Our family there. They come work where ships are. What is word?"

"Harbor? Docks?" Maria interrupted.

"Yes, harbor. They bring boxes from ships. One have rats. Jesús find under house here. Two day after he very sick. After closed in, I see much killing rats and then know why Jesús gone."

"And your brothers?" Maria asked, inching even closer until their knees were touching. "Where are they now?"

"Trouble at harbor. They lose jobs. They go back Hermosillo before Jesús sick. They afraid we all sent Hermosillo if they found. So they go. Go on train."

Maria leaned forward again and asked, gently, "Were your brothers sick when they left?"

"They cough, but they fine. They just leave to protect us."

Maria picked up the drawing and handed it back to Mrs. Lajun. "Please look at this for me. Please. Look at the homes and the names. Do you know if Jesús or your brothers were with any of these people when they were sick? Take your time."

Mrs. Lajun looked at it for about a minute before handing it back to Maria and saying, "No. Brothers work night and sleep day. No others. Just us. Jesús, sick so fast he go to bed. Next hospital. Then die. See no one."

"You're sure?" Maria asked, trying to hand the drawing to her again. Mrs. Lajun brushed it aside and stared out the window.

Maria stood up and said, "We will leave now. Thank you. Please, Carlita, you must take care of yourself."

"Why?" was all Mrs. Lajun responded.

"Because of your son. I promise you I will find out where he is and let you know. I will do that. You must take care of yourself for him. He will need you, and you will need him."

Mrs. Lajun put her face back in her hands. This time she didn't cry.

....

Robert was the first to speak as we made our way back to the car. "Hermosillo. I don't know where that is, but I sure hope there aren't many rail stops between here and there. When we get back to the hospital, we're going to have to get in touch with that town, although I suspect they already know what we're going to tell them. And we'll need someone to look up the rail stops. There will be a lot of telephone calls to make."

"It's worse than that," I said, stopping at the end of the walkway. "The brothers worked at the harbor, and they were here illegally. We'll never find out which ships they worked for. That means the spread could be anywhere in the world right now, and no amount of warning will make a difference."

Maria, who had been quiet to that point, finally spoke up. "I agree that's all important, but there isn't much we can do about that now. But, we *might* be able to do something here. Jesús wasn't the first, so we were wrong about that. The brothers were Adam, and that means we still need to find Cain. And I don't think Jesús was, either. They didn't have contact with the others, so we need to keep searching. That's the Samarano house next door. There may not be anybody there. Both parents died, and two of their sons. Another son is still at the hospital, barely hanging on. When we visited this house before, Mrs. Samarano said something about relatives living with them. I think a sister and her family. Maybe they're still there. I've got to check."

"And if they're there, I suppose you want us to keep our mouths shut again," Robert said as we headed that direction.

"Worked in there, didn't it?" she replied.

A larger "I" had been painted on the Samarano door, and it was evident by the black residue all across the base of their house that a fire had been used to clean out everything underneath. Maria knocked on the door. No answer. She tried again, louder this time. Still nothing. We were just about to leave when we saw the doorknob slowly turning. The door opened just a crack, and a voice inside said, "What do you want? No one is sick here. Please go away."

"We're here to help," Maria said, using her foot to pry the door open a little farther. "I'm Nurse McDonnell from Los Angeles County Hospital. These are doctors who are helping me. We need to ask you some questions to see if we can stop the illness before more become sick. I know you would like to help with that, so I'm asking you if we can come inside for just a minute or two. Please. We need your help."

A short, thin woman about forty opened the door far enough to look at all of us. She wore a white cotton dress with small red flowers around the waist. Her face was angular, stern, and when she spoke her English was polished.

"How could I help?" she asked while fully opening the door. "I know nothing."

Maria smiled at her and said, "You may know more than you realize. Please, I ask just a moment of your time. May we come in?"

She stepped back and said, "Just for a minute. Follow me. I'm making the noon meal for my husband and my children and Raul. We'll have to talk back here."

She led us into a small kitchen area at the back of the house. I felt the heat from the pot belly stove against my arm as we moved past and tried to position myself out of the way.

"My husband and the boys are out back trying to repair furniture the police smashed. You can sit if you want," she said pointing toward Maria. She said nothing to Robert and me.

"What are you cooking?" Maria asked, pointing to the pots on the stove, two of which were boiling.

She turned, snapped a wooden spoon repeatedly into her hand, and said, the sarcasm apparent, "A delicious meal. I call it Quarantine Stew. I've got potatoes that aren't close to ripe. Rice that won't soften no matter how long it's in the pot. Tomatoes so full of worms they seem more like meat than vegetable. This clump is supposed to be smoked ham, but I couldn't swear to it. And did I forget the curdled milk?"

"I'm sorry," Maria responded. "I know the quarantine is hard. When we leave, I'll see if I can have some food sent to you."

"This *is* the food that was sent to us!" Her voice rose as she threw the spoon into the sink. "This is the help we've received. And nothing else—unless you count the spraying they did on all my walls. Don't you smell it? My children can barely sleep at night. They can barely breathe."

Then, after realizing what she had just said and looking at Robert and me, she quickly added, "They're *not* sick—just sick of the smell. That's what I meant. They're fine."

"I'll still see if I can have some other food sent to you," Maria said. "What's your name? I'm sorry I didn't ask before."

"Valentina Delgado. Lucena was my sister. We came to live with them almost a year ago when my husband broke his leg and lost his job with the railroad. He's still not getting around well enough to look for more work. Now that his parents are gone, we're taking care of little Raul. We still don't know what happened to his brothers. They were all taken to the hospital, but no one has told us anything. I pray for them every night, but I don't know if they are alive—or dead. Do you know?"

Maria did know, and I expected her to share the sad news, but she did not. "I'll look at the reports when we get back to the hospital" was all she said. Quickly changing the subject, she handed Mrs. Delgado the drawing and asked her to study it carefully.

"Please look at the names and look where the houses are—the blue marks. Do you remember if any of these people were in this house? Please think carefully."

Mrs. Delgado barely glanced at it before placing it on the table as she moved to stir the pots on the stove. She smiled and asked, "Want to stay for supper? The portions will be small, but we'd be glad to share what we have."

"Maybe another time," Maria said, picking up the drawing and handing it to her again. "Please. I know this is not pleasant, but it could help others. I'm asking for your help. Look at it. Hand me the spoon. I'll stir."

Mrs. Delgado walked to the table and sat down. Her lips moved as she read each name. Then, using her index finger, she pointed to several of the blue circles before sitting up rigidly and crossing herself three times in rapid succession.

"¡Madre de Dios!—Mother of God!" she shouted, throwing the drawing to the floor.

"What—what is it?" Maria asked moving toward her. "Tell me!"

Mrs. Delgado's face turned bright red. She looked at the potatoes boiling over but didn't move. Finally, she said, her voice rising, "I know these families. Almost all of them were here. At Guadalupe's wake. I remember. I remember that night. I remember them. They were here!"

Maria immediately responded, "There was a wake for Guadalupe? Here? How could that be? We didn't . . . "

"That idiot Jacobs!" I said so loudly everyone was startled. "Our pathologist. I told him not to release any of the bodies, but he did it anyway. Mrs. Delgado, this is important. Are you absolutely sure the families on the drawing were here for the wake? You're sure?"

She nodded.

"Then I have just one more question. Please think carefully. Were there any other families here that night that aren't on the drawing? Look at it again."

A tear ran down her cheek as she ran a finger up and down the streets. "I don't remember. I don't think so. I . . . I just don't know." She walked to the stove and moved the potatoes to the side to cool. Turning to me, she asked, "Do you think . . . ? Is it possible . . . ?

Robert then spoke, gently. "Were the boys already ill at the wake?"

"Two of them, Gilberto and Arthuro. Their cough was very bad."

"I think we can go now," Maria said. "Thank you, Mrs. Delgado. We'll let ourselves out."

As she started to leave, Maria turned and said, "I'll see about more food. I'll do my best."

Robert and I followed her outside. Just before we got to the car, we removed our masks and gloves. I stepped on the "I" at the curb and said, "Jacobs. That son-of-a . . . I made myself clear to him—as clear as I could be—but he still . . ."

Maria said, "I've been around him enough to know he hates this neighborhood and everyone in it."

"Could he have done it on purpose?" Robert asked, leaning against the car. "Nobody could be that bad."

"You don't know Jacobs," I said, kicking the bumper.

We stood in silence at least a minute, all staring at the Samarano home. Robert finally spoke. "This is the 'Death House'—that's what we call it in an outbreak like this. We'll do more checking, but I'd have to say this is it, the main source of the spread. As it turns out, it wasn't a person we were looking for at all. This house—this is our Cain."

Maria sat on the front fender and stared off in the distance. Finally, she said, "How can we be sure?"

Robert replied, "We'll send the interns and nurses back here to go to the blue houses to check and see if anyone there is ill. At the same time, they can ask if anyone knows of others who were at the wake. Once that is run down, it shouldn't take long to finally put a stop to this. We may not like what this quarantine has done to these people, but I'll say one thing. Cubicle isolation—keeping everyone inside the homes—usually does the job. It's hard for a disease to spread if people aren't around others."

"Are you serious?" Maria asked, turning toward him. "You think this might end the spread, that this could be over soon? What about the people in the blue houses? If they had contact with others, then no telling how far this has gone. There could be dozens more cases we don't know about yet."

"I don't think so," Robert replied. The quarantine happened very fast, so I doubt those who attended the wake had time to get sick and then pass it along to others outside their homes. We'll likely find a few more family members with it, but that's probably all. At least I hope so."

"Then we need to get our people out here again as soon as we can to go into the blue houses," I said. "I can't believe we could be this lucky, but if we are, this'll close the door. And I want to go on record as saying the person to be thanked most here is Maria."

"Me? Why me?"

"Because if you hadn't charted the victims and drawn the map of their homes the way you did, we'd still be shooting in the dark. It's one thing to have a list of those who were ill. It is entirely another to add the geography—to see where they all came from. That was a fine idea, and if it truly does lead to the end of this, I'm going to see your method shows up in a medical journal if it's the last thing I ever do. No, that wasn't just a fine idea—it was a great idea."

"You're giving me too much credit," she said, staring back at the Samarano home. "Robert would have come up with something himself. I know that."

"I probably would have," he said, smiling at her. "By then, who knows what might have happened. I'm proud of you, Maria, and you should be proud of yourself."

Pointing at the homes up and down the street, she replied, "I'm proud of *them*. Think of what they go through. Think of what they put up with. Think of . . ."

She didn't finish the thought, but she didn't need to. Robert and I knew what she meant.

To lighten our somber mood, I said, while moving around to my door, "I don't know about the two of you, but I'm tired and, believe it or not, I'm hungry. There's no time to sleep, but I'm going to make the time to eat. I can't remember the last time I had a decent meal, and my stomach's rumbling like a freight train. Let's get back to the hospital and order the interns and nurses to get back here right away to the blue homes. Then, I'm going to Morg's. Want to come along? We better eat something. I'll treat."

"I have a better idea," Maria said, stepping back to the curb. "I know another place."

She pointed ahead and added, "Mrs. Delgado said the portions would be small, but that's fine with me. I think I'm going to take her up on the offer for some of that Quarantine Stew. There's another type of healing that needs to take place around here, and we just might be able to start it. At least we can try. Care to join me?"

Robert looked at me and smiled. "That's a pretty fine idea. I'd like to do that—if she'll have us. How about you, Matthew?"

"Morg's will have to wait for another day," I said to Maria. "I'd be honored to share their meal. Lead the way."

Maria slipped between us, hooked her arms through ours, and led us back up the steps.

....

CHAPTER 22

Passage

November 3
4:37 P.M.

Our meal with the Delgado family had been fulfilling in so many ways. Mrs. Delgado had done a masterful job of making her Quarantine Stew not just edible but even quite tasty. At the same time, our visit with them helped us see the extent to which the community was suffering at every turn during the outbreak. Mr. Delgado explained to us that with so many homes damaged or destroyed, those who were displaced were now filling the homes of friends and others willing to take them in, making life pretty uncomfortable and miserable for all. At the same time, even though supplies were being regularly brought in, food and fresh water were still in short supply, causing many to go to bed hungry at night. We also learned the children were most frightened of all. At first, they were happy they were being kept home from school, but as the days passed, they saw in the faces of their parents the fear, uncertainty, and terror building up. Their nightmares and cries in the night testified to that.

It was hard to know how to respond to what we were hearing. Outside of the medical arena, it didn't seem there was much else the three of us could do. The best thing we could think of was shared by Maria. We'd do our best to make others understand that better communication needed to be built between and among all groups, and not just during times of emergency like this. The Macy Street area was truly an island, an island many in Los Angeles chose not to see or have anything to do with because of stereotypes and fear, due to the lack of interaction of any sort. Therefore, we knew our promise was one we'd have a difficult time keeping, but someone had to take the first step, and with Maria's help we could give it a good try.

Before we left, Mrs. Delgado thanked us, not for the medical help being provided, but more than anything just for sitting with them and listening. That made me most sad of all—that more "listening" hadn't been done before. If it had—on both sides—many of the problems facing us now might have been averted.

It was a somber ride back to the hospital. To my relief, Maria and Robert seemed to bury the hatchet during the ride. Not a bad or snippy word was spoken between them.

As we entered the hospital, Maria turned to me and said, "Now I think I can go home and sleep. I'll be back in a few hours. Can you do without me that long?"

Before I could respond, I saw Dr. Barton rushing toward us, waving a clipboard above his head. Maria saw him too and said, "Well, maybe the sleep will have to wait. Want to bet on it?"

"Dr. Thompson, you're here!" He paused, caught his breath, composed himself, and continued. "Father Brualla and Chief Alexander took terrible turns for the worse right after you left this morning. Respiration, heart rate — everything started crashing. I did everything I could, but Chief Alexander passed right at noon."

"And Father Brualla?" Maria asked, stepping next to me.

"I'm afraid he's not far behind. His lungs and heart are both failing quickly. He's been asking for both of you. Hurry!"

"Let's go," Maria ordered, taking my arm, her grip tight.

"Robert," I said, as we started down the hallway. "I'd appreciate it if you'd make the rounds."

"Go," was all he said before taking the charts from Dr. Barton's hand.

Halfway down the hall, Maria grabbed gloves and masks for us, and we put them on while walking. When Maria and I entered the room, Father Mendez was seated next to the bed and holding Father Brualla's hand. He looked up and whispered to us, "He's not asleep. He's praying. Please give us a moment."

Maria crossed herself, closed her eyes, and tilted her head. I waited a few moments before stepping forward. Father Brualla finally opened his eyes, saw me, and said, his speech labored, hoarse, "Matthew, you must not worry about me."

He motioned for me to move closer. Father Mendez stood up and pointed to his chair. I sat down. Father Brualla continued, "I no longer need this body. I will soon be judged by the Lord, and I hope allowed to heaven." He turned his head and coughed roughly several times, blood dripping down his chin. When he was able, he spoke again, this time his breathing somewhat improved. "I have tried to live my life for this and have made my pilgrimage best I knew how."

He actually smiled, reached for my hand, and squeezed it. "I have so many questions for our Savior."

He took in a deep breath, turned his head even more toward me, and said, "I wish you a long life and happiness and grace."

After another series of wracking coughs, he added, his breaths labored, "Please watch over my neighborhood as you can. They are good people, their hearts, their souls. I know this, as do you. And please help Father Mendez. He will need you. I have explained to him what you and I have done these many years. Peace be with you always, my dear friend. Always."

Raising his hand just slightly, he pointed to Maria. She stepped to the edge of the bed. "You, my child, you are not lost. Remember that, always. The Holy Spirit is with you. Make your journey worthy. And look to the Blessed Mother. She will guide you."

Then, looking at Father Mendez, he closed his eyes and said, "I am ready for the Last Rites, to submit myself entirely to the will of God. It is time."

As Father Mendez knelt, Maria took my hand. "We should go," she whispered.

Once back in the hallway, she looked at me, tears streaming down her cheeks, and said, "I'm so tired. So tired."

At that moment I didn't care who saw us. I wrapped my arms around her and hugged her tightly as she sobbed against my shoulder. "I know," I said, "I'll miss him, too."

We stood there at least a minute before she finally stepped back and wiped her eyes.

"I'll drive you home," I said, handing her my handkerchief.

"Thank you," she said, dabbing at her cheeks. "That would be good. But I warn you, I live on the edge of downtown. That's a long way from here."

"That's fine. My house is that same direction, so I'll drop you off and slip by my place on the way back. I could do with a little rest myself before coming back. Robert said he wants to stay here, so he'll keep everyone moving. Let's get out of here."

Once we were seated in the car, I noticed she still had tears running down her cheeks. As we slowly pulled away from the curb, I said cautiously, "You two were getting pretty close."

She looked out the window and said, "It's more than that. It's not just him. It's what this is doing to all those families. The men, women, and children at the hospital. Our treatments don't seem to make too much difference in who lives and who dies. Poor Mrs. Samarano and her unborn baby and her little boy. All gone. And Mr. Samarano so worried about them, and then he gets sick and dies."

Her voice trailed off. "I know," I said. "I keep thinking about the little boy Chief Alexander tried to help. We never found his family. It was good Father Brualla was there to comfort him. He was all the little boy had at the end."

"I remember he kept asking for Father Brualla at the hospital. Poor thing. I felt so sorry and sad for him."

We drove in silence as we made our way across Alhambra and the upper rim of the quarantine area. Off to our left, guards were still clustered every hundred yards or so. Some had their rifles resting on their hips and aimed toward the neighborhood. Others seemed to be preparing for an evening meal. We saw no fires or smoke anywhere.

Once away from the Macy Street area as we continued our way toward downtown, it was as if we had entered another world. We passed block after block of comfortable homes with well-manicured lawns. Children were playing ball and chase games in the street, stopping to scurry to the side only when cars approached. A trolley car clanged by, stopping to drop off men on their way home from work. Many businesses were still open on both sides of the road. I noted a baker, florist, sundry store, tailor, all with customers coming and going.

As if reading my mind, Maria asked, "If the rest of the city knew, do you think they'd care?"

"Maybe. Right now, those who do know about this seem more concerned about their precious city's reputation. If one of them or their family members got sick, then the suffering would matter. Then they'd understand what is happening to these poor people. But, we can't let the plague spread, so we may never know."

Maria looked back out the window and said, "There's so much along here, and there's so little there. How will this ever change? Can it? Do you think there's a chance?"

"If there are enough of us who care, there will. This isn't a new problem. It's one that has been around forever. The real questions are: How to get those who are perfectly comfortable to care about those in need? Or help those they don't understand? Or those they don't seem to have much in common with? I don't know the answers, and I don't know who does, but we have to try."

"I agree with everything you've said, but after what we've gone through the past few days, I'm more angry and confused than ever. There are too many who will never change no matter what happens. Think about Chief Barker. I've known a lot of people like him. Do you see a man like that ever truly helping others? I don't. So, what do we do about the Chief Barkers of the world? Like you, I don't know the answer. And I believe we have to help. But I don't know how. At the same time, I know from now on I'm going to carry Father Brualla's words with me and try to make the journey better, for me and for those we help. I'll be forever grateful to him for that."

A few moments later, Maria pointed ahead and said, "My street's coming up. Turn right at the next corner. It'll be the third house on my side."

When I stopped the car, she turned to me and said, "Thank you."

"For what?"

"For everything." She leaned over and kissed me gently on the lips. Then, after she opened the door and stepped outside, she turned toward me again. "I'll see you tomorrow. Take care of yourself—for you and for me."

Before I could say anything, she was halfway up the sidewalk. I waited to make sure she got inside, then pulled away from the curb and drove slowly to my house. That evening, for the first time in a long time, my rest wasn't fitful. I was asleep the minute my head hit the pillow.

....

CHAPTER 23

Inside the Circle

November 4
6:45 A.M.

Mayor Burgess was demonstrating he could, if it suited his purposes, keep a meeting quiet. Whereas the first meeting to discuss the outbreak had filled his council chamber with those representing the major offices of the city, those before him now numbered just six: Charles Hornbeck, Dr. Thompson, Dr. Miller, Raymond Butler of the Greater Los Angeles Economic Progression Council, Jackson Demeter from the Chamber of Commerce, and acting-Police Chief Walter Chalmers.

As soon as all were seated, Major Burgess stood and said in a subdued voice, "You may be wondering why only you are here today. I'll be brief. First, I need reports from all of you. Second, I'm sure you know that word has leaked out about our little problem, and I felt it best to be careful about who knows what at this point. So, after I hear what you have to say, I'll decide who else should be given information—and how much. There's still so much to do, and we have to be careful moving forward. Therefore, I insist what we talk about now stays inside our circle here until it's time to share with others."

He sat back down and studied their faces. After a few moments, he said, "Before we begin, I'd like to give special thanks to Charles and County Hospital. And the doctors, Dr. Thompson and . . . I'm sorry, I've forgotten your name. You're the one from San Francisco, right?"

"Sir. I'm Dr. Miller."

"I knew it. Just couldn't recall it. Thank you for coming here to help us."

"Glad I could be of assistance, but Dr. Thompson here deserves the real thanks. If he hadn't acted quickly right at the start, there's no telling what would have happened."

Mayor Burgess nodded and faced Dr. Thompson. "I was told just a few minutes ago that Father Brualla passed last night. He was a good friend of yours. So sorry."

"Thank you, your Honor. He was a great man, and I'm going to miss him more than I can say. And I know what he'd want me to say today. He'd say it's the neighborhood we should now be concerned about. He held it together, gave the people hope and cared for their needs, spiritual and otherwise. He'd want all of us now to do that, and I hope we can."

Mayor Burgess looked around the table before replying, "We lost others, too, who will be sorely missed. The doctors know, but the rest of you probably don't, that Chief Alexander also died a few hours ago. He was on the job only a short time, but he already knew the importance of protecting his city, no matter the cost. He made the ultimate sacrifice, and when this is all over, I plan to have a public ceremony to honor him and present his family with the special medal of valor I would have given him.

"And let's not forget Chief Barker. He, too, was injured while on duty. A bad concussion that has, I'm sad to say, left him blind. We don't know yet if he'll ever regain his sight. He, too, will be recognized for his bravery and dedication."

Dr. Miller kicked Dr. Thompson under the table after the Mayor's last remarks. Dr. Thompson turned toward him, making sure no one else could see him, and rolled his eyes. He then turned to the group. "Sir, I hope the same can be done for Ed Armbruster, our senior ambulance driver. He organized transporting many of those who were ill from the neighborhood to the hospital. He, too, caught the illness and is still receiving treatment. We don't know if he's going to make it."

"I will keep him in my thoughts and prayers, as I know we all will," Mayor Burgess replied. He turned to his right and said, "I'm not sure if you know him, but this is Walter Chalmers, a veteran of over ten years on the force. I've asked him to step up as acting Police Chief for now. He has big shoes to fill, and I know he'll do a fine job."

After everyone congratulated Chief Chalmers and wished him luck, Mayor Burgess said, "This meeting was really Charles' idea—and a good one at that—so I'm going to turn it over to him. Charles, the floor is yours."

"Thank you, your Honor," Charles replied. "First, I'd like to thank you and the others around the table for your help and support, both financial and otherwise. And Raymond, I especially want to offer my thanks to you and the Council for your assistance with the isolation wing. However, you haven't seen the bill yet, and it's going to be a *big* one, so you might faint when you see it."

The two doctors smiled politely as the others laughed, which eased the tension that had gripped the room from the start. Raymond then clutched his chest and shouted, "Ouch!"—which set everyone off again—though the look Dr. Thompson shared with Dr. Miller clearly showed the joke was being stretched too thin.

Charles started again. "Thank you for your dedication and the great support you have given to me and our city."

Mayor Burgess applauded and all others followed. Charles continued, "The person we need to hear from most is sitting right here next to me. I've asked Dr. Thompson to let us know where we stand in our fight against this terrible illness. Dr. Thompson, please tell us what is happening."

Dr. Thompson stood and walked slowly back and forth on his side of the table as he addressed the group. "I, too, want to thank everyone for the help that was provided. What Mayor Burgess said earlier is right. We have a lot left to do. I'm going to tell you where we are right now, and then I'm sure some of you will have opinions about what we should do next."

He took a sip of water, and continued. "I'm pleased to say we can finally offer a ray of hope. I don't want everyone to get too excited just yet, but yesterday was a breakthrough. We admitted just one new patient suspected in the pneumonic state. Just one."

Everyone applauded again, but Dr. Thompson waved his arm and said, "It's too early for that. But I'm hopeful. You see, Dr. Miller and I believe we found the source of the outbreak and, when we did, we were able to track the progression. So, yesterday we sent doctors and nurses into the neighborhood again to visit all the homes that were somehow associated with the initial outbreak. We did this to make sure there are no more who were ill there and to see if we can finally put a halt to the spread. We found the one person yesterday, but in large part because of the cubicle isolation we imposed in the quarantine area, there may not be others—at least not in the neighborhood."

"It sounds like you've stopped it," Mayor Burgess said, banging his fist on the table. "Good work, Doctors!"

Dr. Miller jumped in, "We don't know that for sure—not at this point. What Dr. Thompson is saying is that typically there are patterns to the spread of illnesses like this. They aren't always apparent or easy to follow, but we may have caught a break this time. It's still too early to tell, but, like Dr. Thompson, I'm growing more hopeful."

He looked directly at Charles, "The death toll stands at forty-four, and we still have several we're treating the best we know how. Since, the number we're treating has shrunk to this point, we can soon start thinking about shutting down the isolation wing and just keeping a few rooms set off at the end of that hallway. However, before we do that, I'd strongly suggest that the quarantine of the neighborhood be kept in place for at least three to four more weeks."

"That long? If there are so few cases now, why would you want to do that?" Jackson Demeter asked. "The Chamber of Commerce would like all indication of this illness wiped away as soon as possible. The city's reputation is at stake. We tout our city as the 'healthy' city. We can throw that campaign away if we don't get back to normal as fast as we can."

"I know many feel that way," Dr. Miller responded. "But, even though plague has been around for hundreds of years, there's still so much we don't know about it. I've helped out with more outbreaks than I care to admit to, and I still don't understand about such things as why the incubation period seems different from one outbreak to the next and why certain people become ill and others don't when they all seem to have had the same contact. We still don't know for sure the best medicines and course of treatment to follow at the different stages of the illness. That's why I think we should err on the side of caution and take the time to make sure this has completely run its course in that neighborhood."

Noticing their skeptical faces, he added, "You gentlemen wouldn't want to go through this again, would you? Let's give a little more time here, and then we'll be sure. I don't think you need me here anymore, so if Dr. Thompson and Mr. Hornbeck will let me go, I will get on a train tomorrow morning, so I can go back to sleeping in my own bed. I'm ready for that."

As everyone laughed, Mayor Burgess started the applause again. He thanked Dr. Miller and said, "Can't say I'm sorry to see you go, Doctor. That may sound bad, but I think you know what I mean."

"I do, your Honor. And I won't miss you either."

Mayor Burgess smiled and saluted him. Dr. Miller saluted back, but then, his face growing serious again, he said, "Oh—one more thing. I'm not leaving until all of you hear it."

He placed his hand on Dr. Thompson's shoulder. "We discovered something that I think is going to surprise many of you a great deal. It seems like all I've heard since I've been here is how the Mexican community caused all of this—that it was somehow all their fault. Well, guess what? The plague didn't come from Mexico, and it didn't come from that neighborhood. And it didn't come from the Devil. We were able to track it down, and it came on a ship that docked at the harbor here."

There were shocked looks and whispers all around the table. "That's right—the harbor. And from the harbor to the neighborhood. So, the Mexicans didn't cause this—not by a long shot. As a matter of fact, in a way, you owe them a debt of gratitude. Why? Because we now know there should be better scrutiny of the cargo and crews that come off the ships here. *That* is the real danger ahead, and you need to do something about it—and fast."

Everyone started talking at once, but Jackson Demeter's voice carried above the rest. "I find this hard to believe," he said, moving his chair back slightly from the table. "But I still say it doesn't matter how it got there— it still started with the Mexicans. That's where we first found it. That's the truth, and I think that's all that matters."

"You can believe what you want," Dr. Miller replied. "I'm just saying you need to take a long look at the harbor and the practices there."

"Thank you," Mayor Burgess said, banging his fist again on the table and motioning everyone to quiet down. "I'll take that under advisement." He turned to Jackson and asked, "I need to know something else today. What do you and the rest of the Chamber of Commerce think—how bad of a black eye did we get from this? And, what can we do about it now?"

"It's bad," Jackson replied, "but it would have been much worse if the newspapers and radio people hadn't helped keep this as quiet as possible. Whatever you said to them worked because I never saw or heard a thing other than the reports you regularly gave us until someone showed me a New York paper. I don't know who did it, but someone—and I'd like to find him and take him out back of the building—gave out a lot of details a couple of days ago that have apparently spread all over the country. We'll get hurt some in our development plans, in tourism, and in attracting the right sort of people here, but given time, I think we'll be fine. In the meantime, there's already a buzz going around here, and it's just going to get louder. So, we're going to have to do something today or tomorrow to cover ourselves or we're going to look pretty bad, and people will demand answers we might not want to give."

Raymond Butler joined in, "We've already talked this over in the Council. We knew this day would be coming, so we've already come up with a suggestion—a solution if you will."

"And what would that be?" Mayor Burgess asked, picking up a pencil to jot notes on a tablet of paper in front of him. "I'd . . . we'd all like to hear it. Please, go on."

"A radio broadcast. We suggest it be done tonight. Better not wait any longer. We already have an announcement ready to be put in the afternoon papers, so plenty of people will be listening. Six-thirty is a good time. People will be home from work then and can get settled in to listen. The announcement in the papers won't go into any great detail. It'll just say that an important broadcast will take place that will give information about an 'illness' that showed up in our community. Sure, some will be frightened when they see the announcement, especially those who have seen the big city papers, but most will just be curious and will be sure to listen."

Mayor Burgess smiled and said, "And just what would this radio broadcast say?"

Raymond smiled back. "We've already written it out. We'll make sure you see it beforehand in case you'd like to make some changes."

"Sounds good to me," he replied. "What do the rest of you think?"

All agreed it was a fine idea, so Mayor Burgess thanked Raymond and said he'd look forward to seeing the script. Then he asked, "Well, is that about all we need to talk about now?"

When several started scooting chairs back, Dr. Thompson raised his hand and said, "Sir, I'd like to ask one more thing."

There were a few groans as Mayor Burgess asked, the irritation clear in his words, "And what would that be?"

"Sir, what about those who lost their homes, had them burned or torn down? And the people who lived in the field by the railroad tracks? Most of them lost everything. What will be done for them?"

Raymond didn't give Mayor Burgess a chance to answer. Instead, he immediately said, "That was most unfortunate. But, we had no choice. Action had to be taken, and we did the best we could under the very trying circumstances. I agree that we should do something, so we've—that is the *Council*—has already been in contact with Catholic Charities. We're going to work with them to see the unfortunates are relocated, some out nearer the Valley, and others in an area much closer to the harbor, so that all get appropriate housing. That will put them closer to where most of them work, which will be better for them."

"Relocated?" Dr. Thompson asked, clearly irritated. "Why not just rebuild their homes, so they can remain closer to family, their neighbors, their church?"

Here Mayor Burgess jumped in. "Because, Doctor, that area will now forever be known as 'Plague City'—and nobody is going to help them build anything there. No, it would be the right thing, the *Christian* thing, to help them get away from there and the stigma that will always be associated now with that neighborhood. Trust me, relocating them will be the best thing that can happen to them. The very best thing . . ."

Dr. Thompson shook his head. "I don't agree with that. I think—"

Charles Hornbeck leaned over and said, "The Mayor is right. I know why you feel the way you do. But it will be a long time before anyone wants to go to that area again, so a fresh start will help them. Think about it some more. You'll see I'm right."

Dr. Thompson started to speak again, but Mayor Burgess didn't give him a chance. Mayor Burgess looked at his watch and said, "Again, I want to thank all of you because . . . this could have been bad."

Dr. Thompson, still visibly upset, sat forward and said, "What do you mean *could* have? What about the forty-four who are dead? What about those who lost their homes or are still under quarantine? *Could have?*"

"You know what I mean," Mayor Burgess said, sternly. "For the city, for the state. And it *could* have been a lot worse for the Mexicans. A *lot* worse—if we hadn't stepped in and acted as quickly as we did. I think we can all be mighty proud of what we've done."

Shouts of "Hear! Hear!" rang out from all but Dr. Miller and Dr. Thompson. Dr. Miller leaned close to Dr. Thompson and said, "Forget it—for now. They don't want to hear a word you have to say, and they're never going to understand why you're trying. I'm proud of what you and I were able to do, and *that's* what I'm going to be thinking about on my train home."

"And them?" Dr. Thompson asked, pointing around the table as the others stood and started leaving the room.

"What about them? They'll never change."

"*That's* the problem."

Dr. Miller reached out to shake his hand and said, "That's an excellent diagnosis, Doctor. We now know the disease, so we can start looking for a cure. You with me?"

"All the way," Dr. Thompson replied. "And I can't wait to get started."

He stood and looked out the window at the streets of downtown Los Angeles. While the distance in miles may have been small, he saw more than ever downtown was worlds away from the Macy Street area. Some saw the families in that area as helpless people who could be exploited. Others more sympathetic saw them as helpless people needing charity. Before the divide would end, the families of the Macy Street area needed to be embraced as neighbors, co-workers, colleagues—as just people with the same needs and dreams as anyone.

....

CHAPTER 24

Morg's

November 4
8:43 A.M.

I didn't even notice when she came in. Seated on the cold, metal stool in the autopsy suite, I stared at the two covered bodies before me. When she spoke, I didn't even jump.

"Nurse Adams called me and told me you wanted to do the autopsies yourself," Maria said, gently, touching my shoulder. "I know how close you were to Father Brualla. You shouldn't do this alone. *I* didn't want you to do this alone."

When I turned around, I could see above her mask that her eyes were wet. Handing her gloves, I said, "I don't know whether *we* killed them—or the plague killed them. We just don't know enough about treatments. After hundreds of years of this . . . this killer, we're still just guessing. Mercurochrome, aspirin, raise blood pressure, lower blood pressure, increase heart rate, reduce heart rate, give them stimulants, keep them calm. We might as well put everything on a board and fling darts at it. That would be just as scientific."

Maria started rubbing my shoulders and said, "I don't want you berating yourself. You're right we're still experimenting, but these deaths aren't for nothing. As much as we hate it at the time, through a death we learn more about what helps—and what doesn't. And, sometimes what *doesn't help* tells us the most of all. What's most important is that we don't give up trying to do all we can to stop this illness . . . to help this community. I knew him only a short time, but I think Father Brualla would have said the same thing to you."

I reached up and squeezed her hand. "I was at his church once several years ago when he gave a homily I've never forgotten. That morning, the gospel had been the parable of the Good Samaritan, which I'm sure a Jesuit-trained Catholic girl like you would know."

I smiled, but as I might have expected, Maria saw this as a challenge and took the stance of a school girl as she recited the story.

"Well, of course I know it. It's about loving our neighbors as ourselves. In the parable, a traveler is robbed and beaten and left to die by the side of the road. Two other travelers, including a temple priest, come upon the injured man and pass him by. But the Samaritan stops, dresses the man's wounds, and takes him to an inn to recover. The Samaritan pays the innkeeper to take care of the man and even promises to return and pay for any extra costs. The 'neighbor' to the injured man is, of course, the one who shows compassion—the Samaritan. How's that for Jesuit training?"

"Very good!" I laughed. "You obviously paid attention during class."

"So, go on," she said. "The homily . . . ?"

"The part of the story I had never thought about much before was that Samaritans were considered a low class of people—virtually outcasts. This is what Father Brualla most emphasized in his homily. The one who was considered the lowliest, the most looked down upon had the most compassion for others. The Samaritan helped a stranger when even a priest, who should have known better, turned away. Father Brualla told his parishioners that the Lord had high expectations for them all. Their struggles . . . their search for dignity and respect in a country that did not always welcome them should teach them the importance of compassion. They were to be the good Samaritans in Los Angeles and never pass by someone who needed their help. People left his church that day feeling respected and inspired. Father Brualla was always fighting for respect and understanding for all. And now he's here. His journey is done."

I pointed to the other table. "What a waste. Chief Alexander was only thirty-five years old. Prime of his life. Both died within an hour of each other, and there was nothing we could do about it."

Maria stepped around in front of me. "I don't agree—at least about the *waste* part of what you said. I'm sorry they're gone, but if it hadn't been for them, we wouldn't have found the rats. If we hadn't found them, there could have been new outbreaks everywhere, and think of the deaths that would have followed that. We do the best we can. We learn. We move ahead. We fight, and fight, and fight some more. We win some, and sometimes we don't. Father Brualla would say we should just keep on our journey. We should keep doing our best. I agree with that. Deep down, I think you do, too."

She walked over next to the tables and said, "I'm going to get everything ready. Go get a drink of water. Walk around a little. When you're ready, come back. I'll be here. I'm not going anywhere."

"Thanks," I said, standing. "I'll take you up on that. I'll be back in just a few minutes."

"Good. Take as long as you want."

....

The autopsies showed cause of death as respiratory arrest for both. Everything we had done to prevent that had failed. I was as down as I could ever remember when Maria tried to bring me back up some. She reminded me that Thomas Edison had once been described as a failure by a reporter when he couldn't come up with a light bulb that would work effectively. Edison had said in response something close to, "I haven't failed—I've just learned a couple thousand things that didn't work." Maria's point was well taken, but it didn't do much to lift my spirits.

Neither of us had had any breakfast, so we walked across the street to Morg's for eggs and toast topped with a thick layer of strawberry jam, which I had discovered was her favorite meal. We had just started eating when Dr. Barton came in. I waved him over to our table.

"Nurse Adams told me you were here," he said, pulling up a chair.

"I'm so sorry about Father Brualla."

"Thanks, Tom," I said. "His passing is a loss for everyone." Then, pointing to our food, I asked, "Would you like something to eat—like to join us?"

"No, thank you. I just wanted to see what time you'd like me to have everyone together this morning. Nurse Adams didn't go into details. She just said you had another job for us."

Lowering my voice so that others around us couldn't hear me, I said, "Thanks to the work all of you did yesterday in checking the blue homes, we're now convinced we discovered how the spread took place. Our theory tested out fine. You found one new patient, which was better than we anticipated. However, Nurse McDonnell and I have talked this over, and we think we should do at least one more sweep of the entire neighborhood. It's possible a person from a blue home snuck out during the cubicle isolation and made contact with someone else."

"Check everything? The whole neighborhood? Tom replied, blowing out a sharp breath.

"Everything," Maria interjected. "Every house. We have to make sure. It's a lot to ask of you, but if we don't do this and it flares up again, who's to blame then?"

"I know you're right," he said, leaning back in his chair. "It's just that we're all so tired. I don't know how I'm going to explain this to them."

"You don't have to," I said. "That's our job."

"I'll help the best I can," he said, nodding his head. "But, wow, this won't be popular."

"It's not supposed to be popular," Maria shot back. "What we do seldom is in situations like this, and interns and nurses better get used to it now. That is, if they plan to stay in medicine."

"So, *your* job today is going to be very similar to what we asked of you yesterday," I added.

"You form the teams, and give them their areas. Check on everyone again. You all know what to look for now, so if you think any should be brought to the hospital, get them back here while we still have isolation rooms. Hopefully, you won't find any other cases. Hopefully, all of you will just have a nice, pleasant walk today around the neighborhood." I smiled. "I'm sure everyone could use the exercise, right?"

Tom grinned. "Ok," he said, "I'll go round them up again. When do you want to meet?"

"Eleven will be fine. Let's plan on that. Is that enough time for you?"

"I'll make it so. I'll have them ready."

He stood to leave, but I motioned for him to sit again. "Tom, I want to say something else before you go. I'm not one to give out much praise. I've always figured that as physicians and nurses, we all do what we do because we've been called to this profession, and we don't need to be given thanks for anything. But, I do want you to know how proud I am of you and the leadership you've shown. You're going to be a fine doctor. I don't have any doubt of that."

He shifted in his chair and said, "Thank you. That means a lot to me, Sir. I'm trying my best. I . . . "

After an uncomfortable silence, Maria said to him, "We'll see you at eleven. Make sure all my nurses are there, too."

He stood and, without another word, headed for the door. As soon as he had gone, Maria turned to me and said, "I knew it. You're not half as mean as your bark. If you aren't careful, some of the people around here might actually start to like you."

"You're right," I said, slapping my forehead. "What was I thinking?" Maria playfully hit me with her napkin.

"Okay, that's enough about me," I said handing her the dish of strawberry jam. "Now it's my turn. What about you? Why are you here?"

"I already told you. I didn't want you to go through those autopsies alone this morning."

"No," I said, smiling. "I mean why are you *here*—in California? I've been wanting to ask that ever since we first met."

She paused so long I was starting to think she didn't hear me. When I began repeating the question she finally said, while poking her fork at her eggs, "It's an old story. Nothing new here. I actually started medical school, but I had a little problem."

"I didn't know about the medical school. Why did you stop? What was the problem?"

Taking a bite and while still chewing, she said, "My father."

"I know all about your father. He's respected by everyone. He's one of the best."

"And that's the problem," she responded, reaching for the salt. "I decided I needed to get as far away from him as I could."

"I still don't understand. Why, exactly?"

"His reputation, his shadow. At medical school, I first thought my teachers didn't want anything to do with me because I was a woman. I also thought some of them didn't want me around because, well . . . I'm brown.

"Turns out, neither of those were it at all. They were afraid of me because teaching me put them under my father's microscope. He was trying to help, but he didn't realize by calling my teachers all the time to check up on me they felt he was scrutinizing *them*. Oh, and I'm sure some thought I was there only because he had pulled some strings—that I really didn't belong, and they'd suffer if they didn't bend over backward for me. He did mean well. He was just being my father, and I dearly love him for that. But his shadow was too long. So, I quit, went to nursing school where I didn't bother anybody and, here I am."

As she spread more jam to her toast, I motioned her to lean forward, looked around to make sure others weren't listening, and said, "I think I understand now. I went through the same."

"Your father was a famous doctor?" she asked, putting down her toast. "I thought you said he was a veterinarian."

"Yes, he was—a good one. From the time I was a little boy, everyone thought I inherited his talent. If he wasn't around, I was expected to help every neighbor's cat, dog, or parakeet that got hurt or sick. Got scratched and bit more times than I could count. Animals never did like me."

She started laughing so hard she dropped her fork to the floor and spilled her water in her lap. "Well, I can see there might have been a problem or two with that— if you're not making this all up."

"Oh, I assure you I'm not."

"Yes," she said, reaching for her fork, "Famous fathers are hard to live up to. I guess we have that much in common."

I smiled at her and said, "It's not too late for you to go back to school. Think about that. You already know more than any of the interns we have running around here."

"I've thought of it," she said, turning serious again. "We'll see. Time will tell."

Looking at her watch, she said, "We better go. Thank you for the breakfast. I needed it. But, more than that, I want to thank you for . . . being you. I also don't give many compliments, but you're pretty special, Doctor."

I reached over to take her hand, but she quickly looked around and pulled it back. Shaking her head, she said, "What would people think?"

"I don't care what they'd think," I said, standing. "I know what *I* think, and I think you're more than just special. I think . . . well, maybe someday I'll explain it all to you."

She looked at me, confused.

"Someday," I repeated. "Likely someday soon."

....

CHAPTER 25

Declarations

November 4
6:12 P.M.

I was standing in the doorway of my office and looking up and down the hallway for Maria. I had told her to meet me at six o'clock—not a minute later—because I had something important I wanted to talk to her about. She probably thought I was going to give her a report of the search the interns and nurses had conducted earlier. There was good news there; they had found no new cases. However, that wasn't what I wanted to share with her.

As usual, she was late—I had no doubt just to be ornery. I heard the squeak of her shoes against the newly polished floors before I saw her. As she rounded the corner and entered my hallway, I raised my arm and tapped repeatedly on my watch.

Without saying anything she slipped right by me, sat on the edge of the desk, looked around, and asked, "So, where's your shadow?"

"What?"

"Dr. Miller."

"Oh, he left around noon. Couldn't wait to get home, and I can't say as I blame him. Didn't he tell you he was leaving?"

"No, he didn't," she said, pretending to pout.

"Don't tell me you care?" I teased.

"No, it's not that. It's just . . ."

"I know," I said. "I guess I got used to him, too. He wouldn't be a bad colleague to have around here if you ask me."

"I'll grant you he's a good doctor," she said, unpinning her hat and placing it behind her on the desk. "It's just that he's also a—"

"Don't say it!" I interrupted her.

She stood, walked over close to me, straightened my tie, and asked, "So, how well do you think you know me?"

I reached out and swung the door shut, pulled her to me, and kissed her fully on the lips. She started to back away, but I wrapped my arms around her, drawing her even closer as she did the same. I was breathless when she took a step back and said, "You surprise me, Doctor. I had no idea you knew how to kiss like that."

"I doubt anything really surprises you," I said, moving forward and kissing her again, this time running my hand down her cheek as I did so. This time, I pulled back, looked deeply into her eyes, and said, "I want to ask you something."

When I didn't continue right away, she threw her arms out and said, "Well? I'm waiting."

"Imagine that," I said, tapping my watch again. "*You* waiting for me."

I stepped closer to kiss her again, but this time she held out an arm and repeated, "Well?"

I took her hands in mine, squeezed them gently, and said, "How would you like to make an honest man out of me?"

She stepped back to sit on the desk again but slipped, lost her balance, and started falling to the floor. I reached down, grabbed her arm, and barely managed to keep her upright.

"Have I knocked you off your feet?" I asked, laughing.

"Funny man," she replied, straightening her dress. She studied me a minute before saying, "That was either the worst proposal I've ever heard of in my life or you're losing your mind. Right now, I can't tell which it is."

"Then I'll help you out," I said, kissing her again, deeply, holding her as close to me as I could.

Moving her lips just slightly away from mine, she asked, softly, "Are you serious?"

"I am," I said, brushing my lips gently against hers. "Now it's my turn to ask. Well?"

"Well I'm going to have to think about it," she said, backing away again and crossing her arms. "And if I decide to say 'yes,' you're going to have to ask my father for my hand." She smiled and added, "I'm an old-fashioned girl, you know."

"Old fashioned? You're about as old-fashioned as those new bathing outfits that are supposedly causing men to have heart attacks over at the beach. Ask your father?"

She moved back to me, placed her arms around my neck, kissed me gently, and said, "Maybe we can forget that. But, I'm still going to have to think about this."

"Don't take too long. I don't like to be kept waiting, and I know neither do you. I think I'll just ask you every day until you say you will."

I looked at my watch, and she said, sarcastically, "Oh, am I keeping you from something? Bored with me already? Is this what's going to happen when—"

"I'm not bored! I was looking at the time because I think you and I are going to be mentioned on the radio in a few minutes, and I want us to—"

"What are you talking about? The radio? Why?"

"Because there's *finally* going to be a broadcast about the outbreak. Mayor Burgess sent over a reporter this afternoon to talk to me, and I told him about you and how wonderful you've been during all of this. The reporter said he'd use it during the broadcast."

"You didn't!"

"And I mentioned Robert. And Father Brualla and Chief Alexander. I want people to know what they did. I don't want them to be forgotten."

Holding out my watch again so she could see the time, I said, "Look, Hornbeck has a radio set in his office that he's awfully proud of. He and his secretary are already gone for the day, and guess what I have?"

I held out a key. "I borrowed it from the janitor up there. It's to

Charles' office. We have just enough time to get up there and get comfortable. Join me?"

"I'm supposed to be the sneaky one, just ask anybody around here. Have I rubbed off on you that badly?"

"Maybe some," I said, taking her hand in mine. "And maybe I needed it."

"Let's go," she said, urging me toward the door. "This ought to be good."

....

Charles' radio set took nearly two minutes to warm up, finally humming and crackling. I turned the knob at the far right slowly until I heard a voice, muffled at first, then more clearly as I very slowly turned the smaller knob next to it. The voice then came through loud and clear.

"Here we go," I said, sitting with Maria on the large, overstuffed chair Charles often used to take naps during the lunch hour. She leaned her head against my shoulder as the broadcast began.

> Good evening ladies and gentlemen of Los Angeles. This is
> J.T. Stephens coming into your homes this evening to share a
> story with you, one I'm pleased to say has a happy ending. But,
> this could not have been so without the leadership, heroism,
> bravery, and sacrifice of the highest order everywhere from
> the office of our Mayor down to the doctors, nurses, police
> officers, and firemen who risked their very lives to protect us
> and our city.
>
> Our story begins a couple of weeks back when some day
> laborers from the Macy Street Mexican District suddenly fell
> ill, wracked with fever, chills, pain of the chest and abdomen,
> and stabbing pains in the head. The doctors were at first mystified, unable to diagnose this malady, which had come upon
> these men so swiftly and powerfully. At first some believed
> it might have been a return of the Influenza that carried its

devastation to us a scant half dozen years before. Still others thought it to be a new type of tuberculosis. Yet others speculated a new and deadly form of lung complaint. In the end, all were wrong. All were in the dark until Dr. Jacobs of Los Angeles County Hospital, and one of the true heroes of this story, peered into his microscope, and there, before him, he recognized an enemy so terrible, so formidable, he said it felt for an unbearably long moment as if his heart had stopped beating from sheer fright.

And this enemy? In Latin terminology used in the medical books, it is listed as *Yersinia Pestis*. That, ladies and gentlemen—this *Yersinia Pestis*—is none other than the greatest scourge of the Middle Ages. A killer then of over one quarter of the population of Europe. The means by which the most agonizing of deaths known to man have occurred, deaths so horrific they were in the end gladly welcomed by those afflicted. People of Los Angeles, this deliverer of death identified by Dr. Jacobs was none other than the Black Plague or, as others have called it, the Black Death.

But wait—before fright overcomes you, you must hear the rest of the story. Through the valiant efforts orchestrated by Mayor Burgess, another hero of our tale, a total and complete quarantine of the Mexican district was put into place. As a result, this illness, which spread like a raging fire through this Mexican neighborhood, was contained. Death upon death resulted, but our police, firemen, and skilled medical personnel worked tirelessly to make sure the illness did not spread into the streets and homes of the rest of our great city. And now, thanks to the additional efforts of the Greater Los Angeles Economic Progression Council, our Chamber of Commerce, Catholic Charities, and other organizations too numerous to mention here, it can be said the danger has passed, the enemy has been defeated.

Many are now asking why this illness came to the Macy Street

Mexican District—and from whence it came. We will likely never know the answers. What we do know is our city, our Los Angeles, is, as our Chamber of Commerce is fond of saying, "The Paradise of the West"—where prosperity, health, and family flourish.

Again, a crisis has passed, a tragedy averted. For all of you listening to me tonight, I wish you a pleasant evening and wonderful tomorrows. This is J.T. Stephens signing off.

Maria and I looked at each other, blankly. I shook my head. She blew out a long, loud breath.

"Well, at least they didn't say our names," she finally said, reaching over to switch off the radio.

"Have you ever heard anything like that?" I asked.

"I can't say as I have. And where do you suppose that J.T. Whatshisname went to Liar's School?

"I think we both know where that school is, and we can look right out the window and see the lights of it over there across town."

Maria stood, turned around, and said, "Enough of that for now. It'll still be there tomorrow and the next day and the next. Morg's is still open. I haven't had a morsel since breakfast. How about taking me over there for my engagement dinner? How does that sound to you?"

"It sounds absolutely perfect."

I took her hand, and we headed for the door. Just before I turned the doorknob, I stopped.

"What? Cold feet already?" she asked.

"No, I forgot to do something."

I walked back to Charles' desk, picked up the radio, and dropped it in the waste can behind his desk.

"*Now* I'm ready," I said, taking her hand again.

She squeezed my arm and said, "I believe you are."

....

Epilogue

As horrific as the outbreak was for those within the Macy Street District, the quarantine efforts imposed upon the area helped put an end to the ravages of the plague. Once the Samarano home at 724 Clara Street was identified as the "Death House," the medical community was able to track the spread of the illness and put in place additional isolation procedures. Although only a few cases appeared afterward, some of these occurred in other sections of the city; thus the plague finally did reach the "paradise" so many officials had tried to protect. These new cases were all given immediate attention and the best of care to the point the outbreak soon ran its course.

The problems facing the Macy Street District continued to grow even after the medical crisis ended. City officials and civic groups had done a very good job of describing the outbreak as a "Mexican problem" isolated to this particular section of Los Angeles. Therefore, very few in other parts of the city objected when homes and other buildings were demolished, displacing families in the name of "helping" the community and addressing both health and sanitation concerns. According to some reports, as many as two thousand structures were reduced to rubble and hauled to the City Dump, leaving many families in the community suddenly homeless. Adding insult to injury, because these actions were deemed "emergency" in nature and performed for the "common good," in most cases no compensation of any type had to be given to the displaced for their losses.

Those who were suddenly and without compensation uprooted from their homes were forced to leave, most moving farther east of the city. Others who worked at the harbor looked that direction for housing in the new areas of development there. Many, so frustrated and angry at how they had been treated, decided to return to Mexico.

While most news accounts of the time presented the "sanitation" of the area as a noble and kind action, there were others with less benevolent motives. As the expansion and development of the city continued, land became a more precious and valuable commodity. Some were less interested in the welfare of the community members and more concerned with profits that might come from claiming and developing as much of the area as they could acquire. With so many suddenly removed from the area, the land was there for the taking; however, redevelopment could not begin right away. For a good dozen years, the Macy Street District continued to be known as "Plague City," and it wasn't until memories of the tragic events that happened there started to fade that developers moved forward with their plans.

There can be little doubt prejudice and greed guided the actions of many and demonstrated just how quickly inhumane treatment of a community can be justified and tolerated. However, this story is not without its heroes. Medical personnel faced this deadly plague with limited knowledge and resources, risking their lives to save those in the Mexican-American community. They faced obstacles in these efforts but also brought about long-term benefits that reach us even today.

At the time of the outbreak, much was made of a "plague serum" that many believed would successfully treat the illness. Mulford Laboratories, a division of the H.K. Mulford Company of Philadelphia, Pennsylvania, had developed this serum, but it was still largely untested. After multiple requests from Los Angeles civic and health officials and some unexplained delays, the serum was finally sent by way of cross-country airplane delivery, not a common means of transport at the time. Unfortunately, the airplane involved had mechanical issues at several points along the way. As a result, the serum arrived in time to be used with only one patient. That patient survived, but it was never determined whether the individual had been saved by the serum or the previous treatment and care. Still, in its company newsletter "The Spark Plug," Mulford Laboratories was quick to report: "Los Angeles calls for help and in less than 36 hours the vials of serum were brought to the front lines where the battle is on against the Terror."

How many more lives might the serum have saved if it had been sent earlier? No one will ever know, but more than one historian has suggested the delays in delivery might have had something to do with the fact those afflicted were from the Macy Street District and *not* from mainstream Los Angeles.

While treatments were not always successful, the outbreak did lead to important medical protocols. Medical personnel were able to devise a plan to trace the spread of the illness, which later helped provide a foundation for the creation of modern procedures used to locate the "Index Patient" and "Patient Zero" when outbreaks occur, a process which has saved countless lives. This has become more important as outbreaks of one type or another—SARS, Hantavirus, Ebola, Zika, Typhus, Cholera, various forms of the plague, and so many others on an ever-growing list—continue to impact communities around the world.

In addition, because of the imposed secrecy and resulting media blackout all across Los Angeles, which kept nearly everyone in the dark, this outbreak has been cited time and again as one of the leading reasons the national Centers for Disease Control in Atlanta, Georgia was later created. Up until the 1924 plague outbreak, local groups handled these situations as they saw fit. Once the CDC was created, it became much more difficult for those at the local level to determine who would, and would not, receive treatment—decisions often made based upon issues of race, color, creed, national origin, and even economic status.

And what of Dr. Thompson and Maria McDonnell? Their work during the 1924 outbreak had significant consequences in their own lives.

Dr. Matthew Thompson, forever changed by his experiences during the outbreak, decided he wanted to help others who were isolated and, in many ways, also feared because so little was still known about their illness: tuberculosis patients. He spent a long and rewarding career as a care provider and researcher for a Tuberculosis sanitarium. There, he brought comfort and renewed health to thousands.

Nurse Maria McDonnell, with the urging and support of Dr. Thompson, again entered medical school, this time devoting her all to her studies, finally graduating as Dr. Maria McDonnell, Family Practitioner. Through the years she regularly made trips abroad, everywhere from Mexico to Spain, offering her medical skills to those in small towns and villages where her services were badly needed. In 1930, she and Matthew were finally married. They were devoted to each other and were blessed with long and rich lives together.

Outside of the medical community, Father Brualla represents the compassionate members of the Los Angeles religious communities who came forward in the time of need to offer food and shelter for those displaced during the quarantine. His faith steadfast, he also stood up without regard for his own personal safety and well being, to provide spiritual comfort for and to protect the rights of his parishioners. After his passing, he was interred at the San Gabriel Mission. His legacy continues to this day.

Ed Armbruster, who had provided assistance to over half of those brought to the hospital for treatment, was never able to return to his ambulance. He lingered just over a month, finally succumbing to the illness.

Carlita Lajun's brothers, Antonio and Alejandro, reportedly died in a boxcar while on their way back to Hermosillo. No outbreaks were reported at the time in northern Mexico, so it was assumed they had no contact with others along the way.

Chief Barker never regained complete sight. With visual limitations, he could no longer serve on the police force. He spent his remaining days as a night watchman for the Port of Los Angeles.

Our Lady Queen of Angels, also known as "La Placita," continues to serve as an important symbol for the Mexican-American community. Because of the redevelopment of the surrounding area after the outbreak and the eventual relocation of those who once called the Macy Street District home, today most of those who attend services at the church come from areas all across Los Angeles and surrounding areas. As the oldest church in Los Angeles, Our Lady Queen of Angels also represents the past, present, and future. Over one thousand baptisms take place there every month, with families routinely coming from thousands of miles away because of the church's history and significance. Mass is held three to four times per day, more on weekends and special holidays. Approximately 4,500 attend services each Sunday. In addition to helping the homeless, members of the church provide for others, especially those new to the country, assistance with everything from finding employment to securing health insurance to acquiring a wide range of legal documents.

Today, nearly a hundred years later, what was once called the Macy Street District has undergone an incredible transformation. Macy Street is now gone, replaced by Cesar E. Chavez Avenue, a main thoroughfare through this section of Los Angeles. Most of the other streets within the area were also eliminated when redevelopment finally started. The Twin Towers Jail Complex now stands where Clara Street and the Lujan and Samarano homes were located. Olvera Street, one of the most popular areas of the city because of its colorful shops and restaurants, is close at hand. Businesses and housing of all types dot the area once known as "Plague City." However, this transformation came at a terrible cost that should not be forgotten.

And what of the rats? The disease-carrying fleas may be gone, but rats are still present in full force throughout the area. In an ironic twist of history, these rats are indicative of a plague of another type that is growing around the area once known as the Macy Street District: poverty, hunger, and homelessness. Today, Our Lady Queen of Angels provides meals each morning to over two hundred individuals who are without basic shelter and nourishment. Many believe their food scraps attract rats by the thousands and see this new type of "plague" as an impediment to the construction and improvements already in progress in the area. Plans are currently being discussed to eliminate the rats and relocate the homeless so that the construction will continue as scheduled. This, in many ways, sounds very much like the 1924 situation all over again. In this way, the events in the Macy Street District continue to serve as a cautionary tale.

Finally, Los Angeles is currently home to nearly four million residents and is the second largest city in the United States, behind only New York City. The Port of Los Angeles receives close to forty-five percent of all cargo coming to America; it is now known as "America's Port." Did Los Angeles become the "Paradise of the West" that those in 1924 believed it would become? A lively debate could be held on this issue, especially by officials representing some of the other larger American cities. In the end, however, most would agree Los Angeles is a city rich in its diversity, cultural heritage, and history. As far as being a "paradise," that would, of course, depend upon one's own definition. Many of the problems present in 1924 persist today, but Los Angeles is a progressive city, one constantly moving forward to face these challenges.

As the people of Los Angeles—and all of us—face the challenges of living in a growing, diverse society, we may do well to heed the advice of Father Arturo Corral Navárez of "La Placita": "Live now, with dignity and with respect for all, and celebrate the faith because you are valuable."

....

Photos

1. Downtown Los Angeles, California, c. 1924, the "Paradise of the West."
Courtesy: Sherman Library and Gardens, Corona del Mar, CA

2. Los Angeles Harbor, c. 1924—where the infected rats were brought ashore.
Courtesy: Sherman Library and Gardens, Corona del Mar, CA

3. Our Lady Queen of Angels ("La Placita), c. 1924,
where the ill were also treated.
Courtesy: Archival Center, Archdiocese of Los Angeles

4. Our Lady Queen of Angels ("La Placita"), at present.
Courtesy: Copeland Collection

5. Los Angeles County Hospital—where the plague victims were treated.
Courtesy: Copeland Collection

6. Destruction of building in quarantine area suspected of harboring infected animals, fall 1924.
Courtesy: Copeland Collection

*7. Exterminators hired to hunt down rats and squirrels in
Macy Street Area, fall 1924.*
Courtesy: Copeland Collection

*8. Quarantine guards and demolition crew responsible for enforcing
the quarantine boundaries and destroying structures where
infected animals could hide, fall 1924.*
Courtesy: Copeland Collection

9. Guadalupe Samarano home at 724 Clara Street—the "Death House."
Courtesy: Copeland Collection

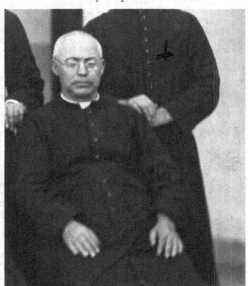

10. Father Medardo Brualla, Our Lady Queen of Angels ("La Placita"),
January 1924.
Courtesy: Claretian Missionaries Archives USA - Canada

Obituary

REV. MEDARDO BRUALLA, C. M. F.

Rev. Father Brualla, C. M. F., one of the assistant priests at the Plaza Church, died last Sunday, comforted with the Holy Sacraments and the prayers of the Church. Father Brualla was born in Spain in 1875. In his early years he became obedient to the divine call and entered the Congregation of Missionary Sons of the Immaculate Heart of Mary. After finishing his studies in the colleges of the Congregation he was ordained in 1900.

While a young priest he volunteered for the African Mission and was sent to that country. But his zeal for souls was not to be matched against the African climate. His health became impaired and he was sent to Mexico. Here he found a fertile field and gathered a rich harvest for Christ in the many Missions where he preached.

The Indians received a good share of his missionary work. He loved this people and always was at home amongst them. There are numerous places in Mexico where he will be remembered.

He came to the United States in 1914 and since then was attached to various parishes in Texas, New Mexico, Arizona, Colorado and California. Four years ago he was appointed assistant at the Plaza Church. He devoted himself heart and soul, to the performance of his parochial duties. His piety, zeal, kindness, humility and self-sacrifice endeared him to all parishioners. Last week while attending the deathbed of a stricken parishioner, Father Brualla contracted the illness that caused his death. He died on the altar of duty and joins the glorious host of Priests, Missionaries and Religious who with unswerving devotion and fidelity, have sacrificed their lives in times of epidemic, war or persecution.

Interment was made in San Gabriel Mission Cemetery. May Father Brualla's soul rest in peace.

11. Obituary of Father Medardo Brualla, Our Lady Queen of Angels ("La Placita"). Note veiled reference to the outbreak.
Courtesy: Archival Center, Archdiocese of Los Angeles

Spanish Glossary

Chapter 2:

Quiñceanera
A party for a girl's fifteenth birthday, at which she is presented to the community and becomes a woman.

¡Santa infiereno—sálvanos!
Holy hell—save us!

Chapter 3:

El médico es mi amigo.
The doctor is my friend.

Por favor, no te preocupes.
Please do not worry.

¿Usted no habla español?
You do not speak Spanish?

Chapter 5:

Gracias mi querido amigo.
Thank you my dear friend.

Nuestra Señora Reina de los Ángeles
Our Lady Queen of Angels

enfermos
sick

Jesús, por favor, es el Padre Brualla
Jesus, please, it's Father Brualla.

Debe despetarse ahora.
You must wake up now.

Por favor contéstame estas preguntas para mí.
Please answer these questions for me.

Chapter 10:

Mi Lucena está enferma, pero mi hijo ... temo ... Por favor, ayúdelo
My Lucena is sick, but my son ... I fear ... Please help him.

El examen fue bien. Vamos rezar.
The exam went well. Let's pray.

Gracias y que Dios te bendiga.
Thank you and bless you.

Chapter 12:

¿Qué es esto? ¿Quiénes son estos hombres?
What is this? Who are these men?

Usted le hizo daño a mi hermano, ¡Mueres!
You hurt my brother, you die!

Por favor, esto va a ir bien.
Please this will be fine.

Chapter 15:

Lo siento, lo siento.
Sorry, sorry.

¡Ustedes son unos demonios!
You are demons!

¡Espere! ¡Hay más!
Wait! There's more!

Chapter 16:

Casa
home

No te preocupes.
Do not worry.

Yo no trabajo. No comemos.
I do not work. We do not eat.

Chapter 18:

¡No más!
No more!

Chapter 19:

¡Ahi está! La gran caja.
There it is! The big box.

Tenemos una vela—y los fósforos.
We have a candle—and the matches.

Chapter 20:

¡Madre de Dios!
Mother of God!

Acknowledgments

This book could not have been written without the generous assistance of many wonderful people, all of whom gave freely of their time and knowledge.

First and foremost, I'd like my wife, Linda, for providing editorial assistance and help gathering research materials, which took considerable time and travel.

The many Research Librarians at the Library of Congress who helped source historical documents and records.

Jason Stratman, Librarian, Missouri Historical Society Library and Research Centere, for helping secure news accounts and biographical information about principle figures in the story.

Dana Peiffer, User Services Lead Support Specialist, of the University of Northern Iowa, for providing the full range of technology support services.

Stan Lyle, Research Librarian, University of Northern Iowa, for help in uncovering a wealth of information about the events of this story.

Gretchen Gould, Collection Strategist Librarian and Library Assessment Coordinator, University of Northern Iowa, for providing Los Angeles maps of the era.

Maryana Britt, Artist, for her inspirational drawings and illustrations.

Douglas Hartley, for his wonderful photographs and image collection.

Juan Carlos Castillo for serving as Editor of the Spanish portions of the text.

Anna Sklar, Los Angeles Historian, for help locating specialists with special knowledge of the history of the events in this story.

Eileen O'Brien, Director of Facilities and Operations, Archdiocesan Catholic Center, Los Angeles, California, for information about the history of "La Placita" and the Catholic Church in Los Angeles—and for making the time to show us around the Plaza and Olvera Street.

Paul Wormser, Library Director, Sherman Library and Gardens, Corona del Mar, California, for his wonderful help securing period photographs of Los Angeles Harbor and downtown Los Angels.

Kevin Feeney, Archivist of the Archdiocese of Los Angeles, for providing photographs of Our Lady Queen of Angels and the obituary for Father Brualla.

Msgr. Francis J. Weber, Archivist Emeritus of the Archdiocese of Los Angeles, for providing history of the Catholic Church in California.

Malachy McCarthy, Province Archivist, Claretian Missionaries Archives USA–Canada, for providing the photo of Father Medardo Brualla.

Father Arturo Corral Nevárez, Our Lady Queen of Angels, for his kindness, support, and for providing information about the current help being provided to all in the area by "La Placita."

Michael "Tiger" Forster, Los Angeles Historian, for providing history of the area once known as the Macy Street District.

Chuck Cross, Barry Eastman, and Doug Davis of "Rudy's of Waterloo" for providing a splendid atmosphere for writing.

And a special "Thank You!" to the following for use of their photographs:

Archival Center, Archdiocese of Los Angeles, for Father Medardo Brualla's Obituary. *The Tidings* Volume XXX, Number 45, November 7, 1924, p.13,

And, for the photo of Our Lady Queen of Angels, c. 1924.

Sherman Library and Gardens, Corona del Mar, CA, for the photos of Los Angeles Harbor, c. 1924, and Downtown Los Angeles, c. 1924.

I would also like recognize four publications in particular that helped provide the initial spark that led to my interest in and research for this story:

"Plague in Los Angeles, 1924: Ethnicity and Typicality," by William Deverell. From *Over the Edge: Remapping the American West*. Eds. Valerie J. Matsumo and Blake Allmendinger. (Berkeley: University of California Press, 1999, 172-200).

Whitewashed Adobe: The Rise of Los Angeles and the Remaking of Its Mexican Past, by William Deverell. (University of California Press, 2004).

The Centers for Disease Control and Prevention "Plague Homepage" (https://www.cdc.gov/plague/index.html). Note: This site has an incredible variety of information about the history and transmission of the plague.

"The Pneumonic Plague Epidemic of 1924 in Los Angeles," by Arthur J. Viseltear (*Yale Journal of Biology and Medicine*, 1, 40-54, 1974).

Finally, I'd like to thank Rosemary Yokoi, the best editor I've ever known, for her guidance and support of this project.

Thank you, and bless you all!

About the Author

Jeffrey S. Copeland is a professor in the Department of Languages and Literatures at the University of Northern Iowa, where he teaches courses in literature and English Education. He has authored numerous books, including *Inman's War: A Soldier's Story of Life in a Colored Battalion in WWII*; *Olivia's Story: The Conspiracy of Heroes Behind Shelley v. Kraemer*; *Shell Games: The Life and Times of Pearl McGill, Industrial Spy and Pioneer Labor Activist*; *Ain't No Harm to Kill the Devil: The Life and Legend of John Fairfield, Abolitionist for Hire*; *I'm Published! Now What? An Author's Guide to Creating Successful Book Events, Readings, and Promotions*.